# Dawn's Early Light

Elsie J. Larson

THOMAS NELSON PUBLISHERS
Nashville • Atlanta • London • Vancouver

Published in Nashville, Tennessee, by Thomas Nelson, Inc., Publishers, and distributed in Canada by Word Communications, Ltd., Richmond, British Columbia, and in the United Kingdom by Word (UK), Ltd., Milton Keynes, England.



All of the characters in this book are fictional and have lived only in the author's imagination, except for those few historical people readers will recognize. The story idea is the author's own and never really happened.

**Library of Congress Cataloging-in-Publication Data**

Larson, Elsie J.
Dawn's early light / Elsie J. Larson.
p. cm. — (Tides of war ; bk. 1)
ISBN 0-7852-7688-2 (pb)
1. Japanese Americans—Evacuation and relocation, 1942–1945—Fiction. 2. World War, 1939–1945—Oregon—Fiction. I. Title. II. Series: Larson, Elsie J. Tides of war ; bk. 1.
PS3562.A7522D38 1996
813'.54—dc20 95–24380
CIP

Printed in the United States of America

1 2 3 4 5 6 7 - 02 01 00 99 98 97 96

*This book is lovingly dedicated to my husband, Richard,*
*and to his boyhood best friend Masaru Uyeda,*
*whom Richard never saw again*
*after the United States internment*
*of all citizens of Japanese ancestry.*

# PREFACE

A few years after World War II, I met my husband, Richard, and learned about his friend Masaru Uyeda. They had kept in touch throughout the war while Massy was interned and then moved to the Midwest on work release. When the war ended Massy wrote to Richard, "I'm on my way home."

Richard never heard from Massy again and didn't know how to search for him. He still sometimes dreams about his friend who mysteriously disappeared.

As for me, I never knew any Japanese people, and for a while after the war, I felt the internment simply had been a wartime necessity. As I learned more about it, however, I rejoiced with Richard as citizens of Japanese descent began to receive justice and their civil rights.

Tulelake was real, and the details about life in the project are as real as research can make them. Quotations from famous people are usually accurate in content. Much of the war news—dates and facts—comes from Lowell Thomas's radio reports, as published in his book, *History the Way You Heard It*.

EJL
*Gresham, Oregon*
*March 1995*

## *THE SECOND SUN*

*Hope is a second sun*
*that we insist upon within our sky.*
*the power the heart knows how to generate*
*from the fierce fires of need*
*has placed it there.*
*We live and move beneath its subtle light,*
*determined it shall be unique*
*and never set.*
*When any flowering corner of our life*
*threatens to die,*
*our thoughts alight like agitated birds*
*among the withering buds*
*and point their wild beaks upward*
*asking, asking . . .*

—June E. Foye

# CHAPTER 1

Jean Thornton's engagement ring sparkled back at her as she reached for the morning newspaper. Some days it was her bridge to sanity. Being a visible link with Dave, the ring gave her courage to do what he would want, build a life for herself now that he was gone.

Six months had passed since he'd been killed at Pearl Harbor, and still, each morning when she woke up, she had to face the loss of him all over again.

In her grandmother's high-ceilinged Victorian kitchen, she sipped her morning coffee while she scanned headlines. The war news was as frightening as ever.

"May 23, 1942—Port Moresby, Australia. Japanese planes bombed the port again, inflicting heavy damage. If the Japanese invade, orders have been given to destroy everything before retreating."

"Jeanie." Her grandmother brought her own coffee and sat at the breakfast table across from her. Her white hair, already in a smooth chignon for the day, set off the anxious line of her striking black eyebrows. "Is everything all right?"

*No!* Jean screamed on the inside. *Without Dave nothing will ever be all right again.* Aloud she said, "Sure, I'm fine. Just tired from cramming for finals, and the news is scary."

Grandmother continued to pursue her bent to anxiety. "I wish you wouldn't dwell on the war news so much; it can only make you feel worse. I know what it's like to lose someone close. You just have to look for some good things in life and make up your mind to go on somehow."

Jean retreated behind simple agreement. "I know."

"I realize you can't believe it now, but your grief will ease, and it won't mean you love Dave any less."

"Yes." Jean swallowed the last of her coffee. "I have to leave now—nine o'clock exam." She picked up her purse and notebook, but paused long enough to say, "Please don't worry about me."

Grandmother raised her chin. "Might as well tell the rain not to fall."

★

The month of May always turned the Willamette Valley into an ocean of green leaves alive with singing birds. Jean strode down the tree-arched sidewalk along Center Street, oppressed by such burgeoning life. How could everything go on as if nothing were wrong?

The perfume of blossoming honey locust trees set her heart to aching. *Last May, with the air filled with this sweetness, Dave proposed, and we thought we had a lifetime for loving.*

Now he was gone. All they would have shared, all he could have done with his bright mind and desire to help others, had been snuffed out by a Japanese bomb. On December 7, while Jean was finalizing their Christmas wedding plans, Dave had gone down on the battleship *Arizona.*

*He never had a chance.* That thought had become like a theme song for her grief. She stifled a sob. She must not think about how he died now; she was almost to school. Pulling out a handkerchief, she dabbed at her eyes.

Her shortcut through the state capitol grounds led her past the bench under the upside-down tree, with branches that looked like tangled roots, where she and Dave had met. Remembering, she could almost see the way his eyes crinkled at the corners with that first slow smile and feel the warmth of his strong hand encircling hers.

When she reached the street, she noticed a group of students on the other side, milling around at the edge of the university campus.

Angry shouts suddenly split the air. She froze for a second and then ran across the street to see what was happening.

Fifteen or twenty Willamette University students, mostly men she knew, crowded around someone or something.

As she drew near, their shouts separated into words.

"Dirty yellow Japs!"

"Why don't you go back to Japan where you belong?"

Her stomach lurched. *A mob here? On our campus?* And then she thought, *Well, why not here?* Several Japanese men had remained on campus after the attack on Pearl Harbor, finishing their education while many other men had dropped out to enlist. Three of Dave's friends had enlisted as soon as they'd learned of his death.

At the edge of the angry group, she spied one of her sorority sisters. "Caroline! What's going on?"

Grief twisted Caroline's features. "Ken Morgan just learned that his brother was killed in action in the Pacific."

"Oh, no! Not Andy!"

Caroline nodded. "I guess Ken's about out of his head, and I think the rest of these guys have just been waiting for an excuse to blow up. Pete Layton accused the Japanese students of spying . . . says he saw them hanging around the railroad line north of the station with sketch pads. They denied it, of course."

Jean stretched to peer over the wall of broad shoulders. She glimpsed the alien-looking faces of four Japanese men, standing at bay. Their cheeks were flushed, but their expressions remained impassive.

"Somebody could get hurt," she ventured. "Maybe we should try to stop them."

Caroline raised her eyebrows. "You want to try?"

"I guess not. I don't blame the guys. Every time I see one of those Japanese students, I get mad. If they were loyal to America, you'd think they would do something to show it."

Above the shouts of accusation, one of the Japanese men yelled, "What do you think you're doing? We're Americans, just like you!"

In a flash, Ken punched him in the face. The man fell backward. Another Japanese man slugged Ken. He doubled over.

Rodger Bennett, Dave's best friend, was still on campus because his football injury had made him 4F, physically unfit for military service. In spite of his game knee, he leaped on Ken's adversary. Another Japanese man laid into Rodge.

Everyone jockeyed for positions and started swinging.

Someone standing next to Jean screamed, "No! Stop!" Jean clapped a hand over her ear and whirled around. Helen Kagawa, the only Japanese woman on campus, stood there. Her oval face and reserved expression had always reminded Jean of a Japanese dancer doll. Now, with her mouth in a grimace and her eyes wide, she looked as if she'd donned a mask for a Greek tragedy.

She grabbed Jean's arm. "Do something. They'll listen to you."

Jean pulled away. "No, they won't. They won't listen to anybody now." Jean only knew Helen by name; they'd shared some classes. Although Jean lived with her grandmother, her social life centered around the Delta Gams, while Helen lived in the only girl's dorm on campus and had nothing to do with sorority life.

Helen's face twisted like a frightened child's. She looked from Jean to Caroline and back again. "Please help. They might listen to all three of us."

Caroline shook her head.

"No," Jean said again. "They won't."

"You just don't want to!" Helen accused. "You don't care!"

With a jolt of surprise, Jean realized Helen was right. Deep down, she wanted to pound and hit those Japanese faces herself. Watching them fight gave her the first relief she'd felt since Pearl Harbor.

Helen's mouth tightened into an angry line. She turned and ran toward Eaton Hall, the stone building in the center of the campus that housed the administration office.

"We'd better get out of here," said Caroline. "We could be suspended right before graduation."

"Yes, even though we haven't done anything. Head for the Cavern."

Caroline took off running. Jean tightened her grip on her notebook and raced after her. By the time they reached the basement door of Waller Hall, the dean of students charged down the steps of nearby Eaton Hall with Helen at his heels.

Jean and Caroline darted into the student hangout, the Bear Cat Cavern. Out of breath, they ordered coffee and slid into the corner booth where Jean always had met Dave.

She glanced at the diamond ring on her left hand and touched it. She'd never removed it since he placed it there.

"Jeanie," Caroline's voice called her back. In her "I-know-best" tone, she said, "You really should put Dave's ring on your other hand."

Jean bit back an angry retort. "I suppose I should," she said quietly, "but I just can't do it yet."

"You've got to start living again. It's as if you died with him."

Jean thumped her fist on the table. "Part of me did die with him!"

Caroline blinked and then reached across the table and gave her arm a sympathetic squeeze. "I'm sorry. I'm such a clod. It's just that . . . we used to have such fun, and this morning, out there with that mob, is the first time I've seen any life on your face since Dave died."

Jean looked away. "You're right. I did feel alive. If I were a man, I'd have waded right into the fight. That doesn't do much for my self-respect. I always thought I was a fair-minded person."

"Of course you are. It's just the war and all. If I lost my fiancé, I'd be angry too."

"Thanks for the vote of confidence," Jean said wryly.

"Any time. You're beginning to sound like your old self. Maybe you need to get into more fights."

"Oh, sure. Grandmother would have kittens if she knew I was even near this one." She glanced at her watch. "Oh, I've got to get to my English lit final. See you later."

"Sure. Good luck."

On the way to her classroom, Jean examined her awakened feelings. *Anger is better than sorrow . . . or emptiness,* she decided. When she began her test, her mind felt clearer than it had in a long time.

★

After Jean finished her exam, she found Rodger Bennett outside the test room, lounging against the wall, hands in pockets, as if nothing unusual had happened. At the sight of her, his gray eyes came alive, he straightened his long frame, and smiled. “Hi. How did your final go?”

“Okay. Well, you sure look great!” A bruise smudged his left cheek, and a small, jagged cut gave his lower lip a lopsided pout. “Did you get in trouble for fighting?”

“Yeah, but I got off with a warning. Did you hear what happened?”

“Anybody within a mile should have heard.” She gave him what she hoped was a motherly look. “That wasn’t too smart, you know.”

“Yeah, I know. Something just snapped, and I started swinging.” He brushed back his hair with one hand, disclosing scraped knuckles and swollen fingers.

“Was anyone else hurt?”

“You kidding? Those Japs won’t be in school for the rest of the week.”

“How about the other guys?”

“A few nicks and bruises. Jeanie . . . will you have dinner with me?”

Something in Rodger’s tone made his invitation sound like a date, and she hadn’t dated anyone but Dave since she had fallen in love with him.

Rodge reacted instantly to her hesitation. “Hey, I know you don’t feel like dating. I didn’t mean a real date, just a little graduation celebration and a chance to sit and talk in a nice place.”

Rodge was like a brother. He and Jean had never dated, although they’d been good friends since Parrish Junior High days. “Well, sure,” she said quickly, “but I’m tied up tonight.”

He gave her a surprised look.

“Uncle Al is taking me to dinner for my graduation. He flew in this morning on a military plane and has to go back to Washington, D.C., in the morning.”

“Well, Senator Moore has seniority over me, for sure. How about tomorrow night?”

“I’d love it.”

His craggy face softened with pleasure. “I’ll be at your house at seven. Now I’ve gotta run. Calculus finals beckon.”

★

At the end of the afternoon, Jean walked home from her very last exam, thinking about her uncle, Senator Al Moore. She would soon be a college graduate because of him. He had paid for her four years at Willamette.

After her mother died when she was eight, her father had left her with her sister, Evelyn, and her husband, Joe. She'd scarcely known her grown-up sister, who had married long before Jean reached school age. Neither Joe nor Evelyn had wanted her, and her father sent a few postcards and then nothing. *I felt like a piece of garbage,* Jean remembered.

Fortunately, soon after her ninth birthday, her mother's mother, Elizabeth Moore, whom Jean had never met, had sent Uncle Al to find her. And then everything had changed for the better.

Now, at the sight of the Moore home ahead of her, Jean's grateful thoughts returned to the present. The turn-of-the-century house stood like an elegant old lady, surrounded by frivolous young society women. Jean felt the house reflected its owner more than any inanimate object should. Even its windows seemed to look down on the world like Grandmother's eyes, with lowered lids. But inside, it was a warm, secure home.

Elizabeth Moore was an austere, dignified woman, but for all of that, loving in her own way. Jean had learned to read the carefully controlled nuances of her affection and to trust her.

*Grandmother and Uncle Al gave me a chance to do something with my life. And now with Dave gone, the prospect of teaching is the only thing that keeps me going.* During her practice teaching, she'd discovered a satisfying talent for helping children learn.

Jean climbed the proper wooden steps of her grandmother's house and opened the never-locked door. Slipping inside, she quietly closed it, shutting out the afternoon sun. The click of the latch reminded her that she was also closing the door on her college days.

A giddy uncertainty swept over her. As yet she'd received no answer to the four applications she'd sent out to school boards in Oregon. At the time she mailed them, a deadening lethargy had robbed her of strength. Should she send out more?

Jean started up the curving staircase, longing for an undisturbed rest before Uncle Al arrived. Just as her foot touched the second step, she heard her grandmother call, "Jeanie, is that you?"

*Who else would it be?* Jean wondered wearily. *If only she wouldn't hover over me.*

"Yes. I'm going up to soak in the tub. I'm really tired."

★

At 6:30, Jean came downstairs ready for dinner with her uncle. In an off-the-shoulder floral print dress, with a touch of rouge, fresh lipstick, and her light brown hair swept up, she knew she looked better than she felt.

Al Moore stepped out of the parlor to greet her, every inch the dignified senator in his impeccable dark suit and tie and with every iron gray hair on his head in place. A sudden smile softened his lined face. "You look so much like your mother tonight! I'd forgotten how pretty she was. I used to have to protect her from the boys." His smile faded. "I'm afraid I haven't done so well by you."

"Uncle Al, I'm not a high-school girl," she said.

With what she considered his politician's smile, he said, "Quite so. According to you, you've been grown up since you were thirteen."

This man, almost as formal and correct as his mother, was so different from her father, and the difference had made Jean trust him. He had stood up for her whenever Grandmother had insisted on really old-fashioned standards. He could charm his mother into or out of anything. Jean was sure Grandmother knew exactly what he was doing and actually enjoyed the process. She was so proud of her son.

*She's a proud woman, period. No wonder Mama couldn't face her after eloping with Daddy.*

From the doorway behind Uncle Al, Grandmother asked, "Where's your coat, Jeanie?"

"I'll get it," Jean said, knowing it was pointless to argue that it was a warm night. She turned and ran back upstairs.

The drive to the Marion Hotel was brief and silent. Uncle Al seemed preoccupied. In the restaurant, after they were seated, he cleared his throat and fumbled in his pocket. "I can't be here for your graduation." He handed her an oblong white velvet box. "Your Aunt Esther would have wanted you to have this. It was her favorite. . . . I gave it to her when I won my first senate race. Sorry I didn't have time to get it wrapped."

She opened the box and lifted out a sapphire pendant. "Oh, thank you!"

"Esther never liked diamonds. That's why I had it designed with pearls."

"It's a dream of a necklace." She fastened the chain around her neck and lifted the jewel for another look.

He smiled warmly. "Think of it as Aunt Esther rooting for you."

"I wish she were here. . . . I hate cancer."

The lines around his eyes tightened with pain.

Too late Jean recognized her insensitivity. "I'm sorry. It's just that I still miss her so much."

"So do I," Uncle Al said quietly.

A waiter appeared. Jean ordered a petite filet mignon. Her uncle chose a sixteen-ounce porterhouse steak. When the waiter left them alone, Uncle Al said, "Jeanie, Esther and I always knew you'd do well in school, but we worried about how you were feeling. You were such a private child. How are you doing now . . . really . . . on the inside?"

Jean fought a lump in her throat. Sympathy always undid her. She swallowed hard. "Well, I'm past the stage of thinking I can't live, but nothing matters much. Grandmother says that feeling will pass." Avoiding his eyes, she folded and unfolded her napkin. "Has it for you, Uncle Al?"

He leaned back, taking his time to answer. "Yes. There comes a time when life seems worth living again. It probably happens differently for each person. I discovered a new sense of purpose when the president sent me to Germany before the war on my first fact-finding assignment. I realized, because of my friendship with Esther's cousins in Berlin, I could do something no one else could do quite so well at that time. After I returned home, my sense of purpose continued."

"I wish I could find something like that," Jean said doubtfully.

"You will," he assured her.

His mention of the German cousins reminded her of her

French cousin, the only daughter of Esther's sister Ruth. "Still no information on Giselle?"

"None. I'm hoping they simply can't communicate because of the occupation."

"You think they're all right then?"

"As all right as anyone who's living under the Nazis."

"It's so awful. Last time she wrote to me, she was trying to persuade Claude to flee and fight for his country from England. The girls must be nine and eleven by now." Before the war, Giselle had spent many summers in Salem, and Jean had grown closer to her grown-up cousin than she'd been to her own sister, Evelyn.

Giselle taught Jean to speak French, and it became their language for private conversations. She said Jean spoke it as well as any French girl. That experience led Jean to study both French and German in high school and college. She had hoped to visit the cousins in Europe after college and maybe even get a temporary teaching position in Germany or France. So much for that. Now her whole hope was that the families were safe and would survive the war.

The waiter placed their dinner before them. Jean discovered she really was hungry.

While they ate, Uncle Al turned to war news. "Everyone's afraid of sabotage, especially on the West Coast. General DeWitt, the head of the Western Defense Command, feels no one of Japanese ancestry can be trusted. When he testified before the House Naval Affairs Committee last month, he made a valid point. Second- and third-generation Japanese, who are citizens by birth, are still aliens by culture. As he put it, 'A Jap is a Jap.' I'm inclined to agree."

Jean gazed at him in concern. "You think they're all a danger to us?"

He didn't answer her directly. Instead, he said, "These people are welded together by traditions that we, as Americans, can't begin to understand. They've never assimilated our ways. Many still worship the emperor." He paused to drink his coffee and then added in a genial tone, "It's a case of different beliefs and attitudes. Some of them are in touch with their homeland and support the Japanese empire."

"I've wondered about that. So it's really true?"

He nodded. "And if some are supporting Japan—if any are—we can't take a chance." Keeping his eyes on hers, he said soberly, "Earl Warren capped it for me. As District Attorney for California, he's running scared. He says that the very fact that no sabotage has occurred yet is evidence that restraint is being used until a carefully orchestrated effort can create havoc."

Jean said slowly, "Some of the guys on campus accused the Japanese students of planning to sabotage the railroad tracks."

He straightened and asked sharply, "Does anyone have hard evidence?"

"I guess not, but a bunch of guys beat up on the Japanese anyway. One of my friends had just learned his brother was killed in the Pacific. I think he started the fight."

"Was anyone hurt?"

"Only cuts and bruises."

"Another reason why the Japanese must be relocated—to protect the innocent. Those Japanese students may finish this academic year by special permission, but they'll soon be safely interned."

He ate his last bit of steak and laid down his fork and knife. "I was glad your grandmother couldn't join us. There's something I wanted to talk to you about tonight, without her . . . ah . . . knowledge."

He peered at her from under brows as black as Grandmother's, but much more imposing because they created thick shade over his deep-set eyes. "I've persuaded the president that we have not yet identified all the Japanese in this country who are dangerous. A few have been jailed, but we must uncover those who may be temporarily biding their time in the relocation centers and move them to more secure detention."

He glanced around, lowering his voice. "I have the go-ahead to line up people I can trust and place them in civilian jobs inside the internment camps. Their real purpose must remain secret: they'll be fact finders, like I was in Berlin." He paused, as if expecting her to comment.

Before she could collect her thoughts, he asked, "Jeanie, would you consider teaching children in a Japanese internment camp?"

# CHAPTER 2

Jean stared at her uncle while the implications of his job offer sank in. "You mean you want me to . . . to become a spy?" The last word leaped from her lips as an exclamation.

"Shh. Not so loud."

Agitated, she lowered her voice to a stage whisper. "But that is what you mean. I'd spy on the Japanese, while teaching their children."

"You'd be fact-finding. All you'd have to do is find ways to be among the Japanese people on a regular basis and report to me on their morale and behavior. If you heard anyone speak against our government, I'd want a detailed report with their names and quotes. With your talent for linguistics, you might even learn some Japanese."

The situation stirred Jean's interest, but she said, "I don't think I could sneak around spying on anyone."

An impatient frown creased her uncle's brow. "Forget spying. What I'm asking you to do is only a fact-finding mission. But our safety on the West Coast may depend on those facts, because the relocation centers are not secure prisons. Determined people could escape and seriously cripple our defenses."

"You make me feel like we're living with a time bomb."

"Couldn't be much more urgent. General DeWitt says that air raid scare in Los Angeles in February was no hoax—that five Japanese planes did fly over. Right now we're sitting ducks. A few traitors could guide enemy planes in by radio.

Think what they could do to Bonneville Dam, the rail lines, the shipyards, the harbors. California could be the next Pearl Harbor."

Newsreels of Japanese planes bombing Chinese villages and strafing peasants in rice paddies had given Jean nightmares during grade school. Now the terror from those dreams clawed its way back into her mind.

Uncle Al must have sensed her growing fear, for he said, "I don't like to frighten you, but we've got to face reality. This war will demand every ounce of our effort if we are to win it."

"*If* we are to win! Is there really a doubt?"

"Jeanie, listen, and don't repeat this to anyone." He leaned close and spoke in a more guarded tone. "Our navy was nearly wiped out at Pearl Harbor. General DeWitt still says Jap reconnaissance planes flew over Fort Bragg the night of December 8. We don't have enough trained men in the army to make a stand anywhere. You saw what happened in the Philippines. So far, the Japs are winning every battle. They're pushing into Alaska. If they're smart, they'll attack the Pacific Coast soon."

Jean shuddered. She'd heard other people say things like that but had marked it off as war hysteria. Hearing this now from her astute uncle, who knew what went on behind the news reports, changed her whole way of thinking. He wouldn't spread rumors or frighten her unnecessarily. "I had no idea things were this bad," she admitted.

He finished his cooling coffee, leaned back, and said quietly, "Then you can see that uncovering possible enemies, even in the internment camps, is important."

She nodded slowly. "Yes, I can."

"Will you take that teaching position then?"

"I . . . I don't think I could do what you need." She hesitated. "No matter what you call it, I'd have to live a double life, and I'm the world's worst liar. Dave could always see through me when I tried to keep things from him."

"That's because he loved you," Uncle Al said gently. "I hope you won't be offended by this, but I've seen you keep things to yourself all the years I've known you. You really do it very well. You've often fooled your grandmother."

She glared at him and started to deny it. "Uncle Al . . ." She could go no further. What he said was true. When her mother had been so ill, Jean had learned to hide her fears rather than worry Mama. And when Mama died, Jean hid her grief to make it easier for Papa. And when Papa left her and her sister didn't want her, Jean had kept her shame to herself. She had never meant to be dishonest, but now she felt exposed and ashamed again. She could feel her cheeks burning.

"Jeanie," her uncle said softly, "it's all right. I've done the same thing myself. Sometimes it's the only way a person can survive. But don't you see? That habit of keeping things to yourself can now help you serve your country. You have a chance to fight for all that Dave died for."

*Maybe it would help,* thought Jean. *So why am I stalling?* She pushed aside her anxieties, straightened on her chair, and met his sympathetic eyes. "Okay. If you think I can do it, I'll try."

★

The next morning Jean awoke to bird calls from the old maple tree outside her open window. She stretched drowsily and wondered how much longer she could doze. Then in midstretch she remembered. She had accepted Uncle Al's offer to teach and be a fact finder at Tulelake, the war relocation center in northern California. Her eyes flew open and she sat up.

Uncle Al had made it clear that the secrecy of her mission must begin immediately. She was not to tell anyone, including Grandmother, that she would be doing anything more than teaching. Although she had years of practice keeping many feelings and thoughts to herself, now she would have to learn the art of conscious, consistent deception. She couldn't imagine what this would entail, but the challenge pulled her out of bed like a battle cry.

By the time Jean finished her morning shower, she knew what she must do to prepare. While pulling on a brightly embroidered peasant blouse and skirt, she rehearsed her plan. First, as Uncle Al had advised, she would mail her application for teaching at Tulelake to the address he'd given her. Then, if she was to teach the children properly, she'd better learn all she could about the Japanese people. And once her application was accepted—Uncle Al had said he'd guide it through the proper channels, whatever that meant—she'd have to start preparing for her assigned class age.

When she walked into the kitchen for a cup of coffee, her grandmother, wearing a freshly ironed apron over her faded gardening dress, glanced her way and then gave her a second questioning look. Jean braced herself to answer her questions without revealing anything she should not, but Grandmother only said, "Good morning. Would you like some French toast?"

Jean had been skipping breakfast more often than not, but Grandmother never gave up asking. *She likes to feed people,* a small voice reminded Jean. *Keep her happy, and she will not probe.* Jean said, "Yes, thanks. I think I would."

Her grandmother's smile erased the sad lines around her eyes as she handed Jean a cup of coffee. Jean sat in her usual chair at the breakfast table and took a swallow of the fragrant brew.

Grandmother, who preferred to do all the cooking herself, whipped eggs for the toast and called over her shoulder, "You must have had a good time last night."

"Yes, I did." To lead her to a safe subject, Jean volunteered, "Uncle Al gave me a gorgeous sapphire necklace that had belonged to Aunt Esther. His gift made me miss her more, and yet at the same time I felt closer to her."

"He showed me yesterday. Esther would be glad you appreciated the memento." She brought a plate of hot, buttery French toast and set it before Jean along with a small pitcher of heated maple syrup.

"Wow! You're splurging your red ration points to cook in this much butter," said Jean, as she tasted Grandmother's confection.

"You haven't used your share lately, and anyway, to see you looking better calls for a celebration."

"Do I look better?" Jean peered at her reflection in the mirror in Grandmother's old china closet. To her dismay the wavering reflection made her look more than ever like Grandmother—same greenish eyes and black brows that were set too straight to be glamorous. She couldn't tell if she looked better than yesterday, but she realized for the first time that her chronic lethargy was gone.

"Completing school is more of a relief than I expected," she offered, still intent on steering the conversation away from her dinner with Uncle Al. She had asked him to break the news about her job at Tulelake after she was hired. Grandmother would not like the idea, but Uncle Al, without too much fuss, could probably persuade her the position was respectable and safe.

Fortunately, Grandmother seemed to accept her light assessment of why she felt better and asked no questions.

After breakfast, Jean walked downtown to pick up her new suit for the baccalaureate service and then spent the day at the Delta Gam house with her sorority sisters. Of those who were graduating, most were hoping to go into war work of one type or another. Several were going into nurses training, but some wanted to work in the shipyards in Portland and others were going to apply at Boeing in Seattle.

*Women doing men's work?* Jean listened quietly, realizing they would all be filling needs they'd never have dreamed of a year ago. She made encouraging comments, but when asked about her own plans, she only said she wanted to teach if she could get a position.

When she and Caroline were alone in the kitchen, fetching colas for the others, Caroline said, "I'm so glad you're aiming to teach. I was afraid you'd sit around moping all summer and lose your chance for a position this year."

"What you said to me the other day in the Cavern made me think," Jean lied. "I still can't take off Dave's ring, but I am going to start living again."

"Good! I'm glad if what I said helped. At the time I could have bitten off my tongue."

Jean staged a smile and instantly felt like a fake and traitor.

Later, on the way home, she told herself, *My little lie to Caroline didn't make me a traitor. What I said was for the good of Uncle Al's mission and for her good too.* In her mind she replayed the other things she'd said and done at the sorority. With a surprising tingle of excitement, she decided her first day's efforts at deception had worked pretty well and had not been too difficult.

She felt very much alive, as if a painful knot inside her had unraveled, although she still missed Dave as much as ever.

She could imagine Dave smiling over her new mission, his dark blue eyes shining with approval. He had expected the war, and before any of his friends had thought about it, he had enlisted, saying college could wait. If Dave could, he'd be cheering her on, saying, "You can pull this off, Jeanie. Sink a few Japs for me, hon!"

*I will, Davy. I will for you.* She blinked back her tears, not wanting to attract attention on a public sidewalk.

★

That evening, true to his word, Rodger knocked on the front door at seven. Because of gas rationing, they walked downtown. The Golden Pheasant Restaurant was not many blocks farther than the campus, and it was a pleasant evening.

After they'd settled at a table beside a bamboo plant and had received their egg flower soup and hot tea, Rodger, who usually spent a lot of time listening to Jean, started talking nonstop. "I haven't said anything before, but I went to a specialist in Portland, and he says my leg has mended so well there's nothing to keep me from enlisting. He mailed his report to the navy, and they agreed. I'm going in right after graduation. I wanted you to celebrate with me."

She tried to smile. "That's great . . ." A fog of dread choked off her words. Rodger was her only friend who truly shared her grief, and he had comforted her and never tired of talking about Dave. Now would he be killed too?

Rodge broke into her thoughts. "Now I can do something for Dave. You are glad, aren't you?"

She cleared her throat. "I know this is what you've wanted, but it scares me. I've been counting on the fact that you would stay safe."

He smiled with obvious relief and then said slowly, "One thing I want to talk about before I leave . . . I know it's too soon, but I . . . the war . . ." He floundered, then forged ahead in a tone of desperation. "I can't leave without asking if there's any chance that someday you . . . and I . . . well, you seem to like me. Do you think . . . you could ever love me?"

An ache swelled in her chest, wrapped tentacles around her throat, and squeezed. She didn't want to hurt him, not this dear friend who had sustained her during her worst grief, but she could never love Rodger, who'd always been like a brother. Maybe she could never love any man again. Raising her eyes to his, she felt her face betray her.

He looked down at his soup and said in a light tone, "That's okay. I know how you feel about Dave. You two had something special. And anyway," he said with a ragged laugh, "how could you go for a guy like me—the proverbial bull in a china shop."

"Oh, Rodge, don't say that. Any girl in her right mind could go for a guy like you, but for me, there's only Dave. I'm sorry."

The waiter brought their plates heaped high with Chinese vegetables, chicken, and rice. When he left, Rodge, undeterred by the interruption, said, "Dave was lucky. I hope you realize that he knew how lucky."

"Thanks. You always seem to know what I need to hear."

"Right! The reader of broken hearts, that's me." He made a sad clown face, as only he could do.

To please him, she laughed.

He picked up his tea cup and held it out toward her. "So let's celebrate my enlistment and your graduation. A toast to us."

"With Chinese tea?"

"Sure. And when I'm out to sea, I'll remember this warm send-off."

They clicked their handle-less cups together as he declaimed, "Here's to us. May we grab hold of our new beginnings and run for a touchdown."

She hadn't thought of graduation as anything but an end. Without Dave, she'd had no compelling goal beyond finishing school. *But now I do have a purpose—a new beginning. I wish I could tell Rodge about my fact-finding mission.*

Instead, she said, "To us and our new beginnings."

★

The day of graduation arrived more swiftly than Jean had expected. Her long series of final good-byes to friends started with Rodger immediately after the graduation ceremony. Impulsively he bent down and kissed her cheek. "Will you write to me?" he asked.

"Of course. And Rodge . . ." She wanted to say she'd be praying for him, but what good would that do? Even if there was a God, her prayers for Dave had not helped him. "I'll be thinking about you and wishing you the very best," she said lamely.

"Hey, kid," he said gently. "Don't worry about me. I'm the bad penny that always turns up. I'm going to get a few Japs for Dave and a few for myself and when it's over, I'll be back. Right?"

"Right," she affirmed.

Then other friends crowded around with good-byes, coming between her and Rodger.

Caroline gave her a farewell hug. "Let's keep in touch."

"Okay," Jean promised, returning her embrace, but even as she agreed, she knew their paths probably would lead them far away from each other.

Slowly the crowd dispersed as the graduates went their separate ways. Jean fought a lump in her throat; this parting was a small death. She would never see most of her friends again, and if she did, none of them would ever be the same.

Her grandmother tugged at her arm. "Come, Jeanie. The ladies are waiting for us out at the curb with the car." Grandmother's widowed friends had insisted on taking her out to dinner.

Jean drew in a deep breath and followed Grandmother.

During the dinner, in such staid company, Jean concentrated on making Grandmother proud and as far as she could tell, she was succeeding. Finally dessert was served.

Mrs. Dorset, whose round face reminded Jean of an aging Raggedy Ann doll, leaned over and touched her hand. "Jeanie, have you decided what you want to do?"

"I'll teach, of course. It's what I've wanted to do ever since grade school."

"And do you have a position?" asked Mrs. Whitman, the bejeweled empress dowager of the group.

"Not yet." *What would she say, if I told her I plan to teach in an internment camp?* Imagining her look of carefully controlled shock, Jean smiled.

"Well, I'm sure you'll have no difficulty," declared Mrs. Whitman, returning her smile. Like Mrs. Dorset, she reached across the table and patted Jean's hand. "It's so nice to see you happy again, dear. With your courage you'll go a long way."

Jean resisted the impulse to pull away from her touch. *I still miss Dave so much I could die, but no one wants me to show it. Not even Rodge anymore.* Well, here was one more way she could practice deceiving. She said, "I'm not brave at all, but I am feeling better . . . more like myself."

All the ladies nodded in approval.

★

On June 22, Uncle Al called before breakfast. "Jeanie, you're on for Tulelake. I just saw your civil service acceptance. You'll be receiving a notice in the mail soon."

"Thanks for letting me know. Will you break it to Grandmother now?"

"Sure, but there's something I want to tell you first, just in case you still have any doubts about the importance of what you'll be doing. But don't tell your grandmother . . . or anyone. What should be known about this will be on the radio and in the papers today."

He lowered his voice, although he was calling from his private office. "Last night the Oregon coast was shelled by the Japs, up near the mouth of the Columbia River. No one was killed, not much damage done—that much will be in the news. What won't be said is that submarines successfully shelled a radio compass station in British Columbia and a freighter off the Washington coast. The ship didn't sink, but is damaged. We don't know yet if this was done by one sub or a group, but the boss doesn't want the Japs to know how near they came to wiping out the navy direction finder at Fort Stevens in Oregon. They knew exactly where to aim. It's obvious they had inside information—"

"You think there's a fifth column here?"

"The FBI hasn't identified one, but someone obtained and sent detailed information. Your mission at Tulelake will help put a final stopper on the possibility of passing on this sort of information."

"I see," she said, sobered more than ever.

"Call your grandmother now, but remember to keep all this to yourself. From now on, you will be privy to information no one else can know, and you've got to acquire the habit of acting as if you know nothing more than the general public knows."

His warning erased all of his assurances that she wouldn't really be a spy. Her mission was becoming more covert by the day. "I will. Good-bye, Uncle Al." She called Grandmother to the phone and then slipped upstairs, out of sight.

Soon Grandmother demanded, "Jeanie! Jeanie, come down here."

Jean felt nine years old again, coming down the stairs to such a summons.

Grandmother sputtered, "A prison camp! You have no idea . . . the deprivation . . . the lack of privacy . . . and sanitation. . . . You don't speak Japanese!" She went on and on, listing her worries, as if cataloging the decline and fall of civilization. In her distress she paced back and forth in the hallway. "You should have discussed this with me. What do you know about teaching Oriental children? Why would you even want to teach the children of enemy aliens?"

"They need a teacher; I've been trained to teach. And it will be good experience for me. I may even be able to learn some Japanese."

Her grandmother shook her head in disbelief. "And for what purpose? You'll rue the day."

Finally, seeming to accept the inevitable, she announced, "Well, you're welcome back here, the minute you change your mind. This will always be your home."

"Thanks, Grandmother. You've been so kind to me already." Jean would have thrown her arms around her, but the Moores were not the hugging type. Instead Jean said softly, "I'll always think of being with you as home."

Tears brightened her grandmother's eyes. "You're a good girl, Jeanie." She turned and made a dignified, but quick retreat. Her downstairs bedroom door clicked shut.

Jean knew she would come out adjusted to the idea.

In the meantime, Jean picked up the newspaper, retreated to her room, and curled up on her bed to read. Since talking with her uncle, she'd anxiously followed the news. The Japs were still bombing the outer islands of Alaska, but the U.S. had sunk more Jap ships at Midway Island than they'd first reported. Jean wondered painfully how many sailors had died in the battle. Soon, Rodger would be out there.

★

Regardless of her hidden mission at Tulelake, Jean intended to do as well as she could in the classroom. She spent her remaining days at home preparing visual aids and flash cards and teaching games for second graders, her assigned class. She also spent hours reading library books about Imperial Japan, Shintoism, ancestor worship, emperor worship, and Buddhism. Still, the complex culture remained a puzzle to her. How could she teach children whose parents she could not understand?

The last week of August, Rodger called. "I wanted to say good-bye."

Her heart sank. "You're being shipped out already?"

"We don't know when and couldn't say if we did, but we've finished basic training here. I sure miss you, Jeanie."

"I miss you too," she said, before she stopped to think how he might react.

"You do?" His voice rose hopefully.

"I . . . I miss your understanding and encouragement," she said quickly.

"Well, thanks, I guess." He laughed and then asked seriously, "How are you doing?"

"I'm okay. I've landed a teaching position, so I feel like I have a purpose, and I've been busy getting ready. How about you?"

"Great! I got through basic without a single pain in my leg. Can you give me your teaching address?"

"No. Soon as I can, I'll let you know."

"Where will you be?"

"A place called Tulelake in California."

"Tulelake? I didn't think there was anything there, besides that Jap internment camp."

"That's where I'll be."

"You're going to teach Japs?"

"Only their children. Second graders."

Except for some kind of background noise, the line fell silent.

"Rodge? Are you there?"

"Yeah. . . . You're teaching enemy aliens after what they did to Dave?"

The aching lump was back in her chest. Of all people, Rodge was questioning her judgment. "We're not at war with their children or, for that matter, with most of the adults in the relocation centers."

"Yeah, but after Pearl Harbor, you can't trust any of them, so why help their kids? You could have your pick of any number of good schools."

Just in time, Jean bit back the impulse to tell him her special reason for going to Tulelake. She took a deep breath and made her voice come out cool and calm. "Tulelake is a unique teaching opportunity. And if Dave were here, I know he would understand." *If I could tell you the truth, so would you,* she added silently.

"I don't know about that. Didn't he ever tell you what the Japs did in central Oregon? It's illegal for aliens to own land, and yet they got around the law by buying up prime land in the names of their underage children. I think Dave would tell you they're no more American than their cousins in Japan."

"I'm sorry you disapprove because this is what I want to do. Please, let's not argue."

"Okay, okay. I'm glad you found something you want to do, even if I don't understand," he said without enthusiasm.

"Thanks, Rodge."

Background noise on his end of the line obliterated his next words. "Hey, I've got to go!" he called in a louder tone. "My buddies are waiting for the phone. I'll send you my new address. Take care of yourself, Jeanie."

"You do the same. Be careful!" His receiver clicked almost before her last words were out.

She hung up, feeling miserably let down. *I knew lying*

*wouldn't be easy,* she thought, *but I never guessed how bad it would hurt.*

★

Rodger's reaction gave Jean some second thoughts about what she was getting into. After a while, she decided she could handle his misunderstanding and Grandmother's worries, but she felt more and more troubled about the idea of spying.

That night she climbed into bed still weighing reasons for and against her decision to spy. The imperative of war clearly canceled out her reservations over the playacting she'd have to do, and yet, she hated to think of how she would not be able to be aboveboard with anyone . . . but if she could save lives . . . Finally, sleep caught up with her.

In the morning, with a clearer mind, she had to admit that her secret mission violated something deep within her. *What will happen to me if I live a lie day after day?*

*Spying in wartime is necessary and even honorable,* came an opposing thought that sounded like Uncle Al.

*Maybe I just fear failure. Dave always said the way to get around that is to go ahead and do what you fear.*

As she gazed at his smiling photo on her dresser, she could almost hear him saying, "You can do it, Jeanie."

That settled the matter. She was not going to agonize any longer. She had accepted the responsibility, and she would see it through.

★

On Friday, Augu[illegible] Jean left home in the middle of the night in order to a[illegible] Tulelake before nightfall the next day.

As the inter[illegible] rolled out of the Salem, Oregon, depot, she wav[illegible] andmother and Mrs. Whitman, who had chauffeured her a[illegible] her heavy bags. Once out of their sight, she leaned back. She might as well relax as best she could on this long ride. The bus, scheduled to stop at every little town for nearly 400 miles, could not exceed the wartime speed limit of 35 miles per hour, which was supposed to save on tires and gas.

A dark-haired young woman with a pompadour sweeping her hair away from her face and securing her sausage shaped curls behind her ears occupied the aisle seat beside Jean. Between snaps of her chewing gum, she asked in a friendly manner, "Going far?"

"Northern California."

"I'm on my way to San Diego. Gonna marry my guy before he ships out."

The girl's announcement instantly triggered pain. *If only I had married Dave before he left. . . .* "That's wonderful. Congratulations."

"Thanks. What are your plans?"

"I'm going to teach. Second graders."

"Really? Gee, I'd never have taken you for a teacher. You going to one of those one-room schools in the mountains?"

"No. I guess there are lots of kids. The town has over 15,000 people."

"That big? What's the name of the town?"

Jean hated to say, but knew the girl would find out when they got there. "Tulelake," she said casually.

The woman stared at her. A puzzled frown creased her forehead. "That must be near that Jap prison camp."

*Well, here we go again.* "No, not near . . . it is the camp."

The woman stopped chewing her gum and turned to stare at her.

"It's really a relocation center," Jean said quietly, "not a prison camp."

The woman eyed her with open hostility. "You're going to teach Jap kids? What kind of an American are you anyway?"

Jean wanted to yell, *I'm the same kind you are, and I'm doing this for my country!* Instead, she said stiffly, "The children are not our enemies." She turned her face to the window and hoped that would end the conversation. It did.

After a while she leaned back and closed her eyes, pretending to sleep. As the bus rumbled south, her anger cooled, and she wished with all her being that she could trade places with the other girl and without anything to hide, simply be on her way to marry the man she loved.

# CHAPTER 3

When Jean stepped off the bus at Tulelake, late afternoon sun seared the top of her head. She squinted into the glare. According to Uncle Al, the camp had been in operation for five months and was still under construction.

His comment had not prepared her for the miles of stark military barracks spreading across the high desert. Guard towers loomed at intervals along an endless fence around the perimeter. In the closest towers, she could see the soldiers with guns, watching. Railroad tracks skirted the base of a rocky butte across the highway from the camp. A siding track ran over the highway and into the camp where several freight cars full of coal stood waiting to be unloaded. Beyond the camp, flat land swept onward, a broad lake bed of gritty soil lapping at distant cliff shores.

The bus driver set Jean's two heavy suitcases beside her, climbed back into the bus, and drove away. The gate into Tulelake, manned by armed guards, reminded her of the state penitentiary in Salem. She leaned over, gripped her suitcase handles, carefully straightened, and staggered toward the gate. While two of the guards stayed at their posts, a third soldier with an MP band on his arm strode toward her, smiling. "Need some help?"

"Yes, please."

He took her luggage. "Private First Class James Duggan at your service."

"I'm Jean Thornton. I've come to teach the children."

Stubble on his shaved head glinted copper below his cap. Freckles and sunburned nose confirmed he was a redhead. Friendly blue eyes searched her face. "You're one of the first teachers to get here." He gestured toward a clump of large barracks joined together in an "L" shape. "That's the administration building. You're supposed to go there first. Where you from?"

"Salem, Oregon."

He marched back to the sentry post, balanced by a suitcase in each hand. Jean followed, feeling like a misfit in this military establishment.

"Never been to Ory-gone," Private Duggan said over his shoulder. "I'm from Iowa, where the corn grows as high as these barracks. First time I saw this place, I thought nothing could grow here, but would you believe it? These Japs have grown acres of vegetables for the mess halls and have even shipped some to other internment camps. Fields are off that-a-way outside the camp."

Jean eyed the high fence and the guard towers again. "You mean the internees get out of here to farm?" she asked in surprise.

"Yep. There ain't no place much they could escape to. But then, I don't think they want to—it's safer for them here. A lot of people don't like the idea of Japs running around loose."

"I found that out." She told him about the reaction of her seatmate on the bus. "After that, I didn't tell anyone where I was going."

"If you go into the towns around here, you'd best keep mum too," he advised. He stacked her luggage against the gatehouse. "You can go ahead and check in, and I'll bring your bags soon as I get permission."

She followed his advice, and sure enough, by the time she finished signing her employment forms, her suitcases were waiting for her just inside the front door of the administration building. A silent Japanese man carried her luggage to the former MP barrack that would be her home until the teachers' apartments could be completed.

This barrack also looked unfinished. She'd heard of tarpaper shacks, but she'd never been in one. The inside was oven hot, in spite of several open windows. A row of army cots lined both walls the length of the fifty-foot room. Her feet left tracks in a gritty dust that covered everything. The planked floor let in streaks of reflected daylight. Jean hated to think what else they might let in. She set her possessions on a cot near the middle of the building and pushed the window above it outward at the bottom as far as it would go.

The stifling room drove her to look for the shower building. Latrines and showers also were in wide-open barracks, with no partitions for privacy.

When Jean returned to the dorm she was relieved to see another teacher, claiming the cot beside hers. Her hair was as blue-black as the Japanese internees, but her skin was paler than Jean's. Her blue eyes flashed with a quick sense of fun. "I'm Mary O'Leary. Just came in on the train," she said. "From New York, I mean real New York, upstate, not the City. Met any promising men yet?"

Jean found it easy to laugh at the prospect of suitable men in an internment camp. "I did meet one. Private Duggan. Nice guy. Not my type, but I'll introduce you."

"Swell," said Mary. "I'll return the favor when I can. What this place needs is a good party. Do the men get any time off for fraternizing with us?"

Jean chuckled. "I don't know, but I'm sure you'll find out." Their conversation was interrupted by another arrival, a tall woman with sun-streaked brown hair and a California suntan. She dumped her luggage on the other side of Jean's cot. After greetings and introductions, Ann Smith, who said she was from Los Angeles, asked, "Where do we hang our clothes?"

"These footlockers seem to be the only place to store anything," Jean said.

"At least it's temporary," said Ann, "and no worse than summer camp." While she packed shoes, books, and cosmetics into the wooden chest at the foot of her bed, she asked, "Do either of you have any Japanese friends?"

Jean shook her head.

Mary said, "Golly, no. I never saw any Japanese people until I went to the City when I was sixteen. Don't know if I did then, 'cause I can't tell one Asian nationality from another."

"Well, I have," Ann said. "That's why I'm here. I despise what's been done to them."

"You do?" said Jean and then wanted to bite her tongue for sounding so surprised.

Ann studied her. "You think it's okay that thousands of innocent people have been forced into concentration camps in the United States?"

"I think it's necessary," said Jean.

"Can you imagine how you'd feel if this had been done to you and your family?" She swung her arm in an arc that encompassed the whole of Tulelake project.

Jean couldn't. And anyway it was beside the point. Relocation was necessary, and she was glad it had been done quickly. Ann seemed to be out of touch with reality. But then, Ann did not have a senator for an uncle. "Right or wrong," Jean said matter-of-factly, "that's the way it is. And I'm here to help the kids, if I can."

"Yeah, I guess that's the way I feel too," Mary said, studying Ann with obvious curiosity.

Ann turned her back and began to lay her clothes out on her cot. "From what I hear, we don't even have supplies—no paper, no books, and no blackboards."

"No books or paper?" Mary squealed. "How can we teach?"

Ann swung around and peered at her through the thick lenses of glasses that gave her eyes a faraway look. "That's what I've been wondering. You gals got any ideas?"

Jean shook her head. "No, but I'm sure glad I made flash cards and a few learning games this summer." Half to herself, she added, "I hope the children at least speak English."

"They most likely will," said Ann.

Mary muttered, "I can't believe no books."

"I hate not being prepared," Jean worried aloud.

Ann pulled a large bath towel from her suitcase and laid it beside her clothes. "You sound scared. You afraid of these people?"

"I think I am," Jean admitted. At least that was an easy truth.

"Then why on earth did you come here?"

Mary volunteered, "I wanted to see the world and at the

same time do something useful. I felt sorry for the kids, being rounded up and torn from their homes and friends."

Jean tossed out the half-truth she'd given Rodge. "I wanted the experience. I'm hoping the challenge of teaching kids who are in a difficult learning environment will help me become a better teacher."

Ann smiled. "Well, you're going to get your wish, first crack out of the box. I wish I'd had the foresight to prepare stuff before I came." Glancing at her watch, she asked, "Which way to the showers?"

Jean showed her.

Mary grabbed a change of clothes and towel and followed Ann.

Musing about how different the other two teachers were from each other, Jean decided both were nice, but she was more drawn to Mary. As for Ann, Jean sighed in frustration. Ann had reminded her that she should keep opinions about the internment to herself. For the sake of her fact-finding mission, she should appear to be as sympathetic to the internees as Ann obviously was. In the future she would listen carefully to Ann and not only agree with her, but try to reflect her attitude.

Before Mary and Ann could return from the shower, Jean slipped Dave's ring off her finger and placed it in an envelope at the bottom of her foot locker. If her grief were known here, it could make her friendly advances toward the Japanese seem strange to some people. From now on, her mourning would be as private as her mission.

★

On September 1, teacher training began. Among other things, Jean learned that the internees, under the Caucasian project leader's supervision, were allowed to form a simple town government, based on block leaders. Internees staffed a volunteer fire department, a hospital, a mimeographed daily newspaper, a few co-op stores, and a few beauty shops. She was surprised at this freedom inside wire fences with guard towers but could see the wisdom of keeping people organized and busy without a lot of soldiers watching from within the project. There would be three elementary schools, but a single high school.

Jean learned also that there were three variations of being Japanese in America: *Nisei, Issei,* and *Kibbei.* The Niseis were American citizens by birth. Most of the Niseis seemed to be younger than thirty. The Isseis had been born in Japan, and therefore were enemy aliens. The older parents and grandparents made up the Issei group. The Kibbeis were American citizens who had been born here, but sent back to Japan for their education. Many would be the same ages as the Niseis, but they were thought to be less Americanized. For Jean, that was a point worth remembering.

At the end of the day, Jean visited the barrack that was to be her classroom. It was as welcoming as an unfinished barn—the inside walls were just bare boards and studs. The internees at the furniture factory hoped to have simple tables and chairs completed for the first day of school, September 15. Three empty potbellied stoves stood like sentinels down the center of the building, their black pipes punctuating the open-beamed space to the roof like giant exclamation points. Jean inspected one stove, and then leaned against its cool metal to survey the room. *What on earth can I do to make this place interesting? Or at least not forbidding?*

A light rap sounded at the open door. Jean turned. A slender woman stood silhouetted against the sunlight. Jean walked over to greet her visitor, hoping it was the mother of one of her future pupils. "Hi!" she called as she approached.

When she reached the woman, a familiar high-cheekboned Japanese face greeted her. "Helen Kagawa!" Jean exclaimed. "You—here?"

Helen gave her a curt nod. "I'm your teaching assistant." She obviously had not forgotten those last moments on campus, when Jean had refused to interfere with the men's fight.

"Well," Jean said. "That's great. I didn't know you planned to become a teacher," she added awkwardly.

"I am a teacher," Helen corrected.

More awkwardly, Jean said, "Oh. I didn't know you graduated."

"Because of the curfew for Japanese people, I wasn't allowed to attend the ceremony." Helen's face remained expressionless.

With her oval face defined by a widow's peak and framed by smoothly drawn back hair, she reminded Jean more than ever of an elegant geisha doll. Totally embarrassed, Jean said again, "I didn't know. I'm sorry."

Now Helen's brown eyes glinted with anger. "All the other Japanese professionals here—nurses, doctors, dentists, lawyers—are allowed to work at their professions, but I'm not allowed to teach the children. I decided at least I could assist. If you'd rather have someone else, you can ask."

"Not at all. I mean, I'm glad to have you. It's nice to have someone I know."

Helen turned away from her and scanned the bare room. "How do you plan to make this place look like a schoolroom?" she asked in an accusing tone.

Jean blew up inside. She glared at Helen's back and clamped her teeth together. *For the sake of Uncle Al's mission, I've got to make peace with this woman, and it's not going to be easy.*

By the time Helen faced her again, Jean could say, "Helen, I'm sorry about what happened at Willamette that day. It must have been terrible for you, and I did nothing to help you. I've no excuse. . . . Can you forgive me? I really need your help now." It was a long speech because Helen's face remained so cold that Jean felt compelled to try harder and harder to awaken some hint of acceptance. She failed.

Helen shrugged. "I said I'd help. Tell me what you want."

Jean took a deep breath. "Can you meet me here tomorrow afternoon? I'll bring some magazine pictures and word cards to hang on the walls and you bring whatever you can scrounge for autumn decorations."

Helen nodded, and without another word, she left.

★

The next afternoon, Jean and Helen worked together peaceably enough, but Helen remained distant and had little to say until Jean asked about the Labor Day celebration that was being planned for the following Monday. Helen began to relax.

Encouraged by the growing conversation, Jean asked, "Do you know any of the girls who are running for queen?" Simple line drawings of the candidates' faces had been published in the mimeographed daily paper, *The Tulean Dispatch.* Photos weren't possible because the internees' cameras had been confiscated.

Helen answered, "No, but my brother Tom knows three." The hint of a smile softened her cool expression. "He gets around, as far as the girls are concerned."

"Are you doing anything special on Labor Day?"

"Not me, but Tom will be in weight lifting. After rooting for him, my little sister Margie and I will probably just walk around and visit the other demonstrations and exhibits."

When Jean first learned about the camp's Labor Day celebration, she was surprised that such a thing would be allowed. Her principal had explained that the young people needed such outlets, and that maintaining order required doing everything possible to keep up the morale of the internees. Ann said it was the humane thing to do. Jean guessed all these reasons made sense, and she wanted to see for herself what the internees had devised. "Could I go with you?" Jean asked hesitantly.

Surprise flashed across Helen's face. "We'll just have simple, homemade stuff—the best we can do without any resources—to remind us of how things used to be, because even here, the children need to keep traditions. I can't imagine why you want to go. It would probably bore you."

"I'd like to get to know the people, if I can. Don't you see, if I'm to teach, I need to know as much as possible about the families? Watching parents with their children may give me a feel for how to communicate with them."

Helen stared at her. "I doubt it'll help much, and I don't think you will like the truth if you find it, especially if you're around my brother Tom. He and his friends are pretty outspoken."

"I wouldn't mind," Jean said more confidently than she felt. "I'm sure anything I can learn will help me to be a better teacher."

Helen gave a half smile that was neither friendly nor unfriendly. She said, "If you really want to do this, I'll come by your apartment on Sunday after church to tell you where and when to meet me." She started to say more, but she hesitated. And then, quite abruptly, she asked, "Or maybe you'd like to go to church with us too?"

Caught off guard, Jean stammered, "I . . . I don't think so, but thanks for asking." She could imagine the discomfort of having to sit in an unfamiliar Buddhist service. It would be bad enough to be stuck in a Christian one. Now that she was away from her grandmother, it was a relief not to have to listen to Sunday morning platitudes.

After Helen left, Jean wondered why her assistant had so unexpectedly decided to ask her to their church. *Did she invite me to test me, or has she begun to accept me?* Nothing in her manner gave Jean a clue.

Now that it was too late, Jean realized she should have accepted Helen's invitation. It could have been a step in the right direction for fact-finding.

★

Jean had not walked into the residential section of the project, beyond the route to and from her classroom. On Labor Day morning she set out with Mary and Ann to watch the internees' parade and flag dedication ceremony. In lieu of streets, government designers had created wide dusty fire breaks that separated the endless identical clusters of tar-paper-black barracks. The buildings were numbered, and so were the areas, but Jean felt lost. Fortunately, Helen had drawn a small map for her. Everyone in the project seemed to be celebrating for the holiday. Walking among them made Jean feel as if she had entered a foreign country. At the outdoor stage, however, the internees presented a surprisingly patriotic opening ceremony and then, with a great deal of ingenuity, they staged a colorful parade. The all-Japanese population and the ugly buildings seemed utterly incongruous to the festivities.

Back at the staff mess hall after lunch, Mary asked if she could return with Jean to meet Helen for the afternoon activities.

"Sure, but I thought you had a date," said Jean.

Mary shrugged cheerfully. "Your friend Duggan weaseled out of it. Says he pulled guard duty. He asked me out for tonight, though, so I want to hang around here instead of going with Ann and the girls on the bus to Klamath Falls."

"You're stuck with the box supper then." Food service

people had been allowed to prepare the boxes so they could have the rest of the day off.

"Our gourmet picnic," said Mary without rancor. "You've got to hand it to these cooks. They're as good as any dime-store chef in the nation."

Laughing, they picked up their evening meal and hiked to the flagpole on the far side of the project to meet Helen.

When they found her, she waved and came to meet them. Giving Mary a brief smile of welcome, she said. "We've just got time to see Tom lift weights."

Away she strode, so fast they were hard put to keep up. Finally, she pointed out a barrack. "This is the place." She led them inside.

The heat indoors was already building up to afternoon intensity. A young man lay with his back on a low, wooden bench while his feet remained on the floor. His face glistened with sweat as he slowly hoisted a bar with large round weights on each end. A small audience crowded around. All conversation stopped while he strained to the peak of his press. Slowly he lowered it back toward his chest. Then two men ran forward, relieved him of the weight, and placed it in a holder above his head. Everyone applauded enthusiastically. Jean discovered she'd been holding her breath.

The man sat up briskly and bounced to his feet. At Jean's side, Helen said, "That's Tom. Come on, I'll introduce you."

Jean stared at him in surprise. He was slim for a weight lifter, above average height, and astonishingly handsome. She couldn't decide exactly why. He had the same widow's peak and high cheekbones as his sister, and his lips were almost as curved and full as hers, but firmly masculine. His features taken separately were strong, but not unique, and yet, blended together, the effect was striking.

Someone handed him a towel. He wiped his face and hands and stepped over to speak to an older couple. Then Tom glanced toward them. When his eyes met Jean's, he seemed to freeze, as if he thought he knew her. His smile faded. Ever so briefly he eyed Jean with an expression of . . . distrust . . . dislike?

# CHAPTER 4

Jean returned Tom's stare, wondering why he looked so unfriendly. Helen had warned her that he was outspoken, but . . . no, he was smiling again, a friendly smile aimed at her and Mary, and then he turned toward his sister.

Helen stepped close to her family and said, "This is my father . . . my mother . . . my sister, Margie . . . little brother, Peter, and," she waved with a teasing flourish, "my big brother, Tom. These are two of our teachers, Jean Thornton and Mary O'Leary."

The parents smiled and bowed slightly. Margie, a young teen, smiled broadly. Peter, five years old but small enough to be four, said, "Hi!"

With mock formality Tom said, "May you enjoy your visit in our charming town. I regret we cannot wine and dine two such lovely guests."

"We Irish have a saying," said Mary. "'A crust of bread and good company are better than a banquet with royalty.' Care to join us for dinner?" She held up her boxed supper.

Tom chuckled. "Sure."

"We're going to visit the other exhibits this afternoon," Helen explained.

"If you wait until I'm done here," said Tom, "I'll come along. With Fuj, Tad, and Yosh, of course."

"The four musketeers. Okay," Helen said. In the presence of her family she laughed with easy good humor.

Jean marveled at the change in her.

Tom turned to Jean. "And does Miss Thornton speak or only watch from her ivory tower?"

Jean blushed; she hated blushing. She had no quick retort; she hated feeling tongue-tied.

Mary came to her rescue. "Jean in an ivory tower? You've got to be kidding!" She rolled her eyes and raised her eyebrows in clownish surprise.

Everyone laughed.

Jean collected her wits. "She who says little seldom finds foot in mouth."

Tom gave her a mock salute. "Touché!"

"Oh, for pity's sake!" Margie burst out. "Speak English!"

Jean and Mary laughed at her "typical little sister" act. At the same time Jean realized that she had been supposing "speak Japanese" would have been more in character. She glanced at Tom to find him watching her. The hint of a smile gave his mouth a friendly boyish look, but she suspected if he said anything, she would not enjoy it. He raised an eyebrow and turned back to watch his competition struggle with the weight he had successfully pressed.

Jean had never been a weight lifting fan. She was surprised to find it so interesting. It was a wonder that these slim men, some no taller than she, could be so strong.

During a break, Tom brought a small weight and laid it in her hand. She almost dropped it, but he already had his hand under hers to catch it. Smiling, he took it back. "Heavier than it looks, isn't it? Wait until you see Tadashi do the overhead. He lifts more than twice his own weight."

An hour later, Tom was announced the winner in the bench press. His friend Tad was the winner in the overhead lift.

Tom stretched and looked smug. He brought his buddies to Mary and Jean and introduced them. Tadashi—Tad—was medium height and blocky as a football player, and Yoshio—called Yosh—was tall and slim, like Tom. Fuj was short and sturdy.

"Okay, ladies," Tom said, "lead the way to the exhibits."

Margie knew where everything was. With the dispatch of a tour guide, she led them from one barrack to another, to see exhibits of woodcarving, drafting, *ikebana,* dance, drama, Red

Cross sewing, Red Cross first aid, furniture making, agricultural displays, and exhibits by 4-H, Boy Scouts, and Camp Fire Girls.

The men drew the line at the fashion show and left to pursue interests of their own. At suppertime they returned to watch the talent show with Helen, Jean, and Mary while they ate their boxed suppers. Tom and his friends joked and cut up like college men anywhere.

Jean felt fleetingly disoriented. It almost did not seem like an internment camp. Tom was charming and fun and sometimes he seemed to anticipate her very thoughts. She wondered why she'd thought at first that he didn't like her; he seemed to enjoy her company now.

Because there was no single building large enough for all the young people, the Queen's Ball, set for 9 P.M. was to be held in three different barracks. Well before that time, Jean began to shiver. With the sun gone down there was frost in the air, despite the hot days. "I didn't bring a sweater. I think I'll go back to the dorm now," she announced.

Mary said, "Me too. I've gotta see if Private First Class Duggan shows up to take me to the rec room party or not."

"We'll walk you back," Tom volunteered.

"There's no need—" Jean began.

He glanced at her sharply. "You're right. You're safer here than on the streets of a free town . . . because everyone here is law abiding." His voice suddenly sounded angry, but his face was a careful mask. Jean didn't know what to say. Mary, too, remained silent.

Margie, who had been talking with Helen on the side, exclaimed, "I wish I could go to the dance!"

"You're too young," Tom said abruptly.

Margie glared up at him. "I'm sure glad you're not my father."

Tom returned her frown for a second, then a smile tugged at the corners of his mouth. "So am I!" He reached out to thump her on the top of her head with his flat palm, but she ducked away.

"She's not much younger than I was when I went to my first dance," Tad remarked.

"Don't encourage her," said Tom.

Yosh said, "Tad, you actually went to a high-school dance?"

"My freshman year," Tad replied. "The school was so small, I made the football team right off. On a night a lot like this one, I made my first touchdown. Everybody cheered and pounded me on the back. It gave me the confidence to ask a swell girl to dance with me after the game—she wasn't Japanese. One of the seniors cut in and said she was his girl. She said she wasn't, but he made a scene and called me a lot of names and we ended up fighting. I learned during the fight that all the guys agreed with him."

Tom, his voice on edge again, said, "Maybe we should change the subject. We may be embarrassing our teachers."

"I'm sorry about Tad's experience," Jean said. "But I'm certainly not embarrassed. It makes me angry."

"Are you angry also about the innocent American citizens and women and children and old men who have been imprisoned here?" Tom challenged.

"Tom," Helen cautioned, "Jean and Mary are here to help."

Fuj slipped his arm around Helen and said, "Yeah, Tom, don't take out your frustration on the ladies."

"Hey, watch it!" Tom exclaimed, but he was not looking at Fuj or Helen. He made a sudden dive behind Jean. She spun around in time to see him snatch a toddling girl baby from the path of a running boy. Tom cradled her protectively in his arms.

Before anyone could speak, the baby's mother, only a step away, exclaimed, "Oh, thank you! I didn't see him coming!" She took the baby, whose face had begun to pucker with fright.

"That's okay," Tom said. "Glad to help." He scanned the clusters of people around them, apparently looking for the boy who had almost run down the baby.

Frowning, he said, "This place is ruining our families. Kids have no work, and pretty soon no discipline. They're losing respect for their parents, so why should they respect anyone else? They need good teaching now more than ever. How can we expect that in an internment camp?" he asked of no one in particular. Jamming his hands in his pockets, he turned to

Jean. "We're here because of racial prejudice. Why are you here, Miss Thornton?"

He caught her off guard. Her heart leaped in fear, although she knew he couldn't possibly suspect anything about her arrangement with Uncle Al. She also realized at that same guilty instant that she was very glad he couldn't guess it. All four of these men, even if they were loyal citizens, would be furious if they knew about her assignment.

In the face of her silence, Tom pressed the issue he'd brought up. "A lot of people are saying teachers who would come here aren't good enough to get a job anywhere else, that they must have been drafted."

Jean said, "That sounds as bigoted as the people who abused Tad at that high-school dance."

"Straight shot!" said Fuj. "Tom, we've got no call to judge the teachers that way."

No one spoke for a few steps. Then Tom came to a halt, and they all stopped. Turning to Jean, he said, "Fuj is right. I don't know what gets into me. It's just that this whole mess makes me so mad. . . . I shouldn't have taken it out on you. I apologize."

"I think I understand," she said, and it was almost the truth. "For the record, you can tell parents that we teachers care about the kids and we want to do our best for them. As for me, however . . . I realize I have a lot to learn in order to be the teacher they deserve."

Mary exclaimed, "This is getting too serious for me! What do you men do for fun around here?"

The rest of the way, they talked baseball and then, finally, about their work in the project. Fuj drove out to the farms every day, and Yosh worked in the furniture factory. Tad cooked in a mess hall, and Tom divided his time between the hospital and the fire department.

"Two jobs? You really must like to make things hard for yourself," teased Mary.

"I like to be where the action is. Fortunately we don't have fires every day, but in the hospital, on my days off, the nurses can always use an extra pair of hands and a strong back."

"Tom took premed," Helen inserted, "and then he changed his major just before graduating."

"To what?" asked Jean.

"Journalism," said Tom.

"Journalism!" Jean exclaimed. "That doesn't seem to go with being a fireman or nurse's aid."

Tad broke in, "None of us are doing what we would like to be doing. It's things like baseball that keep us sane."

The evening ended on that sober note. They had reached the teachers' dorm.

★

The next day Helen met Jean at her empty classroom. They planned a few combined activities to reinforce their formal lesson plans: Helen to use music and drama, and Jean, arts and crafts.

As their ideas expanded, Jean grew excited. "Two heads are so much better than one. We'll really make it fun for the kids."

"I hope so. . . ." Helen wrote in her music notebook furiously, then said slowly, "Jean . . . about the way Tom acted last night. I . . . I expected . . . no, I hoped he'd blow up at you. But now, I see what a cheap thing I did. I think he almost forgot who you are. You see, you look a lot like a Caucasian girl he once loved. While she was stringing him along, she secretly got engaged to someone else. He hasn't been serious about a girl since."

*That explains a lot,* thought Jean. "Well, thanks for the initiation!" she exclaimed wryly. "So why are you telling me this now?"

"I'm not sure. I guess after I thought about it, I wanted you to know Tom isn't such a jerk."

*Family pride,* thought Jean. *No concern for my feelings, just family pride. She and Grandmother have at least one thing in common.* The thought of what her straightlaced grandmother would say to being compared with a young woman, whom Grandmother considered an enemy alien, struck Jean as impossibly funny. She chuckled to herself.

Helen gave her a puzzled look, and then her cheeks flushed

with anger. Before Jean could explain, she snatched up her notebook and left.

Jean called after her, "Helen! Wait! I wasn't laughing at you." She ran to the door, calling, "Please let me explain."

Helen had disappeared. Jean thought, *Now I've got that fence to mend. When will I learn? Well, for what she pulled, she deserved it.*

A few minutes later, on the way to her dorm, Jean thought about Tom's betrayal by a Caucasian woman and his anger over the internment. He could be hurt and angry enough to want to aid Japan. He would bear watching, and she should probably make some notes on him as soon as she could engineer some privacy.

★

No matter what friendly advances Jean made, Helen remained cool, but she was an exemplary assistant teacher. For that, Jean was grateful.

At last, on September 15, school opened. The first day Jean was almost too nervous to eat her breakfast. She reached her classroom early and propped the door open to welcome everyone. The children arrived by twos and threes, the girls in freshly starched cotton dresses and the boys in neat shirts and carefully pressed pants held up by clip-on suspenders.

Helen showed them to their chairs while Jean greeted the mothers who had brought them.

Soon every one of the fifty-three children on her roll were seated. As she'd expected, she had no books to offer them, except some of her own old storybooks she'd asked her grandmother to send. Other supplies consisted of a three-inch stack of eight-by-eleven scratch paper and twenty-four boxes of crayons.

Jean had hoped until the last minute she might receive an adequate supply of paper and crayons by this Monday morning. Now, because of her optimism, Helen had to fold and cut the papers in half to make them last longer and break the crayons in half to provide some for each table. While she did so, Jean introduced a word game the children could play without paper or a blackboard.

From that hectic beginning, Jean's day went from bad to

worse. Japanese, she decided, would not be as easy to pick up as German and French had been. She couldn't pronounce, remember, or spell her pupils' surnames; Tokuno and Tokiryo, or Uyekawa and Uyetake, jumbled in her mind with Matsuhara and Matsushira. Worse than that, when the fifty-three glossy black heads bent over their papers, they all looked alike. Some of them looked alike even when they raised their faces to gaze at her. She confused Grace with Hisayo and Itsuo with Fred.

*How can I be so undiscerning?* Helen had no such problem. By the end of the day, Helen was calling many by name.

The children were obedient and orderly but asked no questions and volunteered nothing. Jean tried everything she could think of to stir their interest, but they remained reserved and overly cautious.

By the end of the first week, Jean was exhausted and disheartened. After the children left Friday afternoon, she complained to Helen. "How can they learn when they just repeat what I say . . . with no questions . . . no enthusiasm?"

"They're doing all right. You just need time to get to know them."

"I suppose that's part of it, but with so many kids, it'll take me forever. It would do them good just to get out of this bare classroom." An idea blossomed on the edge of her thoughts. "I wonder if we could take them on an outing—a field trip?"

"Where to?"

"Oh, somewhere outside the fence. The men go to the farms, and the young people have been allowed to go out on hikes."

"Yes, but our kids are too little for that. They could get hurt, and anyway, they're doing fine for their first week. Some are just shy, and all of them are more respectful than the children we worked with for practice teaching."

Jean sighed and held her aching head. "I suppose you're right. Maybe I'm the one who needs a day out of here. Still, they would have fun on a simple nature hike." She slowly straightened in her chair. "I'm going to ask for permission."

"You're the teacher," Helen muttered and began to sweep the room.

Jean jumped up and caught hold of the broom handle, pulling her to a halt. "Helen, you're the teacher, too, whether the principal thinks so or not. Don't you see what fun it would be for them? We can ask several mothers to help us—that way we can get acquainted with them too. Please help me do this."

Helen's frown smoothed. She shook her head in amazement. "I can't believe I'm agreeing to this. You could sell an Eskimo an icebox."

"Not me. Fact is, you're a good teacher who can see the value of an activity that will stimulate learning."

Helen ignored Jean's intended compliment. "You'll need a lot of luck to convince our principal."

"Maybe, maybe not." Jean wished Helen would soften up. Now that she was getting to know the girl with the geisha face, she felt they could have been good friends . . . in another time and place.

★

As it turned out, Helen was mistaken about the principal's reservations. Mrs. Smith thought it was a good idea. The next Wednesday, Jean and her class, with the help of Helen and five mother volunteers, marched out the sentry gate to explore the lower slope of Castle Rock, the picturesque bluff across the highway. Each child carried a tiny drawing board that Yosh had cut from scrap lumber in the furniture factory. The mothers carried the paper and crayons.

At the base of Castle Rock, Jean called everyone into a circle for final instructions. "This will be like mountain climbing," she said. "Stay close to your mother-leader. Wild things will run from us, but remember to watch for scorpions and spiders just as you do at school and at home. Look before you step or touch or sit."

As they moved away to explore, Jean went from one group to another. Using an old nature book of her own, she told them about the plants and insects they found. Soon from all sides she heard calls of: "Teacher, what's this? " and, "Teacher, look what I found!"

They picked up handfuls of tiny seashells from the sandy shale. Jean put them in a bag to take back to the classroom.

Finally she asked the children to choose suitable large rocks to use for desks and to draw a picture of something they had seen for the first time. While they worked, she and Helen walked from one to another to observe or assist. Some of the children showed great facility with their hands. Others struggled to draw.

"If it's hard to draw the shape, think more about the colors," she urged. "Do the colors first and then the lines."

"Teacher?" one boy, Masaru, asked shyly. "Can I write, instead of making a picture?"

This was what she had hoped for, the budding of independent creativity. "Yes, you may," she said, pleased to encourage him.

After a while she glanced at her watch and was surprised to see they'd been out for an hour and a half. "Come line up!" she called, "It's time to go back for lunch."

When they were in an orderly line, she counted heads. Twice she was interrupted by questions and had to start over, but at last she finished and came out with the correct number. They marched back down the slope with three mothers leading and the other two in the middle, while she and Helen brought up the rear.

Suddenly a high-pitched scream came from behind them. Jean whirled around. Masaru! Off to the right, about fifty yards away, half concealed by rocks. How had she not missed him?

He stood stiff, arms crossed over his chest, as if to protect himself. His shrieks were bloodcurdling. Jean cried to Helen, "Keep the children here."

She scrambled across the slope. A few feet from Masaru, she stopped in midstride. In front of him, at the base of a rock, slithered a rattlesnake.

# CHAPTER 5

The sight of a rattlesnake within striking distance of Masaru froze Jean in her tracks. Revulsion and terror gripped her.

Masaru had quieted to shuddering sobs.

"Masaru," Jean said firmly. "Don't move. Be quiet and don't move."

Trembling, he obeyed.

She stepped toward the snake. "Stay still," she repeated softly.

Masaru held his shaky stance.

The snake turned its triangle head toward Jean while she spoke in a low singsong to Masaru, telling him to step back slowly. He obeyed, and the snake did not turn toward him.

"Take one more quiet step back," she murmured. At the same time she stepped sideways away from Masaru. The snake turned its whole body to face her. "Now, Masaru, slowly turn around."

He did.

"Now run," she ordered in a stage whisper, keeping her eyes on the snake.

Masaru took off. The snake, remaining focused on her, raised its head, flicked out its tongue, and began to gather itself into a coil. She stepped back . . . one step . . . another . . . and then she spun around and fled.

Ahead of her Masaru stumbled and fell. She rushed to him, knelt, and gathered him in her arms. "My leg," he whimpered. "It bit my leg."

She laid him down carefully and pulled up his pants leg. Two fang marks on his calf were swelling already. His face looked gray, and his hands were cold. She had no snakebite kit, only a Boy Scout knife in her shoulder bag.

Keeping her voice steady, Jean said, "Masaru, I know it hurts, but please don't be afraid. I'm going to take care of you." She slit open his pants leg, and quickly slashed a strip of fabric from the hem of her cotton skirt. "I'm going to tie a tight bandage around your leg and then I'm going to fix the bite. Just try not to be afraid."

He nodded. Scared as he was, he continued to do exactly as she said. She wondered briefly how many children of her own culture would have such self-control. No. Each one would be different. It wasn't a cultural thing. She tied the cloth tightly above his knee, and then opened the small blade of her knife. *How am I going to do this?*

In eighth grade she'd taken a first aid class and remembered she had to cut at least one-fourth inch deep on the fang marks. Swiftly she made the first cut. Masaru screamed and fainted. She quickly plunged the blade into the other mark and began to suck blood and spit it out. After a while she realized Helen was standing beside her.

"I sent Mrs. Kimura to the hospital for help," Helen said. "The other mothers are taking the children back to the colony. Mrs. Hirata and I will help you carry him."

"Good," Jean gasped. "I've sucked out as much poison as I can."

They took turns carrying Masaru, still unconscious, down the slope of loose rocks and shale.

They had no more than staggered to the edge of the highway when a car inside the camp roared toward the gate, paused for an instant at the sentry post, and then swung across the road and braked in front of them. Tom Kagawa leaped out. He checked the tourniquet on Masaru's leg and felt the pulse in his neck.

Taking the boy in his arms, he climbed back in beside the driver. Over his shoulder, he ordered, "Get in back!"

The women climbed in.

As worried as Jean was about Masaru, she still felt a

reprimand in Tom's tone. *He's going to blast me for not taking better care of the children. And this time he's right.*

Heartsick for Masaru, Jean leaned forward and searched his pale face for any hopeful sign. As she watched, his eyelids flickered open. He stared blankly at Tom, and then he grimaced with pain and began to cry. With one hand, Tom cradled his head and smoothed his hair. "It's okay. . . ." He glanced at Jean for help on his name.

"Masaru," she supplied.

"Masaru," Tom said in a firm, calm voice, "we're taking you to the doctor. He'll make you feel better. You're going to be okay, little brother."

The boy's cries subsided to hiccuping sobs.

"We're almost there, Masaru. Soon you'll feel better," said Jean, leaning over Tom's shoulder.

"Teacher—" He started to cry again. "I didn't mean to get lost, and when I tried to catch up, I didn't see the snake."

"Oh, Masaru, that's all right. I know you did the best you could."

The car pulled up to the hospital, another complex of tar-papered barracks. Tom jumped out with the child in his arms and dashed inside. The women clambered out of the backseat and followed him. Apparently forewarned, Mrs. Ito, Masaru's mother, was there waiting. She darted an accusing look at Jean and ran at Tom's heels into the emergency room.

Jean turned to Helen. "She must hate me for letting her son be hurt."

Helen said, "You mustn't blame her. She's very upset."

Mrs. Hirata said nothing.

Jean made no effort to defend herself. "I should have missed him when I counted the children. He wouldn't have been bitten if only I had counted correctly."

Mrs. Hirata looked ready to agree. Helen glanced at the mother and then said to Jean, "You did the best you could. I should have counted too."

It was gratifying to have Helen defend her in front of Mrs. Hirata, but Jean knew Helen's real feelings. She had not wanted to take the children out in the beginning, and she had been proven correct.

Shaking her head in remorse, Jean pressed her lips together to keep them from trembling. She had no idea whether a rattlesnake bite was life threatening for a child his size.

A nurse brought Masaru's weeping mother back to the waiting room. She asked the waiting women, "Would you stay with her until her husband comes?"

Near hysteria, Mrs. Ito pointed at Jean. "Not her. Because of her, my son may die!"

Mrs. Hirata took her by the arm. "Come, sit down. Kenji will soon be here." She looked at Jean and rolled her eyes toward the door.

Helen whispered, "It would be better if you leave."

Jean jogged the mile and a half to her classroom, not knowing whether the children had been returned to school. They hadn't. No doubt all the parents were hearing the frightening story of what had happened to Masaru.

She hurried back to her principal's office to report. Mrs. Smith paled as Jean delivered her account, but she said, "It's as much my fault as yours; I gave my permission. I thought the snakes would be hibernating by now. I'll tell the parents I'm responsible. However, in the future, we shall both be much more careful."

Jean nodded vigorously. "Yes," she agreed. Silently she added, *I won't ever take the children out again.*

"You go to your dorm and try to relax. I'll run over to the hospital to see if there's anything I can do, and I'll make sure you receive a report on the boy's condition."

Jean left and distractedly wandered to the post office to pick up her mail. Her Uncle Al had written, using a small plain envelope, instead of his office stationery. A V-mail letter—thin wartime stationery of one page that served as its own envelope when folded—was addressed in Rodger's handwriting. She carried both letters to the dorm without opening them. The rest of the teachers were still in class. She could read in private, a rare treat.

★

Jean sat on the edge of her cot and slit open Rodge's letter, taking care not to cut where his writing should be on the inside.

In smaller than normal writing he said, "September 3, 1942: Dear Jean, even though we're busy with ——————"—a phrase had been blacked out with heavy permanent ink by a censor—"I've had a lot of time to think. I hope you can forgive me for questioning your decision to teach the internees' kids. I was a jerk to be mad at the kids. They can't help what their parents do. And it is so like you to want to help them. That's what I love about you. Sorry. That just slipped out. The problem is, I love you and miss you so much."

*Oh, Rodge, please don't love me.*

"It's rough out here"—the next three sentences were blacked out. "Dear Jeanie-with-the-light-brown-hair, the longer we're apart the more I know you're the only girl for me. I promise not to mention this again, but I have to say it now, because we're ——————." The rest of the sentence disappeared under the censor's ink.

Jean held the paper up to the lightbulb in her desk lamp, trying to see the hidden words. Nothing showed. She reread the parts that had been spared. The danger she sensed between the lines made her shiver.

"Lots of the men are homesick and talk about their hometowns and home cooking and their girls back home. Jeanie, I'm only homesick for you. Sometimes I pretend you're my girl, and I dream of you, like in Stephen Foster's old song, imagining you'll be waiting for me. Please forgive my rambling about this. I promise I won't hold you to anything you say in my daydreams—Your Old Faithful Bad Penny, Rodge."

Her tears turned his writing into a blur. He was headed for battle—maybe fighting right now. *He could die like Dave. Oh, Rodge. I wish I could be your girl.*

She wished it so much, she couldn't answer his letter right away. She didn't have the heart to say what she should to keep from leading him on. She folded the V-mail carefully and tucked it in her footlocker beside the Bible her grandmother had sent with her.

Ripping open the second letter, Jean scanned Uncle Al's bold handwriting. Until her move to Tulelake, his personal letters had always been typed by his secretary. Now, in addition to his privately written notes, he had asked Jean to burn them as soon as she'd read them.

"September 17: Dear Jean," he scrawled in a black ink, "I hope you're not too uncomfortable in your new home. The Boss," he used his code name for the President, "asked me this morning if I had any word from you. Your last note didn't tell me much. I need specific details.

"These are trying times. The news from the front isn't good. The Germans are inside Stalingrad now. I don't know how the Russians can hold out. And just tonight I learned that the Japanese have been able to get reinforcements onto Guadalcanal, which means our men will face terrible odds when they attack. We must control that island before we can take back any part of the South Pacific.

"This is all just to say, send me every detail you can right away, even if you feel it isn't much. You and I can make a difference in this hell called war. Affectionately, Uncle Al."

Jean carried his letter to the stove, tossed it in, and touched a lighted match to it. Might as well answer right now, she decided. Writing would help pass the time while she waited to hear about Masaru. She pulled her writing pad from her footlocker and sat cross-legged on her cot with her plumped-up pillow for a lap table.

Struggling to keep her thoughts off Masaru, she told about meeting Helen's family and chronicled the Labor Day celebration. "The Kagawas have invited me to their apartment to visit, but I haven't been there yet. The morale in the project—that's what all of the teachers call the residential area of the camp—seems to be good. A lot of these people look upon being here as their contribution to the war effort. By peacefully obeying the government, I mean. There are some who are angry, but I think they are in the minority. I'm enclosing reports on the young men I've met who seem worth watching. Helen's brother Tom, for instance. He's intelligent, aggressive, and seems chronically angry."

She paused, remembering his accusations. "He flew off at me soon after we met. He thinks Americans should be ashamed of imprisoning the Japanese and frequently says so. His buddies are just as upset." She quoted the biting remarks she could remember, adding, "I hope I can come through with what you need, but so far I've probably made that task more difficult."

She told him about her disastrous field trip, explaining, "Tom looked angry, as usual, when he rushed Masaru to the hospital. The boy's mother blames me, too, and I think a lot of other people will when they hear about it.

"Tom says lots of people are suspicious of the Caucasian teachers, thinking we are the dregs of our profession or we wouldn't be here. Now I've given them good reason to doubt my ability as well as my concern for the children. I'll do my best to make amends, but I'm afraid this will slow down my access to the people and to information."

Several teachers came into the dorm, said "hi," grabbed their towels, and headed for the showers. They apparently hadn't heard about Masaru; at least they didn't say anything.

Jean signed her letter and placed it in a stamped envelope. Glancing at her alarm clock on the dresser, she saw that she could drop it off at the post office on the way to the mess hall if she showered later. Her prompt mailing might make up for the shortage of details in her previous report.

At supper, Jean sat between Ann and Mary.

Between bites Ann said, "I heard about your field trip. I hope the boy is okay."

Jean laid down her fork and sighed. "So do I. I haven't heard a word, and I'm afraid to go to the hospital and ask because his mother was so upset at me."

"That's too bad," Mary said, "but it was an accident."

"I should have prevented it."

Barb, a teacher from San Francisco, seated across from Jean, said, "Well, it does make all of us look bad."

"That's a stupid remark!" snapped Mary.

"Come on," said Ann. "Let's not make a big deal of this. Jean was doing her best. It could have happened to any of us."

Barb shook her head. "Not to me. I wouldn't take my class out on those rocks for anything."

"Neither would I," agreed another teacher farther down the table. "It's hard enough to win the trust of these parents without taking any risks with their children."

Mary jumped to her feet. "Look, you know-it-alls. Jean was doing what we all should be doing—making an extra effort to motivate her pupils. Now lay off of her."

Ann said firmly, "I second that."

Silence fell over the women sitting closest to them.

Jean tried to eat and found she couldn't swallow. After a few minutes, she said quietly, "Mary, Ann, thanks for standing up for me. I really appreciate your loyalty, but I guess I agree with what the others said." She stood up and turned to Barb and her friends. "I understand how you feel, and I'm sorry if I've made things more difficult for you."

She picked up her plate, took it to the dishwasher's counter, and left. Behind her, she heard Mary's feisty voice, again defending her.

As she headed down the plank steps of the mess hall, Mary stormed out. "What a batch of prissy hypocrites! From day one, Barb's mind has been on her next date with the guards more than on teaching these kids. I think that's the main reason she came here. She's having the time of her life every night, playing the field."

Jean smiled. Mary was a party girl, too, but Jean had learned that she was what Grandmother would call a good girl. For all her playfulness, she was discriminating and did not lead the men on to expect anything more than friendship and a sympathetic ear. *Underneath the teasing and fun, she looks at men as seriously as I do.* Aloud Jean said, "Thanks for defending me, but you didn't have to leave your supper. I'm okay."

Mary shrugged her shoulders. "I was done anyway. And except for Ann, I didn't like the company."

"I hope we're not going to have cliques here," said Jean. "We can't avoid each other, and it's so childish."

"Yeah, but cows can't change their spots. Barb is a walking clique all by herself and probably has been since she was three. She needs a verbal swat now and then to keep her in line."

"I'm not good at that. Maybe if I'd lived in the college dorm, I'd do better."

"Maybe, but those who don't have spots can't grow them either."

"You're calling me a cow too?" Jean cried in mock horror.

Mary threw an arm around her shoulder, gave her a squeeze, and laughed. "In a manner of speaking—and me too. Cows are innately nicer than most of us."

Jean chuckled. "I'm so glad you decided to come here to teach. When we get our apartments, will you be my roommate?"

"Naturally. I thought you'd never ask."

★

In the dorm Jean spread notebook papers on her bed and reviewed her lesson plans for the next day. She would use the shells the children had gathered from the sandy soil of Castle Rock for arithmetic. First thing in the morning, however, she'd have to talk about Masaru and try to dispel their fears. *I've got to know how he is. I'll have to go over to the hospital before bedtime, if I don't hear.* She revised her plans and dropped an art project in favor of Helen's music instruction.

The teachers came into the dorm by twos and threes. Several stopped to offer sympathy; others just smiled and went on to their own lesson plans. A friendly atmosphere prevailed, for which Jean was thankful. Barb and her friends remained notable by their absence. But then, Barb seldom studied in the dorm after supper. Mary's assessment of her seemed to fit.

Someone called from the doorway, "Jean, you have company!"

Jean laid aside her papers and made her way down the aisle between the cots. Helen stood soberly on the doorstep. Tom waited a few paces away. Jean searched his face anxiously, but his expression was unreadable.

Helen spoke first. "Masaru will be all right."

"Oh, I'm so glad! I was afraid . . . he's so little, and I didn't know . . ."

Tom stepped forward. "He's going to be fine. The doctors said your quick action probably saved his life. The fangs went deep, but you removed much of the poison before it could be picked up."

"What a relief!" Jean suddenly felt light-headed. Her ears began to ring. Before her eyes, Tom began to disappear into a fog. She sank down to sit on the top step. Tom reached out and shoved her head down over her knees. She instinctively struggled against his grip on the back of her head, but to no avail.

About the time her vision cleared, he let go. "Easy does it. Sit up slowly. You were about to faint."

She straightened up cautiously but said, "I have never fainted in my life."

"Bet you didn't eat supper," said Tom.

"Not much. In fact, I never had lunch either."

"Helen, give her that cookie you were saving for Margie," he ordered.

"Oh no, I'm fine."

Helen sat down beside her and handed her an oatmeal cookie. "Eat it. Margie won't miss it."

"It'll raise your blood sugar and make you feel better in a hurry," Tom explained.

While Jean ate, Helen said, "I thought you'd still be blaming yourself."

"You're right. And you were right in the first place about not taking the children out. It was all my fault. I can't forgive myself and I don't suppose Mr. and Mrs. Ito can forgive me either." She not only wanted their forgiveness, she needed it for the sake of her secret mission.

Tom said, "Mr. and Mrs. Ito attend our church. Why don't you come Sunday and meet them."

Jean cast aside her anxiety about being in an unfamiliar Buddhist service in the Japanese language and said, "I will. Where do you meet?"

"We attend the Union Christian services at number 708," Tom said.

"You're Christians?" Jean exclaimed. Only when she heard herself did she recognize the prejudice of her assumption. Chagrined, she glanced at Tom, hoping he had missed the implication of her remark.

"Did you think we were Emperor worshipers?" Tom asked soberly, but he was fighting a grin.

Jean was glad it was growing dark. Her cheeks burned with embarrassment. She stammered. "No. . . . But I expected you to be Buddhist. They have church on Sunday too," she added defensively. She stood up on steady legs; the cookie had done its work.

Tom said, "More than a third of us who are imprisoned here are Christians."

Jean didn't know what to say. If she expressed her true surprise, it would sound even more prejudiced. Even if she commented favorably, it would sound like a put-down to the internees who were not Christians.

Tom caught her eye and smiled disarmingly. "It's okay. We all have our little prejudices."

"Tom," Helen said in a chilly tone, "we've done what we came for. We need to get home."

"Yes, teacher," he mimicked in a little boy voice. "I'm sure she keeps the kids in line for you."

"Truth is," Jean said soberly, "the children have been so good, I thought they were bored. Helen was right when she said they've been taught to be very respectful and obedient. Masaru's obedience probably saved his life."

"We've got a lot of good kids here," Tom agreed. "I pray we can keep them that way."

He said "pray" with a serious inflection; it seemed like more than a figure of speech. Jean was surprised. He obviously believed in God, but did he actually believe his personal prayers would be answered?

She hadn't been to church since leaving Salem, and she hadn't even thought of praying for Masaru this afternoon. If Dave had not been killed, she would have. *Back then I believed in romance and happy endings—and prayer too.*

That night after the dorm was quiet and dark, Jean silently prayed, *God, if you're there, thank you for saving Masaru. Help him to get well soon . . . and please keep Rodge safe. . . .*

Then her heart cried out, *Why didn't you keep Dave safe?*

She stopped trying to pray. Her mind drifted back to Rodger's letter. What should she say to him? She was too tired to think . . . to decide. She gave up the struggle, and a dulling blanket of sleep fell over her.

# CHAPTER 6

Sunday morning at the Union Christian Church, Jean was the only Caucasian. The church, like everything else at Tulelake, was housed in a barrack building.

When Jean went inside, she saw Mrs. Ito, but there was no opportunity to go speak to her before the service began. Jean shrank down into her seat beside the Kagawas, dreading the moment when she would have to approach Masaru's parents.

The bare walls and the desolate view of the camp through the small paned windows gave her a trapped feeling. She glanced around at the internees. She was in Tulelake of her own volition; the rest of the congregation was not. And yet at this moment, they looked more free than she felt.

To her surprise, the whole service was in English. In fact, it was very much like church had been back in Salem: a few familiar hymns, a solo by a young woman with a pleasing contralto voice, and the inevitable announcements. The sermon, filled with statements of faith, made her angry. These people were as out of touch with reality as her grandmother. Sitting in a prison camp, they talked about the goodness of God and in the same breath said he was all powerful. A good person, if he were all powerful, would not let the war go on. Certainly Dave, weak as he had been, was better than their God. *If there is a God, either he isn't powerful or he doesn't care about us.*

After the benediction, an elderly man in front of Jean turned and greeted her with a warm smile. "How nice to have you with us."

Standing as erect as a young soldier, he was no taller than Jean. Unlike most of the men, he was bald and wore a sparse, short white beard. His tan skin wrinkled deepest in all of the smile lines. His kind eyes behind metal-rimmed spectacles did not hurry to look away from Jean.

Mr. Kagawa introduced her to him. "Miss Thornton, this is Pastor Ichiba, one of our beloved retired ministers. Of course, one such as he can never really retire; he continues to encourage us. Pastor, Miss Thornton is one of our teachers and a former classmate of Helen's at Willamette University."

Pastor Ichiba bowed his head to her in the Japanese manner. "We are very grateful for the teachers who have been willing to come at this difficult time. I hope you are not too uncomfortable."

"Oh, no!" Jean assured him brightly. "And the children are a delight to teach. I just hope I can do well enough for them."

Pastor Ichiba continued to gaze into her eyes. "I'm sure you can and will," he said. "You must not let feelings of inadequacy disturb you. We are all striving to do well in very difficult circumstances, you know." His friendly smile removed any sense of criticism from his words.

Standing beside Jean, Tom said, "Pastor Ichiba, Miss Thornton is troubled about an accident to one of her pupils last week. Would you be willing to ask the parents, Mr. and Mrs. Ito, if she may talk to them?"

Jean wanted to flee. "I don't want to impose on Pastor Ichiba!"

The older man merely smiled wider. "I shall be delighted to introduce you to them. Just wait here a moment. I will bring them." He turned and with numerous stops to shake hands and return greetings, he worked his way through the standing congregation toward Mr. and Mrs. Ito.

Jean flashed Tom a look that she hoped would express her indignation. "I wish you hadn't done that," she said in a low voice.

"I thought Pastor Ichiba's help would make it easier for you."

"I could have done it without bothering him. After all, I've already met Mrs. Ito."

His lips tightened, and his face seemed to close like a book. "My mistake. Of course, you could have."

Helen, talking to another young woman, missed their brief dialogue. She touched Jean's arm, "I'd like you to meet my friend, Betty Shintaku. We've known each other since first grade."

Jean was surprised at how much friendlier Helen seemed here in the church.

*The sermon must have done her some good,* thought Jean wryly, as she acknowledged the introduction. *I wonder if it will last through Monday.*

Betty, in contrast to Helen, was very short and round-faced, with a smooth fluff of a pompadour over her forehead and a bright smile that would do justice to any toothpaste ad. After Betty, there followed a procession of Helen's friends, who greeted Jean warmly. After hearing the first few names, Jean was as confused as she'd been the first day of school, trying to remember the names of her pupils. Across the room, Jean could see Pastor Ichiba talking earnestly with Mr. and Mrs. Ito. As they glanced her way, her discomfort increased.

Two boys who looked to be just entering their teens lingered at Tom's side. They smiled shyly at Jean when he gave her their names. Tom then turned attention to them, speaking quietly.

Jean listened curiously.

"The point I was trying to make, fellas," Tom said, "is that Christ is as much of God as we can comprehend—God focused down to a size we can take in—"

"Miss Thornton," Pastor Ichiba's voice drew her attention away from Tom. "Mr. and Mrs. Ito would like to thank you for taking such quick action to help Masaru."

Masaru's mother and father stood a step behind the elderly man.

Smiling at the calm-faced woman who had screamed at her last Wednesday, Jean said, "Thank me? I'm so sorry he was hurt. Can you forgive me?"

Mr. Ito said quietly but firmly, "There is nothing to forgive. It was an accident. We do not blame you, so you should not blame yourself."

Now Mrs. Ito smiled and added, "I owe you an apology. I was so frightened . . . but that is no excuse." She held out her hand. "Please forgive me."

Jean took her hand and returned her firm grip. "Of course. I don't blame you a bit; I was scared too. How is Masaru?"

"We will take him home as we go from church today. His leg is sore, of course, but the doctor says he may come to school tomorrow. I think he will be more obedient in the future."

"Oh, Mrs. Ito, his obedience probably saved his life. If he had panicked . . . moved wrong . . . I hate to think about it," she said with a shudder. "You should be very proud of him. He's a good boy and so talented. He just lost himself in what he was doing."

Mr. and Mrs. Ito beamed, shook hands again, and excused themselves to go to the hospital.

Pastor Ichiba said, "They are truly grateful to you."

"They're so kind. Thank you for speaking to them first. I was nervous about approaching them."

"I am happy to be of some small use. I hope you have found our worship service beneficial." His eyes asked questions she didn't want to answer.

"I have," she lied easily. Her relief over Mr. and Mrs. Ito's kind reception gave her a lift, despite her irritation with the sermon.

Pastor Ichiba smiled. With an innocent trust that assured her she was playing her part well, he said, "The church comes alive when we most need it. This tragic war and the internment will be a blessing to us, if we can embrace it." His tone was optimistic, and yet there was sorrow in his eyes—as if he were filled with a painful foreknowing. And then it was gone, erased by his warm smile.

His statement startled and bewildered Jean. "Embrace the internment?" she echoed.

"Yes. All troubles are opportunities, if we accept them as from God . . . if we walk into them and embrace them, instead of resenting them and wanting to flee from them."

"Even when things are unfair?" Jean asked uneasily. *Is he some kind of fanatic?* she wondered.

"Unfair things most of all. Troubles always seem unfair because we seldom see what we actually deserve. But we Christians are so blessed. Someday I would like to tell you how much God has blessed me."

"I'd like that," Jean lied. She'd heard "testimonies" when she'd visited a classmate's church in Salem and had hated them. The whole process, a prolonged telling and retelling of past sins, had been embarrassing. Some people apparently had done nothing worse than craving chocolate, while others seemed to relish dwelling on ugliness to show how much they had changed.

Pastor Ichiba grinned impishly. "Do not worry, Miss Thornton. I like to talk about God, not about myself."

The way he said it made her laugh. He had seen right through her and had not condemned her. There was warmth and real happiness in his ensuing laughter.

*I wish I could talk to him,* she thought, *but he's the one person I must avoid. I wouldn't be able to fool him for long about anything.*

Before leaving the building, Jean thanked Tom for asking the elderly man to help her talk to Masaru's parents. "He's an amazing person," she said. "He made it much easier for me, and for them, too, I think."

Tom nodded. "Pastor Ichiba is the reason I became a Christian. I watched him for a long time and finally decided that he was not explainable without believing in the Christ he proclaimed." As he spoke, his face softened with the same strange expression of innocence she'd seen on Pastor Ichiba's face.

She caught herself staring and looked away quickly. She almost wished she had not mentioned him in her letter to Uncle Al. Despite his angry words, he did not seem to be the type to go in for espionage. *But then,* she realized, *he would probably say the same thing about me.*

★

Monday morning Masaru was in class, limping and confined to his chair. His wound and his adventure made him an overnight hero. The other children crowded around him, questioning and exclaiming over his impressive bandage.

"Miss Thornton, did you really cut his leg to get the poison out?" one after another asked.

Each time they did, Jean's stomach lurched at the memory. Nevertheless, she tried to answer them frankly and simply. Gradually she led them into a discussion of what they should do when they were out together again. As they responded to her "what if" questions, she sensed that their experience on the hike had bonded them into a classroom family. Their concern for Masaru and their trust in her filled her with an unexpected rush of affection. Several girls leaned confidently against her and the boys crowded close.

Finally she told them to go to their chairs and remain standing for the flag salute. In seconds fifty-three earnest seven-year-olds faced the flag. They recited the pledge of allegiance and then sang "America" with patriotic fervor.

Helen passed out the arithmetic pages they had printed one at a time on a gelatin mimeo pad. Watching the children eagerly set to work on their sums, Jean decided their trek up Castle Rock truly had awakened them in some way.

Surely, despite Masaru's injury, her plan had helped. Some good had come out of the trouble. But was it worth the cost?

She remembered Pastor Ichiba's cryptic remark about embracing trouble and wondered what he would say. Certainly not that a snake-bitten child was a necessary evil to bring about good. Maybe someday she could ask him.

During the next couple of weeks, many of the parents of Jean's class sent notes, offering to help whenever she wished to take the children on another field trip. Jean planned a simpler hike on level, open ground, and she informed Uncle Al that Masaru's accident had come out all right.

★

In October, high school was dismissed for a few days so the students could help harvest a bumper crop of potatoes. Tulelake shipped out tons of potatoes for the war effort, and their success at farming seemed to raise morale among the internees.

Jean was surprised at this until she remembered her earlier shock over seeing service flags with blue stars, hanging in project apartment windows. Some families had sons who, like

Dave, had enlisted before war had been declared and had continued to serve while their families were interned. Two service flags on her route to school bore gold stars, signifying a family member had been killed in action.

The sight of the gold stars never failed to jolt Jean back to Pearl Harbor Day. She had not hung a service flag for Dave. At first it had hurt too much and now in Tulelake she couldn't. Her memorial to him was private—a storehouse of vignettes. She would always remember the glint of the sun turning his chestnut hair as red as the coat of his sorrel mare, his big gentle hands calming a foal on his dad's ranch, the glow in his eyes when he surveyed their range land from the top of the rim rock, and his joy in the winter snow and spring rain that nourished the land. He'd made the common things in life so wonderful.

★

As the Tulelake farms closed down for winter, internee leaders asked permission to have a harvest festival on Saturday, October 31. The harvest was something to be proud of, something worth celebrating. The Caucasian camp administrators agreed.

Helen said the adults were grasping at anything to keep up morale. School, church, sports, and dozens of special interest clubs flourished, but the internment lay heavy on everyone. People had lost everything. If they were to survive with health and honor, they had to put every effort into not letting their spirits be broken.

Jean reasoned that in wartime, everyone paid a painful price and most people lost a lot, but she didn't say that to Helen.

The morning of the harvest festival, Jean dreamed she was still at Willamette, snuggling close to Dave in the Bear Cat Cavern, warming to his impulsive stolen kisses. "Marry me now," he whispered and drew her closer. She awoke and tried to flee back into the dream, but she couldn't.

Jean glanced across at Mary's neatly made bed. She was already gone to breakfast. She had a date for the day with Jimmy Duggan. They had wanted to set Jean up with a blind date, but she'd gotten out of it without having to lie. She really preferred the harvest festival to dating anyone, especially a stranger.

Jean climbed out of bed, reminding herself that the festival was an excellent opportunity for fact-finding. Helen had remained somewhat friendly ever since Jean had attended church. It had not been difficult to persuade her to let Jean help in a fish pond booth sponsored by the 4-H girls.

★

By the time Jean reached the 4-H booth midmorning, the area between blocks 24 and 25 looked like a miniature county fair. It had filled with almost thirty carnival booths—offering games such as penny throws, ball throws, bingo, ring tosses, and even a Popsicle and mask stand.

The smell of hamburgers sizzling with onions and the tang of hot dogs and mustard drew youngsters like bees to nectar. Those were foods everyone missed and craved because of the stringent rationing of meat. Helen had been complaining about more meatless meals than usual. Project cooks must have been saving ration points for today.

Off to one side shouts of laughter rose from a pen where young men struggled to catch pigs that had been greased for the occasion. In another location Helen's parents and other adults were enjoying a musical program made up of everyone's favorite records.

The fish pond booth was fun. The 4-H girls had wrapped all kinds of donated trinkets. Children were given fishing poles with string lines to dangle over the counter. From a concealed place, a girl attached a wrapped prize to each pole and then tugged on the line to signal a fish had taken the hook.

Jean helped fasten the prizes onto the hooks until time for the Mardi Gras parade, and then everything stopped for the parade. All the colorful costumes had been hand sewn because there were no sewing machines in the project. The amount of effort and ingenuity that had gone into the festival impressed Jean, but she could imagine what some people on the outside would think of such a festival in an internment camp.

When the parade ended, a scarcely recognizable Tom appeared at the fish booth, brightly garbed as a clown. In each hand he held a neatly wrapped hamburger, one for Helen and one for Jean.

"Thanks!" Jean said gratefully. "I don't know when I've

been hungrier." With relish she bit into hers before asking, "Aren't you having any?"

His grin stretched his painted smile. "I already did. Couldn't wait."

He lounged against the booth, talking until Yosh, Fuj, and Tad soon showed up. When he turned to leave with them, Jean felt a twinge of disappointment. She'd hoped he and his friends would spend time with Helen and her, as they had on Labor Day, and possibly introduce her to other young men.

As she watched their departing backs, Tom paused and called back to her, "Pastor Ichiba is leading a Bible study tomorrow night. Maybe you'd like to come?"

Although she'd told Pastor Ichiba she would come to church, she had not returned. No other Caucasians went to the project church, or for that matter, to any project activities. It was a fine line to walk—to be where she needed to be and yet not attract undue attention to herself. And although she no longer valued church for herself, she felt a little squeamish about spying on people who were gathered for worship. Maybe the feeling was a holdover from her Sunday school days.

Well, no matter. She stopped analyzing and replied to Tom, "Yes, I'd like to come."

Jean watched the stage shows in the afternoon and identified a few more men who seemed angry and aggressive. She devised ways to be near them long enough to learn more about them and made a few secret notes when she returned to the fish pond booth.

By five o'clock she headed home for supper. Mary was still out, but Jean switched on her radio to listen to the news while she changed her clothes. Lowell Thomas's clipped words bristled with excitement. A giant air and naval battle was going on in the Solomon Islands.

*Could Rodge be there?* Jean shuddered and flipped off the radio.

Seating herself at her desk, she tried to complete the notes she had scribbled so hastily before she forgot the details. She wrote with a vengeance until she couldn't remember any more and then sealed them in an envelope addressed to Uncle

Al. In another letter to her grandmother, she described the events of the day as if she were a tourist visiting a foreign country, hoping her light tone would ease Grandmother's distress over the living conditions in the internment camp.

Grandmother had been begging her to come home to Salem for a real Thanksgiving. Jean was homesick, but she felt going home now would only prolong her homesickness. She had tried to explain this. She couldn't reveal her other reason—her wish to avoid questions that would force her to lie more than she already had.

★

Sunday evening Jean put on her forest green gabardine suit. She dabbed clear nail polish on the beginning of a run in her best pair of stockings and slipped her feet into low spectator pumps. Brushing her hair into a smooth, turned-under page-boy, she decided not to wear a hat.

Mary looked up from her lesson-planning notebook and teased, "You finally going on a date?"

"No. I wish you'd go with me to this Bible study," she said.

"Sorry, kid. You know we Catholics can be too easily misled." Mary joked about some of the rules she followed, but Jean knew they were important to her.

"Just thought I'd ask. I hate walking in by myself."

Mary opened her mouth, closed it, and then finally said what was on her mind. "Do you really think it's a good idea to mix so much with the internees?"

"What do you mean?" Jean asked cautiously.

"Well, none of the rest of us do, and it sets you up for gossip."

"So who's talking?" asked Jean, trying to sound as if she didn't care.

"Barb and her friends."

"You know she gossips whether she has a reason or not." Jean sensed Mary had more to say. "Is that all that's bothering you?"

"No. . . . I don't think it's safe. You're too trusting. You could be drawn into more than you imagine."

"Mary, stop hedging," said Jean with the first irritation she'd ever felt for her new friend. "Say what you mean."

"Oh, Jean . . . I know it's none of my business, but you could even become attracted to a Japanese man, if you got to know one well enough, and then what would you do? You know you could never marry."

Jean laughed in relief. "Always the matchmaker. I can promise you, that will never happen." Then she sobered and added, "I didn't expect you to be so against mixed marriages."

"Kid, that's the point—you're so naive. The truth is, you can never tell how people may feel about such things, and the way we are in this country, a mixed marriage would not be fair to the children."

"I agree. Sorry I upset you. Do you realize we almost had a fight over something that will never happen?"

Mary chuckled and shook her head. "Whew, boy. You really had me jumping for a minute. I'm sorry I butted into your business. Forget what I said."

"Forgotten," promised Jean, "but thanks for being concerned."

"Any time, pal." Mary closed her notebook and pulled out her compact to refresh her red lipstick. "Time for me to go meet Jimmy. We're catching the bus to K. Falls for a movie tonight—Betty Hutton in *Stage Door Canteen.*"

"How long does the bus take?" Klamath Falls was about thirty-five miles to the north, just over the Oregon border.

"A little over an hour. It makes a lot of stops. Sometime you should come along . . . do you good to get out of here."

"I will—"

From the far end of the barrack one of the teachers yelled, "Hey, Jean, you've got company!"

Jean gave one last dab to her own lipstick and went to see who had come.

Helen stood waiting.

"Am I glad to see you!" Jean exclaimed. "I was just wishing I had company." She added quickly. "It's just that I don't know anyone or what to expect."

"That's what Tom thought."

"Tom?" Jean repeated.

Helen gave a half-smile. "It was his idea for me to come."

"Well, thanks anyway. Do you often do what he wants?"

"Not when I don't want to." This time Helen really smiled.

Jean smiled back. "Come on in while I get my coat. I think it's already below freezing."

"Thanks, but I'll wait here."

Jean didn't argue. Back inside, she slipped into her winter coat and tied a soft woolen bandanna over her hair. Helen was carrying a Bible. Jean thought about Grandmother's Bible in the bottom of her footlocker and decided to leave it there.

On the way to the Union Church, she and Helen discussed lesson plans for the next day. By the time they arrived at the barrack the internees euphemistically called the chapel, the room was full. Jean had not expected such a large attendance on a Sunday evening.

Pastor Ichiba's Bible study turned out to be a teaching sermon. The flow of his words—a colorful interweaving of captivating stories and strong, simple wisdom—fascinated Jean. She'd never heard such a vivid teaching style.

At one point Tom, two seats away, caught her eye, and flashed her a closed-lip smile, as if he understood her appreciation.

Afterward, because it was dark, Tom joined Helen to walk Jean back to the teachers' dorm. He asked, "So what did you think of Pastor Ichiba's teaching?"

"He's good," said Jean emphatically. "He sure made a strong case for telling the truth, hurt or not."

"'Speaking the truth in love' is a good goal," Helen said.

"I disagree," came Tom's voice through the darkness. "Sticking to the truth ought to be a daily standard instead of something to strive for."

"Telling the truth isn't that easy when you know it will really hurt someone," said Jean.

"The truth can never hurt as much as kind lies," Tom said. He sounded angry again.

Jean waited for him to go on, but he didn't.

The wind suddenly blasted them, straight from snow-covered Mount Shasta. They had reached the middle of a fire break, the wide open area between wards of barracks. An icy gust lashed coarse sand against Jean's legs. "If we had snow, this could be a blizzard!" she shouted.

"If it doesn't ease off, we could be caught in a dust storm," Tom called back. "We'd better get a move on."

Jean walked as fast as she could in her dress shoes. When they reached the edge of the project, with her dorm in sight, she panted, "I can make it alone from here. You'd better hurry on home."

They refused to leave her, however, until they reached her doorstep. With quick thanks, she said goodnight and slipped inside. She was the first one back home. A single lightbulb burned in the long room, and the fire had died down. She turned on more lights and, keeping her coat on, shoveled coal into both stoves. Outside, the wind pelted the windows with grit.

As the fire began to relieve the chilliness of the room, Jean decided the time had come to write to Rodge—as Pastor Ichiba had put it, to speak the truth. She lifted his letter from her footlocker and read it again. "I love you and miss you so much. . . . You're the only girl for me. . . . I promise I won't hold you to anything you say in my daydreams."

On thin airmail paper she wrote, "November 1, 1942: Dear Rodge, Winter isn't even here and boy, is it cold. . . ." She told him about a normal day for her and then with difficulty wrote, "I'm sorry I've taken so long to answer your letter, but I needed time to think. This is one of the hardest things I've ever had to do, but for your own good, please don't daydream about me or you'll be cheating yourself.

"I dearly love you as a friend, but as I said before, I can't love anyone the way I loved Dave, and I don't even want to. I know that there's a Miss Right for you somewhere who will love you the way Dave and I loved each other. That's what I want for you."

She brushed sudden tears from her cheeks. It sounded like such a rebuff when they weren't even going together. And yet, after all Rodger had done for her, he deserved better than kind lies. She painfully closed with: "Do you want me to keep writing? As always, Jean."

★

November passed quickly. Piercing cold weather kept the children's cheeks ruddy and made for fast games at recess—tag, Blind Man's Bluff, Drop the Handkerchief, and anything else to keep them moving for fifteen minutes.

At last the teachers' apartments were finished. Jean and Mary moved into the one assigned them, rejoicing over a real bathroom to be shared with only two other teachers. Their end-of-the-barrack apartment was separated from the next one by room dividers and an open walkway. Above the dividers, which did not reach to the ceiling, the building was open, allowing lights—bare bulbs in the ceiling—to shine from one apartment to another. Still, the new quarters gave Jean a sense of a place of her own and a little more room.

The divider walls contained small closets. For each of the teachers, the project furniture factory had provided a real single bed, a simple upholstered chair, a straight chair, a small table that served as a desk, and a dresser with drawers. In the middle of the room stood a round black coal stove with coal buckets, a shovel, and a poker.

On the wall on her side of the room, Jean placed one of her own watercolor landscapes of Willamette Valley hills, an old family photo of Grandmother, Uncle Al, Aunt Esther, Aunt Ruth, and Giselle, and another photo of a group of her college friends that included Dave.

★

As Thanksgiving Day drew near, Jean was glad she had decided to stay at Tulelake. All of the teachers were staying. With gas rationing, driving was out of the question, and public transportation was also rationed. Servicemen and their wives received priority on trains and buses, and anyone else had to wait.

A few days before Thanksgiving, when Jean picked up her mail after school, she found a letter from Caroline and one from her grandmother. Jean sighed. *Grandmother is not going to give up trying to get me home for a few days*.

She opened Caroline's letter first. "I'm marrying the boy next door, before he ships out," she wrote. "I learned from your experience. If he shouldn't come back, I want as much of him as I can have, even a baby, although he wants to wait on that."

Jean smiled, picturing Caroline's happiness. *Good for you!* she cheered silently.

Then with resignation she tore open her grandmother's letter. Scanning the precise penmanship of the first sentences, she winced and closed her eyes.

## CHAPTER 7

Rodger *missing in action?* Jeanie opened her eyes and forced herself to read on.

"Rodger's parents say the ship's captain gives them no hope that he could be alive somewhere. They simply could not recover his body. His mother felt he would want you to know. She said his last letter home was so full of talk about you, they wondered if he had an understanding with you.

"I didn't know what to say. Of course, one way or the other, I knew you'd want to send your condolences."

The letter went on, but Jean couldn't read any further. She shoved it into her coat pocket. Trudging home, she held back her tears. She collected her towel, soap, washcloth, and fresh clothes and headed for the shower, the only place she could go for privacy. She locked the door, leaned against it, and gave way to pain that threatened to choke her.

They said there was no hope, and she must accept the fact, but losing Rodge was almost like losing Dave all over again. Rodger alone had understood her grief. His love for Dave had been an anchor to her, and now, if he had read her last letter, he probably had died feeling rejected. She couldn't bear the thought. She wanted to just give up and walk away from everyone and everything.

Automatically she undressed and turned on the water. Stepping under the warm stream, she let the water course over her face, mix with her tears, and rinse them away. When she was all cried out, she toweled herself dry in the damp cold air of the bathroom, and at last a burning outrage came to her rescue. She wanted to get even with the Japanese who had forced war on the United States and had killed Dave and Rodge and so many other good men.

Anger gave Jean the strength to walk back to her room and continue to play the part her uncle had said would help the war effort. She couldn't bring herself to talk with Mary about Rodge. Somehow she got through the rest of the day without having to tell anyone about losing him.

★

The next day at school, all the while Jean was teaching, her thoughts kept slipping away to Rodge. She remembered him smiling, sympathetic, funny, and sometimes a little cocky.

While she sat at her desk during the children's writing period, the wistful words of his last letter came to her as if she had memorized them. "I love you and miss you so much. . . . I daydream about you."

She imagined him reading her last letter to him. "I can't love you. . . . I don't even want to."

She couldn't keep from imagining how he may have died. It hurt so much. Had she misjudged her affection for him? Could she have loved him enough to marry him?

"Miss Thornton?"

She jumped.

Masaru was standing beside her desk, and beyond him Helen watched her with a puzzled frown. All of the children were staring at her.

"You said you would read to us again," Masaru said, "if we finished our writing in time. We have finished." He placed the stack of papers he had collected in front of her.

She glanced at her watch. Twenty minutes until dismissal. "Everyone is really finished?" she asked needlessly.

Dozens of voices chorused, "Yes, Miss Thornton."

"That's wonderful. Okay. Bring your chairs up and sit close to my desk."

With a minimum of scraping and thumping, they obeyed. Helen handed her the worn copy of *Mother West Wind Stories* opened at her marker. She read as expressively as she could until mercifully Helen signaled that it was time to straighten the room and go home.

After the last child was out the door, Helen asked bluntly, "Are you ill?"

"No. Why do you ask?"

"You might as well not have been here. You haven't heard half of what the kids said to you today." Helen's smooth features did not bend to the concern in her voice.

*She sounds so American, and yet right now she looks so alien.* Jean pushed aside the thought. "Have I really been that bad?"

"The fact that you don't even know it proves my point. What's wrong?" Jean suddenly wanted to tell her. Revealing her tragedy to Helen seemed less traumatic than talking to a close friend like Mary. "I . . . I've had some bad news . . . but I hoped it wouldn't show that much. Were the children upset?"

"No. I guess I'm the only one who is upset. Is there anything I can do to help?" Helen asked slowly.

"No. . . . Yes, there is. I need to talk. I'm used to handling things alone, but this . . ." To Jean's great embarrassment, she burst into tears.

Helen took her by the arm and led her back to her desk. "Come on. Sit down," she ordered. Helen sat beside her, quietly waiting.

Jean tried to stop crying. After a few minutes she regained control, blew her nose, and little by little told her about Rodger, their long friendship, her final letter to him, and the news that he was lost at sea and presumed dead. She never mentioned Dave.

Helen's face softened with sympathy. "If you had told Mrs. Smith, she would have given you the day off."

"I don't know. Rodge and I weren't engaged or anything, and I sent him a letter that was so rejecting. That's like being a traitor to our country in some people's eyes."

"But you told him before he left that you didn't want to marry him."

"Yes, but now . . . I almost feel as if I've made a mistake." Her throat tightened again.

"Losing someone makes us regret some things that we really shouldn't. If he were still alive, would you really want to marry him?"

"I'm so confused. I was so sure I wouldn't, but now I actually don't know!" She wept uncontrollably again.

When she quieted, Helen said, "You need some time off. Let me talk to Mrs. Smith for you."

"No!" Jean exclaimed sharply, then swiftly softened. "Please. I promise I'll do better with the children. It'll be easier, now that you know about Rodge. I don't want to have to talk to anyone else about it."

Helen studied her and then shrugged. "Okay, if that's what you want."

Jean stood up. "Yes." She fingered the stack of papers Masaru had left on her desk. "If you'll grade these, I'll draw up the mimeos for tomorrow's arithmetic and coloring." Her mind was beginning to work properly again. "Helen, you've helped me more than you know. Thanks."

A gentle half-smile curved Helen's lips. "You're welcome," she said and set to work.

Jean, accustomed to watching her grandmother for subtle mood changes, recognized a change in Helen. She had lowered her defenses. It was a relief, even if they couldn't be close friends.

★

Jean would just as soon have forgotten Thanksgiving altogether, but she had to plan special activities for the children, and the teachers insisted on a costume party she couldn't avoid without stirring up a lot of questions.

On Thanksgiving Day the cooks prepared turkey and all the trimmings for the teachers, but it wasn't anything like Grandmother's cooking.

Jean hated the weekend off. She needed to keep busy and couldn't wait to get back to teaching. She washed sweaters, cleaned the apartment, mended clothes, and shortened hems of her older skirts to an inch above the knee—the new length that had become the style after the government said longer skirts used too much fabric.

She wrote to Rodger's parents and let them go on thinking that she and Rodge had been "coming to an understanding." Mostly she just wanted them to know how much she cared for their son and how much she would miss him.

At last Monday came. Jean threw herself into teaching. That evening she dug into the next day's lessons. She'd long ago made the outline, but now she added some new word games. She scarcely heard the knock on the door, until Mary bounced up from her desk to answer.

Ann stepped in. "Hard at it for the second graders?" she teased. She taught high school. She plopped into Mary's upholstered chair and then grabbed at her ankle. "Oh darn! I've got a run. This is my last pair of decent stockings, and I probably can't get anymore. Guess I shouldn't complain . . . at least they'll go for a good cause since we've been salvaging our old stockings for parachutes . . . but don't you hate those cotton-rayon things?"

Mary said, "Yeah. I'm on my last good pair, too, and my one pair of shoes is never going to last until my next ration ticket is good. This gritty dirt is grinding right through the soles."

Jean exploded. "Since when is war supposed to be convenient?"

"Well, what brought that on?" Mary exclaimed. Her startled expression made Jean angrier.

"I'm tired of listening to petty gripes when our men are out there getting shot up so we can be safe."

"My dear Miss Patriotism, where's your sense of humor? Griping is the American way," Mary kidded.

Ann, however, soberly scrutinized Jean. "What's up?"

"Never mind," said Jean, realizing too late that she had overreacted. She still didn't want to talk about Rodge with anyone.

"You're making us mind," prodded Ann.

"Okay," she conceded stiffly. "You're right, and I'm sorry I jumped on you. A friend of mine is missing in action at Guadalcanal."

"Oh, Jean," cried Mary with instant sympathy. "Is it Rodge?" Jean nodded and gave them the few facts she knew. After words of sympathy, a hush fell over them. Finally Ann rose to leave. "When will it ever end?" she said wearily. "I'll let myself out, girls. See you tomorrow."

Mary followed her to the door anyway. When she returned, she asked in a hurt tone, "Why didn't you tell me?"

Jean could only say, "I knew I'd cry all over you, and I just couldn't handle having you feel bad on top of me feeling bad." Beyond that, she wasn't sure why. "Does that make sense?"

"No," said Mary. "Not unless you're my mother. Friends are supposed to feel bad with you. Where did you get such an idea?"

Jean shook her head. "I don't know."

"Well, look, kid. I don't want to make you feel bad either, but I hope I could lean on you if I lost someone."

"I see what you mean. I'd want you to. It was just so difficult to talk about, and it still is. I hope you won't tell the others."

"Not a word will they get from me," Mary promised. "But you didn't warn Ann. . . . Well, maybe she won't think to tell anybody."

★

By the next morning all the other teachers knew. Several with fiancés in the service offered their sympathy and then avoided sitting by her, as if her loss might be contagious. To the other extreme, some gathered around assuming Jean wanted to talk. Jean was glad to escape to school. The children, who loved and needed her, asked no questions she did not want to answer.

After class on Wednesday, on her way to the post office, Jean met Tom, Tad, and Fuj. Fuj, usually affable, wore an angry frown. Tom's eyes also flashed fire, while Tad stomped along as if to punish the sod under his feet.

"Hi. How's it going?" Jean asked, hoping she didn't sound too nosy.

Fuj's straight black brows dropped half an inch lower. "Can you imagine? I just got lectured at the administration building for snaring a wild duck and bringing it home to cook for my grandfather. There are thousands of those birds all over the farms that haven't migrated, and that one little duck gave him a real treat from the usual fare—no slight meant to you, Tad—but you have to admit the mess halls don't serve what you'd call home cooking."

"Well, this whole area is a waterfowl preserve," said Jean. "I suppose they can't make an exception for one grandfather or everyone would be cooking ducks on their heating stoves."

Tom jammed his hands in his pockets. The look in his eyes and the set of his shoulders reminded Jean of an eagle she'd once seen forced to live in a cage. He said, "They're making a big fuss about nothing. People are more important than a few birds. This project food is hard on our grandmothers and grandfathers. I'll bet the military cooks get to prepare a lot more variety for our guards than we ever see."

Jean's anger flared. "If they do, they deserve it!" she burst out.

All three men gaped at her.

Tom raised an eyebrow and wagged his head in disbelief. "I never said they didn't. I just suspect that we could have more decent food than raunchy mutton. Some of the old people can't even chew it."

"Then your cooks should cook it longer," Jean snapped. Having started to speak her mind, she couldn't stop. "You think you've got it so rough, sitting here in camp, while other men are out there dying for us."

"We have not been allowed to enlist," Tom ground out in a threatening tone. "But truth is, a lot of us think a government that imprisons innocent people isn't worth fighting for."

"Yeah," Tad agreed. "We've been fools to think the Constitution included us."

"Aw, come on, Tom," muttered Fuj. "This will get us nowhere."

Tom refused to back down. "Tad's right, and someday I'm going to show them what a Nisei can do."

Jean wondered what he meant by that. He didn't elaborate. Without a good-bye or a backward glance, the men headed back into the project.

*The nerve of them,* thought Jean. *Comparing themselves with our fighting men.*

Later when she calmed down, she regretted her rude behavior. Then on second thought she decided they deserved what she said, and besides, she had gained valuable information—she had provoked them to show their true colors.

Back home in the apartment, she added their comments to her report for the week, sealed the whole thing in an envelope, and ran back to the post office to mail it.

Later, after she calmed down a little, second thoughts struck her. Had she overstated the case? She couldn't imagine Tom or Tad being a threat to national security. On the other hand, she didn't dare let personal feelings influence her report. She returned to the apartment filled with conflict.

Mary met her at the door and gave her a searching look. Whatever she saw led her to say, "Everyone knows about Rodge now. Wouldn't you feel better if you hung a service flag in our window in his memory? I know I would."

"But he's not family."

"The way you feel, he might as well have been. Why not let others share your grief?"

"Sure, and I can say to people who ask about him, 'We were only good friends, but I sent him a get-lost letter.'"

Mary looked stricken. "I'm sorry. I must seem like a real dummy. I didn't stop to think."

"That's okay. I shouldn't expect you to understand all the twists of my peculiar problem."

"You ever going to forgive yourself?"

"I don't know. I feel as if I totally failed him."

Throwing an arm across her shoulders, Mary gave her a squeeze and a little shake. "No matter how you feel, that's not true. If Rodge was worthy of your friendship, he'd be telling you the same thing. Mourn for him, but don't be tacking on uglies that he'd call lies."

Jean burst into tears. She was full of uglies, and most of them had nothing to do with Rodge.

★

By Friday, the children began to ask the same questions over and over, as if their minds were already on the weekend.

Finally Jean couldn't stand it any longer. She banged her hand on the desk and yelled, "Sit down and listen! I will not repeat this again!"

Stunned, they scurried to their seats and folded their hands on their table tops.

She angrily restated the directions for their silent reading period. By the time she finished, their shock was reflected on Helen's face.

*I've got to get out of here and calm down.* Aloud Jean said,

"Miss Kagawa will help you with difficult words." Grabbing her coat, she strode out to the latrine building, which offered no privacy, but there was no other place she could go that would give reason to her exit. She brushed away her tears before she entered; by the time she came out, she had regained control.

When she returned to the classroom, every head was bent studiously over a book. At the end of the reading time Jean said, "Boys and girls, I'm sorry I shouted at you. I was unfair, and I hope you will forgive me."

The children stared at her with more surprise. Jean sent Helen a what-do-I-do-now look.

Helen stepped forward. "Let's sing our new happy song to Miss Thornton. Everyone stand up."

Fifty-three chairs scraped the floor as they stood. They sang and clapped about happy kids and snowflakes and winter fun. When they finished, it was time to straighten the room for dismissal. Then out they marched, as cheerfully as usual.

Jean closed the door and retreated to her desk to collapse in her chair. Dropping her chin to her hands, she said, "I can't believe I yelled at them like that. What's wrong with me?"

"You've been under a lot of stress. I still think you should take some time off. If you tried, you could get home for a week. Surely Mrs. Smith would let me take the class or I could assist while another teacher adds them to hers."

"I can't go home. I'd be admitting defeat to Grandmother. She was so against my coming here." Jean bit her lip. "Oh, Helen, that came out sounding terrible. I only meant she was upset about my being in a prison camp."

"That's okay. Let's talk about you. You need better advice than I can give."

Jean nodded. "I'll go talk to Mrs. Smith."

★

Jean's talk with her principal increased her stress. Mrs. Smith did not understand her reluctance to go home for a few days. Finally the principal agreed, "It won't do you much good if I have to force you to take time off, and maybe you'll be better off staying busy, but you must not let your personal life affect how you teach. I'm trusting you," she tapped her desk with her pencil to emphasize each word, "to practice a professional level of self-control."

After that, in the classroom Jean focused rigidly on the children. They responded by putting forth their usual determined efforts. Everything seemed back to normal, no matter how she felt on the inside.

One day Tom appeared shortly after the children had gone home. Jean was sweeping the floor when he stepped in out of the cold wind. She supposed he had come to see his sister.

Instead, Helen came and took the broom from her hands and said, "Tom stopped by because I asked him to talk with you. When I told him about Rodge, he said some things that I thought might help you. I hope that's okay?" Helen finished anxiously.

Jean wanted to yell, *No, it's not okay,* but Helen's concern stopped her. "I must not be doing as well with the children as I thought."

"You've become so silent. The children don't know what to make of it. They are losing their joy for learning."

At a distance Tom stood awkwardly, shifting his weight from one foot to the other like a schoolboy himself.

Jean shrugged. "I don't know what anyone could say that would help me. This is something I have to work through and live with, but . . ." she waved her hand toward the extra chair by her desk, "come and sit." She sat at her desk, and Helen pulled up her own chair closer.

Tom sat for a moment staring at his folded hands in his lap. When he looked up, his face telegraphed sympathy. "I didn't know about your loss the other day. No wonder you were upset with Tad and me. I'm sorry about what I said."

Jean drew in a tired breath. "I wish I could say the same, but I know I'd react the same way again. I just see red when anyone sounds like they aren't behind our troops."

"Under the circumstances, I don't blame you." Tom went on, "But that's not what I came to say." He shifted, facing her more directly. "I know there's nothing anyone can say that will make you feel better, but Helen thought you should hear what I told her." He stopped and waited for her response.

Silence stretched tightly between them until Jean crossed her arms on her desk and nodded wearily. "Go ahead."

He leaned forward with his elbows propped on his knees, his hands still clasped. His black brows pinched together as he searched for words. "We . . . I . . . can't know what it's really like for you, but from what Helen told me, I think you are blaming yourself unjustly about that letter you sent. First, you don't know if he even received it, but if he did . . . may I tell you how a man might feel about it?"

She swallowed to ward off a tightening in her throat and nodded again.

He straightened and sat upright. "If it were me . . . when I received your letter, I'd go on loving you, in spite of whether or not you loved me. And I'd go on hoping against hope—unless you married someone else—that I could win your love someday. And if a bullet took me . . . Don't you see? Even without warning, my love for you would make my life . . . and my death worth it all."

Jean dropped her face to her hands and closed her eyes. *How can he talk like this one time and sound like a dangerous traitor the next?* She swallowed hard again and drew in a deep breath. Looking up, she said, "I'm just so tired." She pushed a stray strand of hair back from her face. "You're right about how much I blame myself, and even though I still do, you've given me something different to think about."

Tom straightened. "Would you go and talk to Pastor Ichiba? He helped me a lot when . . ." he stopped, as if he had said more than he intended and then finished, "when I was going through a rough time."

"No. I can't," Jean cried vehemently. Canned Christian answers were the last thing she wanted to hear. Besides, Pastor Ichiba was so honest and open, she felt unclean around him. She wanted never to lie to him, but if they were to talk for long, she would have to.

Tom persisted. "If you change your mind, let me know. I can set it up for you. I know he'd like to help if he could."

Getting a grip on herself, Jean explained, "It's not that I don't value his counsel," which was true if he didn't get religious, "but what you've said is probably better for me than anything he could say. I'm glad you came."

Tom stood up. "Okay."

With a teasing smile Helen jumped to her feet and handed him the broom. "While you're here, you may as well help us."

He smiled and quickly swept the day's dirt into the dustpan Helen held for him. Then he filled the stove and banked the fire for the night. In a few minutes the chores were done.

On the cold walk home, Jean thought about Tom's way of looking at a letter of rejection. Could Rodge possibly have felt like Tom? She wished it were so but could not guess.

## CHAPTER 8

"Remember Pearl Harbor," a popular song, had become the nation's battle cry. Everyone had been urged to remember the day that President Roosevelt had said "would live in infamy." Although Jean knew December 7, the anniversary of the attack, was approaching, the impact of her memories crept up on her unawares. Suddenly they were as fresh as yesterday.

At breakfast on Pearl Harbor Day, the teachers took turns describing what they'd been doing when they first heard the news. Jean tried to participate, but she found she couldn't.

She couldn't tell them that she'd been dreaming of her wedding while she sat in church that morning with her grandmother. She'd pictured red and white bouquets of roses on the steps up the platform and the candelabra twined with fragrant evergreens and red carnations. She'd imagined walking down the aisle on Uncle Al's arm. She could almost see Dave standing there, waiting for her with the biggest of his smiles lighting up his whole face.

And then she and Grandmother had come home from church and heard the terrible news. She'd tried to console herself, thinking maybe Dave wouldn't get a leave for the wedding, but at least he was supposed to be on his way to the States. A week passed before she'd learned he had not left his ship, the *Arizona,* which had been sunk in Pearl Harbor.

Now in the evening, the worst moment of this first anniversary of Pearl Harbor Day came, when Mary turned her radio to a song that had haunted Jean ever since she'd first heard the words. "There will never be another you. . . ." *Silly, sentimental song,* she tried to tell herself, but her heart cried, *No, it's true.*

She pleaded a headache and went to bed early. Not only her head was aching—her whole inside was again a wound of loss. The pain was as agonizing as if she had just received that awful telegram.

Long before daylight Jean awoke, armed again with anger. She was angry at the war and at death and at God, if he was in charge. She hated the Japs. *Yes, Japs!* She said it over again in her mind, like swearing. *Dirty yellow Japs!*

Unable to sleep, she grabbed her robe and towel and tiptoed to the bathroom for a shower. The cool night air on her skin brought her sharply awake. While she bathed, she tried to think of more ways to obtain the information Uncle Al needed. She must meet more internees, even though the other teachers did not mix with them.

★

After school that day, feeling as if she were leaping off a cliff into a dark pit, Jean asked Helen, "Would it be all right if I ate supper with you . . . sometimes . . . in your mess hall?"

Helen's mouth dropped open. "Well . . . I suppose so. . . . But why would you want to? You probably have better food in yours."

"I want to meet more people," Jean said with honesty, "and I want to know firsthand how the internment is for them. Would anyone mind?"

"I can ask our block manager," Helen said doubtfully.

★

Later that week Jean joined Helen in the long supper line at the internees' mess hall in the block where she lived. At last they picked up their food and found empty spaces at a table. By this time, the carrot sticks and celery placed on the tables at the beginning of each meal were gone.

When Jean sat down, people nearby greeted her politely and then conversation ceased in favor of eating. The food was simple, but well prepared—not much different from the teachers' menu. Good meat was scarce for everybody. The teachers also had their share of mutton and black codfish when they did not have macaroni and cheese or beans.

"Where's Tom?" Jean asked, not seeing him anywhere nearby.

"He usually eats at a later shift," Helen replied.

"What about Fuj and Yosh?"

"They eat at the mess hall where Tad cooks. I've eaten there a few times. He's a pretty good chef."

"How many shifts are fed here?" asked Jean, glancing around the crowded hall, which hummed with conversations in both English and Japanese.

"Three. About a hundred people each shift. We laugh at the posters that tell us to 'Eat slowly for the sake of your health.' If we ate slowly the later shifts wouldn't be served until bedtime. Even the last shift doesn't linger because lots of the kitchen workers are mothers who want to get home to their children."

Just when Jean had given up hope of overhearing anything of value to Uncle Al, several older Isseis, men who had been born in Japan and were therefore aliens, paused beside her table. They were speaking English in urgent tones to several young Nisei men. The Niseis, born in the United States, were American citizens.

A squarely built Issei with a strong, stern face and iron gray hair said in a penetrating voice, "They have always hated us. Look what your citizenship has earned for you." The wave of his hand seemed to encompass a lifetime of hurts beyond the immediate scene in the mess hall. "You owe America nothing."

Another silver-haired Issei added, "We kept hoping, and now there is no more hope. In America you will never have a chance. At first opportunity, go to Japan. There you will find a decent life." His eyes caught Jean watching him. He switched to Japanese and continued angrily. Jean wished Japanese were not so difficult. She had picked up so few words, she couldn't understand any conversations.

The Niseis were nodding their heads, apparently agreeing with whatever the Isseis were saying.

*No opportunities,* thought Jean bitterly. Because of the

Japan they loved, Dave's hopes and dreams were gone forever. *These men could betray our country and cost us more lives. I've got to find out who they are.* Before the men walked on outside, Jean memorized their faces and casually asked Helen if she knew any of them. Helen innocently pointed out and named two Niseis and one of the Isseis.

As soon as Jean reached her apartment, she wrote down their names and the snatch of their conversation she'd heard. Next time she would get more. Twice she had to conceal what she was writing when Mary came to her desk unexpectedly. The first time her heart lurched in apprehension. She felt guilty, which was idiotic. She was working for her country. Must be jumpy because she hated having secrets. The second time Mary came close, Jean managed to control her nervous reaction and casually slip a fresh paper over her notes.

Jean waited several days before visiting the project mess hall again. She didn't want to arouse curiosity and questions from the other teachers. On her next visit, Helen introduced her to two of the Niseis who had been listening and agreeing with the embittered older men. They were Tom's friends, Frank Ikeda and Akira Miyamoto. In her presence they said nothing incriminating. She went home frustrated. Eating in the project mess hall where she was the alien made her so uncomfortable, and her efforts were not giving her much information.

More often than not, the internees chided anyone who complained about the internment or said a word against the government. The prevailing attitude among most of the adults was as patriotic as Jean's second graders singing "America" and saluting the flag. More than once Jean heard men say with dignity, "We are helping the war effort by submitting peacefully to the internment."

Still, Jean watched and listened for the rare remark that could reveal a person who was against the United States.

★

Sunday morning Jean trudged dutifully to the Union Christian Church, another place where she felt alien, but she was desperate enough to try anything in the hope of getting leads for Uncle Al. Again her effort went unrewarded.

With Christmas approaching, however, the young people were going to meet that afternoon to prepare props for a simple program. Tom had written a script telling the stories behind some Christmas carols and climaxing with a tableau of the manger scene. Jean volunteered to help, hoping that proximity to Tom and the young people could turn up information.

After lunch she headed back to the church. Tom had scrounged scraps of lumber and cardboard. As the writer, he directed the work, advised on the set design, and coordinated the boys' hammering and sawing. Jean directed the stage crew of high-school girls and boys in the construction of cardboard rocks, palm trees, a star, and some sheep. Helen and most of the girls wielded scissors and knives, trimming where Jean marked the cardboard.

"The last time I worked on a set like this I was in ninth grade," Jean said.

Tom groaned dramatically. "That sounds encouraging."

"None of your lip," she tossed back, borrowing one of Mary's favorite phrases. "We created a masterpiece, only to be surpassed by this one."

"I hope you're right," Tom said with a cheerful grin. "We'll have to live with this one every Sunday until Christmas. There's no storage room for stage props."

"But then it won't be a surprise," Jean protested. "Part of the fun is seeing an impressive set for the first time when the curtain goes up."

"The curtain here will have to be in our minds," reminded Tom. "Think of Shakespeare and theater in the round."

"I'll try."

"And remember, it will be the church's holiday decorations," said Tom.

Helen remarked, "I wish we could have some fir boughs, even if we can't have a tree."

"Yes," said one of the girls wistfully. "Last year our whole church was filled with evergreens."

"I'm going to call Grandmother for poster-paint powder," said Jean. "Maybe she could mail us some evergreen boughs."

The girls' faces brightened. "That would be neat!" cried one.

Another exclaimed, "Do you think she can?"

"I don't know, but I'll ask," said Jean, careful not to reveal her second-thought qualms. Grandmother certainly could, but would she want to brighten the Christmas of people she called enemy aliens?

"Hey, Jean," Tom called from where the boys had been hammering. "Come look at this frame, and tell me if it's tall enough to support your palm tree." He'd never addressed her by her first name, and now he'd done it naturally, as if it meant nothing. And yet, she felt as if a wall between them had disappeared—as if a door had opened, and there was sunshine beyond it.

The rest of the afternoon passed swiftly. When Tom called a halt and asked everyone to clean the room for the evening service, Jean was surprised to see the winter daylight fading. She helped sweep the board floor and then excused herself to go home and work on lesson plans.

Back in her apartment, she couldn't concentrate. When she tried, her thoughts and feelings scattered all directions. She'd actually had fun this afternoon, so much so that she'd temporarily forgotten her real purpose for being there. But even more distressing, for four hours she'd forgotten about Dave and Rodge.

★

In mid-December, Jean heard many internees wishing, just like people back home, for a white Christmas. Beyond Castle Rock, Mount Shasta glistened under a fresh mantle of snow, while at Tulelake, although the thermometer stayed below freezing, the wind blew away any dry skiffs of white that occasionally fell.

Helen told Jean that fun in the snow on Christmas would be the most the project children could expect. Mothers and fathers were trying to prepare them for no presents. In the move to internment, families had lost everything except what they could carry in their hands. Now they worked in the project for sixteen to nineteen dollars a month, which left nothing for gifts.

One Saturday Jean and Mary took the bus to Klamath Falls to purchase small gifts for their pupils. Jimmy Duggan and his buddy went with them. Mary treated the trip like a date, but Jean had a hard time even remembering the other young man's name.

Before they could go again, news came in the *Tulean Dispatch* that Nisei servicemen had begun to send presents, and some Caucasian churches and civic organizations on the outside were also sending gifts for the children. All these were being stored in a small warehouse. The little ones would have Christmas surprises after all.

War news, although not reporting momentous gains, gave some hope too. In North Africa, American and British soldiers were forcing the Germans into retreat. And in the South Pacific, General Douglas MacArthur moved his headquarters from the safety of Australia into New Guinea, leading the army in person for the first time since retreating from the Philippines.

Although these good things were happening, Jean remained locked in anger. She continued her fact-finding with vengeance. Each Sunday she attended the Union Church and helped with the program practice. A couple of times a week she ate supper with Helen, listening surreptitiously and learning a few more names.

The week before Christmas, Jean's grandmother shipped her two big boxes of cedar and Douglas fir boughs, stating pointedly that Jean could do whatever she wished with them. Her avoidance of mentioning the Union Christian Church made plain her disapproval of Jean's participation in a Japanese internment camp church. She begged Jean to come home for Christmas.

In the next mail, Jean refused without trying to give a reason. Her commitment to Uncle Al's project consumed her, and until her mission was completed, she would stay in Tulelake. Grandmother and her Victorian house were another world.

Jean now had a more lengthy list of suspects, pieced together by hanging around the post office and getting Helen to take her to other mess halls for supper. It was anything but complete, but she conscientiously mailed a weekly report.

★

Whenever Jean joined Helen for supper, she tried to maneuver Helen to sit within hearing range of young men. Most of their negative remarks, however, sounded like normal frustration over being interned. Frequently someone would tease the bitter person with, "You think you got all the problems here?"

Or someone else would scold, "Come on. We've got to pull together and help each other."

One night when Jean and Helen ate at Tad's mess hall, Tom came in with Frank and Akira, the two Niseis Jean had met after hearing the Isseis urge them to forsake their citizenship and flee to Japan. The three of them sat across from Helen and Jean. In spite of the need to eat quickly, they talked between bites of stew.

Frank asked, "Do you think we'll be sent to Japan?"

Tom laid down his fork. "Where did you get that idea?"

"Some of us are going to ask. There's nothing here for us," said Akira.

Tom openly agreed. "It's true that most of what I believed about America is proving to be a mistake."

Jean's heart sank. She didn't want to listen. After Tom had shown such compassion toward her grief, she did not want to report anything more on him.

"Did you hear about that old Issei at the Jerome Relocation Center, who got shot when he climbed through the barbed wire fence to get a little dog he'd made a pet of?" asked Frank.

"No! Is he all right?" asked Tom.

"He died. The guard said he refused to halt. Turns out he was deaf."

Horror flashed across Tom's face; then it became a mask of bitterness. "They treat us like pigs going to slaughter. You're probably right, wanting to go to Japan. In the end there will be no place for us here. Constitution or no, they'll never give us equal rights."

Helen leaned forward and interrupted. "Tom! You're upset

and with good reason, but you know as well as I do, that we're Americans. We wouldn't fit in in Japan."

"I do *not* know that," Tom grated. "And I'm ashamed to be called an American."

"Meet us in the laundry room by the boilers after supper, Tom. A bunch of us get together to talk where we can keep warm."

Tom nodded grimly. "I'll be there. Tonight I'm off duty from the hospital."

Helen frowned at her brother but said nothing. In a few minutes she finished her meal and sat fidgeting with her fork, obviously wanting to leave.

Jean needed to hear more from Tom's friends, who were still eating. She said to Helen, "You don't have to wait for me. I can find my way alone now."

"Okay, if you don't mind. I need to hit the showers before the evening rush. Have to shampoo and set my hair."

Jean smiled. "Sure, go ahead." With Helen gone, she assumed she could concentrate on the men's conversation, but to her disappointment, they stopped talking, ate quickly, stood up, and left.

Tom excused himself and followed his friends.

Jean wondered where the boiler room was and whether she could at least see who was there. Snatching up her plate, she carried it to the counter and slipped out the door just in time to see the men entering the closest laundry building. She couldn't follow, but must remember which building it was. From her purse she pulled a scrap of paper and made a quick line drawing of the six barracks in view of the door. She was about to mark the one for the laundry building with an "X" when a familiar male voice at her side asked, "What are you doing?"

She flinched as if she'd been struck. "Tad!"

In shirt sleeves despite the cold and still wearing his apron, he peered over her shoulder.

She closed her hand on the paper. "I was making myself a map, so I could find my way," she lied.

"I saw you jump up and follow those guys. Looked to me like you were snooping." He frowned at her with narrowed eyes. "Why are you eating here anyway? You so bored that you enjoy slumming?"

Keeping her head high, she backed away. "I don't know why you're so upset, but I don't have to explain myself to you."

"Yeah? Well maybe you do. Those guys are my friends, and right now I can see trouble written all over you." He grabbed her hand, forcing her fingers open, and took her crumpled note.

People leaving the building glanced at them curiously, but did not intervene. Jean's heart pounded in panic. She was trapped and not a clever liar. "Give that back to me," she demanded. To her despair, her voice quavered.

"Yes, Tad. Give the lady whatever you took from her," said Tom.

She swung around. Tom gazed down at her. "I forgot my gloves. Maybe it's a good thing I did. What's going on here?" he demanded of Tad.

"I think she's some kind of a spy. She went dashing to the door to follow you guys when you left. When I came to see what her hurry was, I found her making a map of some sort. Look." He thrust the note at Tom.

Breathless with fear, Jean watched.

Tom glanced at the paper and turned it over. On the back she had scribbled symbols in her personal code for various types of anti-American talk with an initial to help her remember who said what.

She volunteered, "After I told Helen I could find my way, I wasn't sure how to get to the fire break that leads to my apartment. I had just begun to map the arrangement of the buildings so I could find my way back here, if I got lost."

"So what's the writing on the back?" demanded Tad.

"Notes for school tomorrow," she lied.

Tom didn't even glance back at the code. He said, "Tad, give it up and apologize to Jean. How could you think she's some kind of a spy? And why should anyone be spying on us, for Pete's sake? We're already in a prison." He handed the note to Jean.

Tad scowled. "I think you're making a mistake. I have this gut feeling she's up to no good."

Tom thrust out his chin. "I asked you to apologize."

The two men glared at each other. Their breath formed white puffs in the cold air between them.

Tad's mouth tightened into a grim line. "You made your choice, Tom." He swung around and stomped back into the building.

Tom glowered after him and then turned to her. "I'm sorry, Jean. He's been getting more and more upset over the internment, but to have him act like this . . . I wouldn't have believed it, if I hadn't seen it." He slammed his fist into his other hand and burst out, "This place is destroying us!"

Jean was afraid to say a word. She was safe for the time being, but she knew she'd have to be much more careful in the future.

"Let me walk you home," Tom offered.

"If you can just get me aimed the right direction, I can make it."

He strode beside her, saying nothing. His silence distressed Jean. What was he thinking? Had she caused a serious break in the two men's friendship? Then she told herself that was beside the point. Her purpose was greater than any of their personal wants and wishes.

Jean insisted that Tom leave her as soon as she could reasonably assure him she knew the way. He didn't argue.

She did not want to include him in tonight's report. And yet how could she ignore him while implicating his friends?

Back in her apartment, she decided she dared not leave out Tom's remarks. His volatile reactions had often suggested he could be as much a threat to national security as any of the others. Having watched his hand tighten into a white-knuckled fist tonight, Jean suspected he would fight actively against whatever he despised.

She wrote down everything she could remember and then read over her entire report. Trying to sort out comments that reflected true disloyalty to the United States was difficult. Finally she decided to leave all the negative remarks, but added that Tom did not seem to be anti-American so much as disappointed in America.

The next morning on the way to school, she mailed the report.

# CHAPTER 9

The more excited about Christmas Mary grew, the more homesick she became. "Who would've thought I'd miss my crew of sisters and brothers," she groaned. "I couldn't wait to get out on my own and have a bed to myself, and now I'd give anything to have just one day with them."

She had four brothers and six sisters, all still in school. To get home and back on the train in the few vacation days at Christmas was not possible, even if this had not been wartime.

"You're my only family now, pal," said Mary. "Please come celebrate with me at the Christmas party the soldiers are giving in the rec room." The army guards had invited the teachers for an evening of playing records, dancing, and refreshments.

Jean felt sorry for Mary in her intense homesickness. At the same time, she realized she must do some of the normal things the other teachers seemed to enjoy, if she were to deflate curiosity over how much she fraternized with the internees. "Okay. I'll go," she said.

With a whoop of delight, Mary gave her an exuberant hug.

★

When the party night arrived, Jean donned her blue wool jersey dress and wore the sapphire pendant Uncle Al had given her for graduation. As she brushed her hair up and pinned it into a crown of soft curls, Mary complained, "I'm sorry I asked you. You're going to get all the attention."

Jean smiled at her in the mirror. "Thanks, but you don't have to worry. You look fabulous and Christmas-y too."

Mary's porcelain skin and black hair were more striking than ever set off by her kelly green dress.

At the party, with a couple of dozen other teachers, Jean found herself surrounded by no less than four men at a time, even though she took over the task of running the record player. Tall, short, thick, and thin, they all flirted, happy to just talk if she didn't want to dance.

While Mary danced with Jimmy and anyone else who asked, one young man, whose name was Bob, lingered at Jean's side, saying little. His lips smiled, but his eyes never did. From time to time Jean turned to him with a friendly comment. He responded briefly. Of all the men, only he seemed to ask nothing, but he lingered.

After a while a pushy corporal elbowed his way to her other side, seemingly determined to get her to dance. "Come on," he urged. He held out his arms and sang in what he must have thought was a seductive baritone, "You can't say no to a soldier—"

"Aw, come off it, Anders," said Bob, the quiet one. "She doesn't want to dance, so leave her alone."

Jean blushed. They must think she was a real dud, but she didn't want to be in a strange man's arms. She forced a smile and said, "I'm not much for dancing, but I'd love a sing-along. Why don't you pick some records you can sing to and lead us?"

Anders brightened. "Sure. Let me see what you've got."

He went through the stack and pulled out some. When the record player stopped, he placed his selection on the spindle, announcing, "Hey, you Joes! We're gonna have a sing-along. And if any of you want to do a solo, just come up here and lead out. I'll start us with 'Jingle, Jangle, Jingle.'"

The catchy tune drew them all in. He followed that with a rousing rendition of "This Is Worth Fighting For" and then switched to dreamy romantic songs. Several of the men sang passable solos. Soon someone requested a favorite from a man who had brought his guitar. The evening swiftly turned into a talent show.

Mary and Jimmy came and stood beside Jean. During a lull Mary asked, "Can we sing some Christmas carols now?"

To the accompaniment of a couple of harmonicas and guitars, they sang carols. When they had gone through all the familiar ones, Jimmy turned to Bob. "Sing that carol you sang for us the other night, Bob."

"Yeah, Bob, go ahead," urged another, handing his guitar to the quiet man.

Jean felt sorry they were pressuring him when he so obviously did not want to, but he took the guitar. Strumming, he tightened strings. Then as he stroked some chords, she relaxed. He was good. In a low voice, pure and fluid, he sang an old carol Jean recognized as one Tom was featuring in his Christmas program. Tom said Martin Luther had written it for his own children. "Long time ago / in Bethlehem / the holy Bible says / Mary's boy child, Jesus Christ / was born on Christmas day. . . ." A true musician, Bob's face told her he was lost in the music. Even his eyes came to life.

The beauty of his voice, rising and falling with the lilting tune, twisted her heart. She glanced around at the others who were listening. Their faces reflected the wonder she felt. No one tried to sing along. When Bob stopped, the room fell silent. Then Anders, the self-appointed emcee began to clap. Applause filled the room. "More! More!" called several.

Bob smiled and bowed but handed the guitar back to its owner. "Let's hear the teachers sing," he said.

Ignoring their protests, the men herded the teachers to the record player. The women went into a huddle. "What do we all know?" asked Ann.

They settled on a love song, "Time Was." They went through the sentimental words in unison once and then fell into four-part harmony. When they finished the men applauded, stomped their feet, and yelled for more. "Sorry, but we're going to quit while we're ahead," announced Mary. "And anyway, we're hungry. Where's the food?"

Jean put on a record of Bing Crosby singing "White Christmas," and everyone descended upon the refreshment table.

Bob touched Jean's arm. "I'll get you something. Any preferences?"

"Thanks. I like everything." She watched him thread his way toward the table.

At her questioning glance to Jimmy, he said, "He's from a

missionary family. His mother and sister are prisoners in the Philippines. His father and brother died trying to protect them, while Bob was here, safe in college. Now he's a man with only one goal. All he wants is to get out there and fight. I think he pictures himself marching into the prison camp and freeing them all by himself."

Bob returned with two plates of food. "Shall we sit somewhere?" he invited.

Jean nodded and followed him. He placed her plate on a table for two near the wall and pulled out her chair. "Thanks," she said, hoping he wouldn't leave all the conversation to her.

"You're different from the other girls," he said. "I've been trying to figure out why. It's not just that you don't want to dance. There's something else."

"I'm the only Oregonian here," she offered with a laugh.

But he wouldn't be put off by lightness. "I think maybe you've cried a lot. And the others haven't begun to live."

Looking deep into his eyes, she recognized a fellow mourner. She could tell him the truth. "I lost my fiancé at Pearl Harbor, three weeks before our wedding date. He was supposed to be on his way home."

"I thought it could be something like that." He told her about his family and how guilty he felt about not being there to help them. "I've written my congressman, asking him to get me out of here and into action."

"I feel as if I can't do enough, either, for the war effort."

"Well, you're a girl. There's not much you can do."

"That's not true," exclaimed Jean. "There are ways." She caught herself and added, "In Russia and China, women fight right beside the men."

"Well, I pray to God we never come to that here. All we men need is faithful women to stand behind us."

Jean bit her tongue. Such a nice young man, but all wrong about women just sitting at home waiting. She vowed then and there that someday she would do something important for the war effort that did not have to be a secret. In the meantime she was as good a fact finder as any man could be, even if she couldn't tell anyone.

She changed the subject. "You sing beautifully. Have you had professional training?"

"A little," he admitted. "I had a music scholarship. But that can wait until the war is won."

They chatted until the evening ended, and he walked her home with Mary and Jimmy.

Two days later, Jimmy came by their apartment and said, "Bob's on his way to the Pacific. I wish I didn't feel like he's got some kind of a death wish."

Jean said, "I don't think he has. I think he will do anything to make it into the Philippines to see his mother and sister again."

Jimmy sighed. "I sure hope you're right."

That night Jean wrote to Caroline and told her about Bob, adding, "I'm so glad you're marrying Rudy now. This is no time to postpone being together. Even here, the internees are getting married. They often have to share an apartment with their parents and the rest of the family. It all seems incredibly impractical, but then I guess falling in love never has been practical."

★

On Christmas Eve the long-awaited program was presented. The young people sang like earthbound angels. The set didn't fall down. And Grandmother's Douglas fir and cedar boughs wafted a woodsy fragrance throughout the long room. At the close of the short program Tom had written, Pastor Ichiba came to the front and said, "I have been asked to tell you about my most memorable Christmas. I would have to say my first Christmas was my most memorable."

Jean couldn't remember her first Christmas and wondered what he could say about his.

Smiling, he continued. "My story begins in the summer of the year I was twelve. In my village in Japan we knew nothing about Christmas. My father had died. I had no brothers or sisters, no grandparents, uncles, or aunts. I was fortunate to obtain work in the kitchen of an inn where foreign travelers occasionally stayed. I earned food for Mother and me and sometimes a few coins from kind travelers. In our village, a boy with no family had no future. I began to worry about what I could do to take care of my mother."

With a pang of sympathy, Jean remembered her own fear and loneliness when her father had left her with her sister, who didn't want her. At least she had not had to worry about anyone but herself.

Pastor Ichiba was saying, "One day a stranger came to the inn. His name was Mr. Nagai. He was different from anyone I had ever known. He greeted me with kindly respect and listened with interest. He stayed for many days . . . maybe two weeks and talked with me often. One day when he made me sit down and have tea with him, he asked if my father had told me about God.

"'I know about many gods,' I said confidently, proud to know so much.

"To my surprise he looked sad, but then he smiled and said, 'I will pray that the one true God will reveal himself to you.'

"I remember shaking my head in confusion and stammering, 'I don't know what you mean.'

"He said, 'Don't worry, little one. You will. You'll see.' He then revealed that he was leaving.

"Big as I was, my eyes filled with tears. He had become like a father to me. He politely pretended not to see my weakness and handed me a small black book written in Japanese. He said he would come back again one day and asked me to read the book while he was gone. I bowed low and thanked him and promised I would.

"The book was a New Testament, which I even read to my mother. When I read about Jesus the Nazarene, I understood what made Mr. Nagai different. He was like Jesus.

"Gradually, Mother and I began to pray to the Father of Jesus. I told the Father I loved his Son, and I asked him to take care of Mr. Nagai. Soon Mother and I both became Christians.

"And then the worst possible thing happened. When winter grew cold, Mother fell deathly ill with terrible coughing, and then I did too. I grew so weak, I couldn't take care of her! One morning," his voice broke, "I awoke and found her dead on the other mat. I couldn't even get up to tell anyone.

"I lay there too sick to call out, yet I formed one prayer: 'Lord Jesus, help us.' Through my closed lids I suddenly saw the face of my beloved Mr. Nagai. I fell asleep feeling safe.

"When I awoke someone was holding me. Mr. Nagai had returned. He held me on his lap like a baby and offered me tea. After I drank all of it, he asked how I felt.

"'I'm hungry,'" I whispered.

"He said, 'Good. You are getting better. Do you understand about your mother?'"

"'Yes, she died. I couldn't help her. I was too weak to make a sound when I cried.'"

"'Shinkichi, did you read the book I gave you?'"

"I nodded. 'Mother and I believe in Jesus and his Father.'"

"'Thank God. Then you know your mother is waiting for you in heaven.'" He drew me close and tears coursed down his cheeks. It seemed as if he were crying my tears for me, and I didn't need to cry anymore. My pain over failing my mother eased.

"Finally, he carried me to the inn where I had worked and placed me on a mat in his room. He told me today was Christmas Day—the day when Christians celebrate the birth of Jesus. My first Christmas present was a warm padded kimono he had brought from his journey to the north. After that Mr. Nagai arranged and paid for my mother's funeral. As soon as I was strong enough, he took me to his home in Tokyo to live with him.

"Thus, on my very first Christmas I learned that although sadness may come, the joy Christ brings is deep and everlasting. On this Christmas 1942, although your hearts have been wounded by this war, I pray you may be filled with his joy." He bowed politely and sat down.

In the ensuing moments of silence, Jean felt surrounded by holiness, an unearthly peace that seemed to settle over the room. She sat very still, afraid to breathe for fear of breaking the spell.

In this hush, a young woman stood and began to sing softly in a pure, sweet soprano, "O Holy night! / The stars are brightly shining. / It is the night of the dear Savior's birth. . . ."

The terrible beauty of the birth of Christ struck Jean. The Son of God had come in human flesh, willing to be betrayed, despised, rejected, and killed, because of love. Selfless love, like

Dave's love for his country. *Maybe God really does care. Maybe God is weeping with me like Mr. Nagai wept with Pastor Ichiba.*

★

After the service, Mr. and Mrs. Kagawa invited Jean to their apartment for hot cocoa. "Our dear neighbor back home in Elliston sent us a gift package with cookies and fruitcake," said Mrs. Kagawa. "Please come and celebrate with us."

"I'd love to," said Jean. Even if she had wished to refuse, she could not have resisted Mrs. Kagawa's delighted invitation. She looked happier than Jean had ever seen her.

The tiny apartment was not set up for entertaining, and Jean was the only person there who was not family. They had to sit on the neatly made cots. She met white-haired Grandmother Kagawa, who spoke only Japanese, but smiled and nodded and clapped her hands when she laughed. Uncle Shuji was thin to the point of being gaunt. He grinned and made sly, gentle jokes about everything. Aunt Tatsu was well rounded compared with most Japanese women. She listened to everyone with enthusiastic empathy. Her face reflected her generous feelings by the set of her brows, the line of her lips, and the changing crinkles around her eyes. Jean felt so comfortable with her, she wondered about it, until she realized that Aunt Tatsu's warm concern reminded her of her own mother.

Uncle Shuji accepted a cup of cocoa but refused cake, saying, "No thanks. Taz says I've gained too much weight, now that I don't have to work the orchard," he joked, giving his wife a puckish grin.

She rose to the bait. "Gained weight! I tell him he's melting away on the food here. If I could cook for him, I'd fatten him up again."

"Shuji, Taz is right. You ought to eat home-cooked food every chance you get, even cake and cookies," said Mrs. Kagawa.

He laughed and replied with a wave of his hand. "Curves belong on you ladies."

The women sputtered in embarrassment and Mrs. Kagawa apologized to Jean. "He is too free with his tongue, but we let it go because he's the poet in the family."

"You write poetry? I'd like to read some," said Jean.

Tom laughed. "Don't get him started. He also recites."

"But I'd love to hear some too," Jean protested.

"I'll have Helen bring you some copies," Uncle Shuji agreed, temporarily serious.

The bantering picked up while everyone enjoyed the rare treat of cookies and fruitcake. "Our friend back home sacrificed her own rations of sugar to be able to send this. Such a gift," Mrs. Kagawa marveled.

When Jean finally rose to go home, Helen said, "Tom and I will walk with you, but wait a minute. We have a little gift for you."

"Oh no," said Jean, immediately embarrassed that she had no gift for them.

"Don't worry. It's nothing much. When I said I wanted some token for you, Tom thought of this." She walked to a small table and picked up a miniature pine tree, growing in a flat dish. Velvet green moss carpeted the potting soil. The tree's branches twisted this way and that, creating an exquisite design. "Tom is pretty good at bonsai. He trained this one."

"Oh, thank you. How beautiful," Jean stammered. She cupped her hands under the dish. "I don't know what to say. You've all been so kind."

"You must not feel obligated," said Mr. Kagawa. "We give from joy of knowing you and thankfulness for your teaching here in the colony. You make much effort to know and understand Japanese culture."

"Teaching here is my pleasure, and I'm so lucky to have Helen to help me," she said quickly. Guilt over her hidden agenda almost gagged her. Admiringly, she held up the tree. "I will really treasure this. And tomorrow it will be my living Christmas tree."

She and Helen and Tom put on their coats, scarves, and caps and stepped out into the icy night. Jean had forgotten to wear gloves, so Helen carried the tree in her mittened hands, while Tom opened the door. Outside, the air was still. Their breath made dense white clouds in the light shining from the windows as they walked away from the apartment. Above, glittering stars pierced a blue-black sky. Jean tipped her face up toward them.

"It looks like there'll be no white Christmas tonight," she

said. "Oops!" Her feet skidded sideways on a patch of unexpected ice. She struggled to regain her balance and failed.

Tom, a step behind, grabbed and caught her before she crashed to the frozen ground. With his arms wrapped tightly around her, he carefully straightened, bringing her upright against himself. Slowly he eased his hold but still held her close. His breath was warm against her cheek. His arms wrapped protectively around her seemed like an embrace. Jean suddenly wished she was facing him, wished that she could reach up and pull his face down to hers . . . his lips to hers.

"You okay now?" he said lightly beside her ear.

"Yes," she gasped.

Cautiously he released her. "Maybe we should hold onto each other." He tucked Jean's hand under his elbow. "Helen, take my other arm."

They walked on carefully, saying nothing, for fear of waking the people in the nearby barracks. Their voices, even from the street, could easily be heard through the thin walls. The ensuing silence left Jean with her distressing thoughts.

*How could I feel any attraction for a Japanese man after the Japanese killed Dave?* Although Tom was an American, her sudden desire for him seemed shameful. Tom had been outspoken in his opposition to the United States, while Dave, unquestioning, had laid down his life for his country.

Jean wanted to let go of Tom's arm, but he had her hand clamped tightly against his side. She'd have to explain if she pulled away, and to be so firmly held was a surprising comfort. She dismissed her impulse. For these few minutes, she would enjoy the unexpected pleasure of feeling cared for. Suspending her mental war, she walked along, matching her steps to his.

When they reached her apartment, she took the tree from Helen, thanked them again, and wished them a merry Christmas.

Inside, Mary was still up. That meant explaining the tree and telling her about the evening. Jean hoped she could conceal the disturbing feelings her experience with Tom had aroused. Soon they would fade and reality would return.

A little voice in her head warned, *Those feelings may not go away.*

She pressed her lips together. *They must, or they'll have to be one more secret.*

# CHAPTER 10

After Christmas the snow came at last, softening the stark lines of the blocks and blocks of ugly barracks. Even the metal stovepipes on the roofs seemed less jarring with a soft quilt of snow around them. Castle Rock, covered with snow, tempted the daring to ski down its steep sides. Unfortunately, injuries were frequent.

To Jean's dismay, the days after Christmas did not diminish her attraction to Tom. She felt half-sick from wanting to see him and horrified that she had reported him to Uncle Al, while at the same time she hated herself for both the desire and the guilt.

Every morning, as if it were an icon, she secretly rested her eyes on Dave's photo hidden in the bottom of her drawer with her engagement ring. Each time she gazed at his smiling face, she pledged herself anew to the task of completing her mission for Uncle Al.

As the days passed, however, devising ways to gather information became increasingly difficult. After Tad's accusation, she never dared return to his mess hall or ask Helen to take her to others. Eating at Helen's mess hall gave her nothing new. When she wrote to Uncle Al, she admitted she no longer felt comfortable trying to meet more young men.

In her apartment one evening, while Mary worked on her lesson plans, Jean read Uncle Al's letter responding to her doubts. "Don't worry about meeting new people. What you've already sent may be enough for the Boss. Plans are in the making, based on what you and my other assistants have turned up. Watch for anything unusual, but don't do anything that will trigger more questions."

He was even more upset about Tad's suspicions than she was.

"There's more involved in this than I can tell you," he explained, "and many more people than you and me."

*You already told me that.* She dropped his letter into her wastebasket, carried it to the stove, and tossed in the contents. The fire flared and she slammed the door.

Mary never looked up from her book.

Jean asked Helen's Uncle Shuji to come to class and show the children how to write haiku.

The day he came, six inches of snow fell. Having played in icy fluff all the way to school, the children tumbled into the building with giggles and sparkling eyes. Helen brushed the snow off their boots and coats outside the door with the broom. Still they tracked some in, where it instantly formed puddles, large and small. Jean gave their coats a final shake and hung them on the wall near the stove, hoping they would dry quickly. With measles on the increase, she didn't want any of them to chill next time they went out.

After roll call and the flag salute, Helen introduced Uncle Shuji. Sitting on one of the children's chairs so he could be on their level, he told them a story about a famous Japanese poet and read some haiku he had written for their class. Jean was entranced by the simple beauty of his poems and impressed with his power to conjure up images and meanings beyond the images.

The children listened with rapt attention.

Then suddenly the class cutup began to giggle. Jean, fearing he was laughing at Uncle Shuji or his poetry, scolded, "Osamu! Hush!"

The chubby-cheeked boy struggled for control and pointed. "But teacher, Masuko's coat has sprung a leak."

Following his gesture, she saw a puddle forming under the girl's coat. She went to it, reached into the pocket, and pulled out a handful of slush.

Masuko's two ponytails bobbed as she clapped both hands over her mouth in consternation.

"Osamu," said Jean, "did you put this in Masuko's pocket?" Osamu reluctantly nodded. "I just wanted to surprise her when she put her hand in, but she never found it."

Jean said, "For that you will—"

Before she could finish, Uncle Shuji burst into a gale of laughter. The children took their cue from him and laughed until Jean had to join them.

When they finally quieted, she said, "Osamu, lay Masuko's coat on that table by the stove with the pocket turned out to dry. And don't do that again. If any of you get chilled, you could catch cold, and then you won't get to play in the snow for a long time."

They listened solemnly.

Uncle Shuji said, "Miss Thornton is right. You must take care of yourselves in this cold weather. But if you act wisely, you can have much fun. I've told you how to write a haiku. Now I want you to write about something you saw on the way to school in this beautiful snow. And I shall write about Osamu's snowball."

The children giggled but didn't get out of hand.

He repeated simple rules for composing a haiku verse and printed them on a piece of newsprint.

Jean hung his rules from the front of her desk for everyone to see. "Write quietly, please, so you don't bother others," she said. "If you have questions, you may come and whisper them to Uncle Shuji. When you're finished with your haiku, please make a picture to go with it."

The children labored, counting syllables on their fingers, as Uncle Shuji had shown them. At last they were all done, and Uncle Shuji asked them to take turns reading them to him. Whether shy or bold, they read well and beamed when their classmates applauded.

Jean was astonished at the maturity of their poems. After class was dismissed that day, she said, "Helen, these should be on display at the administration building. Let's mount them on the red construction paper we have left from Christmas."

When they finished the display, she silently read the framed poems. To one girl, the snow was a comforting bandage wrapped around the ugly barracks; to a boy, the fun of sliding on ice to school stirred a wish to return to life before the internment; for another girl, the chimneys on snow-blanketed roofs elicited an image of new, friendly guardians watching over the camp.

Although all the poems expressed fun and appreciation of beauty, they also seemed to reveal hidden pools of fear and pain and loss. She bowed her head over their carefully lettered verses, humbled by how Uncle Shuji had helped her see inside the children. Surely now she could do more to help each one.

She read Masaru's poem again.

*New snow burns my face,*
*my hands, my feet—no warming*
*from this winter fire.*

Among them all, his image of snow touched her most. It seemed tragically mature, for according to Helen, the internment was a burning cold to most adults.

She handed the page to Helen. "Do you think Masaru was thinking beyond the literal words?"

Helen read it again and shook her head. "Not likely. These children are too young to do that."

"But surely it's a cry from some deep place . . . all of these must be. Poor little kids." Tears of sympathy welled into her eyes. "Being taken from their homes and friends must have done things to them that will affect them the rest of their lives."

Staring at her with raised eyebrows, Helen folded her arms and cocked her head to one side. "Probably. And then again, maybe not. Of all the people here, I think the oldest ones suffer the most. Parents shelter the little children, and most people my age are able to make the best of a bad situation. It's even kind of fun being in an all-Japanese town where there's no shortage of dates," she smiled wryly, "even if there's no place to go. But the old people . . . some are literally dying of broken hearts."

"That's too bad." Then Jean corrected herself. "It's worse than too bad!" She stopped, amazed that she was saying the right words without any forethought and that she truly meant it.

Helen gave her a quizzical look and returned to straightening the room.

A few minutes later, before Helen left for the night, she said, "Oh, by the way, Tom said he could come Friday and show the children how to start a bonsai tree, so I told him it would be a nice way to end the day after lunch. I hope that's all right."

"Sure," Jean said, suppressing the tingle of excitement her announcement brought. "Fine. Is there anything we need to provide?"

"I don't think so, but I'll ask him."

After Helen left, Jean pressed both palms to her temples. *This is insane. For my own peace of mind, I shouldn't even be around Tom.* All the same, she was glad he was coming.

★

Friday afternoon Tom arrived promptly at two.

Jean asked Helen to assist him. They gathered the children around a table on which he spread out his tools, tree, and planting dish. Kneeling beside the table, he said, "The tree drinks water and food through its roots. I will remove the largest roots to make it drink slowly and grow slowly. Also the tree will stay happier in a small pot with the big roots gone."

Jean watched his deft movements. His fingers maneuvered the tiny clippers around the fragile roots with the skill of a surgeon. She wondered why he'd dropped premed, when he'd probably make a good doctor. Her eyes moved to his face. While no one was looking, she studied its angular planes, his smooth flat cheeks, the line of his dark eyes and brows, his straight nose, and the chiseled curve of his lips. Why did she find him desirable? A face like his had looked down a bomb sight and released the bomb that killed Dave.

He glanced up at her and raised one eyebrow.

She lowered her eyes to the tree in his hand and kept her attention there. Dave used to sense when she was thinking about him. *But Tom is not Dave,* she chastised herself. *He just happened to look up.* She walked slowly to a vantage point behind him.

He poured a little sandy soil into the dish and stood the tree on it. Then he let several children pour more soil over the roots and pat it down. "Gently," he cautioned. "It's like tucking a baby into bed."

Once the tree was securely set, he turned the dish and studied it from all sides. With quick snips he removed a few tiny branches and shortened two long ones. Then he carefully shaped several short lengths of wire. Tenderly bending the main branches around the wire, he tied them. "The tree will grow the way it's bent, if we hold it there. After a while, we will look at it again and decide where to bend it next."

He handed an envelope to a girl and asked her to sprinkle the contents on top of the soil. It looked like brown dirt, but he explained, "This is dried moss. When you water the tree, the moss will turn green and grow a velvet carpet under the tree."

He pulled a clean rag out of the bag he had brought, wiped his hands, and leaned back on his heels. "Kids, you and I are a lot like trees. If we do something over and over, it becomes a habit. Habits are like invisible wires that bend us. They can help us grow ugly or beautiful. Every time you look at this tree, I hope you will think about choosing good habits."

Jean stepped forward. "Boys and girls, how do we thank Mr. Kagawa?"

They clapped with enthusiasm.

Jean said to Tom, "Thank you for showing us how to start a bonsai tree and for reminding us about habits. We'll be talking about building some good habits next week." Turning back to the children, she said, "Time to place your chairs on your tabletops, and then get your coats on and line up at the door by Miss Kagawa."

Tom helped with the chairs, buttoned coats, looked for mittens, and pulled on boots. When the children finally marched out, Jean pushed her hair back from her forehead and said, "You're a good teacher. You kept the children interested every minute, and even I will remember your little lesson about habits."

"I like kids . . . their imagination and honesty." He smiled. "You do all right with them yourself."

"Thank you, kind sir." She tried to give him her best interpretation of a Japanese bow.

"You'll never get that right," he teased. "You're just not the bowing type."

"So what type am I?"

"I haven't decided yet." He studied her thoughtfully.

"Let me know when you do," she said with a laugh. Her heart, ignoring her resolution not to respond to him, began to race. Turning away, she went through the motions of clearing off her desk.

"See you later, sis," Tom called to Helen, who was dampering down the coal stove for the night. "Got to get to the hospital. We're overloaded with winter illness, and the nurses are about to drop."

Helen came over. "Can they use volunteers like me? I could do chores in the evening that don't take special training."

"Sure they could. Why don't you come and ask after you finish here?"

"Okay."

"Why don't you go on now with Tom," Jean said. "All the papers are ready for Monday, and I'll take today's work home with me."

"All right. See you later then," said Helen.

As brother and sister left together, Jean called, "Helen, will you ask for me too? I could help a couple of nights a week."

"I'll ask," said Helen. The two stepped out and slammed the door against a rising wind.

Jean straightened her desk and slipped the children's papers into a large envelope for carrying home. Seeing the bonsai tree, still on the child-size table, she picked it up and placed it on the front edge of her desk.

*Habits . . . wires bending us,* she mused. She'd been working so hard at trying to be two people. Who was she becoming? When she was with Tom and Helen, she felt like a liar—a traitor.

*But our country is in a death struggle. Dave gave his life. I can't let personal feelings keep me from doing the little I can do.*

She walked home in the cold waning light, feeling more alone than ever.

★

The following week Jean did help at the hospital. On Wednesday, before leaving for her stint of volunteering, she lingered in her room to listen to the evening news. The familiar voice of Lowell Thomas announced, "Red Army forces have battled to within eighty miles of Kharkov in their effort to take back that city. . . . The British Eighth Army drove today to within fifty miles of Tripoli."

"Not a word about Guadalcanal," she complained to Mary. "It's been hand-to-hand combat around Henderson Field for weeks. How much longer can this go on? They claimed the naval battle that took Rodger was a great step forward, and now, two months later, they still can't take that place."

"Well, the Japanese had a long time to dig in," said Mary.

Jean huffed a sigh of frustration. "You sound like my Uncle Al. Mary, do you ever try to imagine what it's like over there for our men . . . the rain . . . mud . . . steaming jungle . . . malaria . . . and snipers calling your name in perfect American English to get you to show yourself?"

Horrified, Mary grimaced. "They're doing that?"

"I just read about it in the paper. They use common names, like Bill, so someone most likely will answer."

Mary asked abruptly, "Have you ever thought about joining the WACs or WAVEs or the Red Cross?"

Jean blinked. "No. I've been so busy teaching, I haven't thought past next week."

"Well, I sent for information. When this school year's over, I'm leaving for one of them. Want to go along?"

"Gee, Mary, I might," said Jean. "Tell me more about it later. Right now, I need to get to the hospital. They'll be preparing patients for the night and could use some extra hands."

Mary shook her head in disbelief. "This is your third night. You sure are burning your candle at both ends for these people."

Jean shrugged. "It's something to do. And they're desperate for help. After you see how much you're needed, you want to go back. Eighty homes are quarantined with measles now. Kids are coming in with complications and older people are showing up with bronchitis and pneumonia after having flu."

"All the more reason for you to stay home and not expose yourself."

"Yes, Mother," Jean said, imitating a popular teen character on the radio.

"Oh, go on. Get out of here."

"I'll stoke the stove for the night when I come in," Jean

promised as she pulled on her coat. They had learned how to bank the fire so the temperature inside stayed above freezing for dressing in the morning.

At the hospital, another complex of drafty barracks, a cacophony of coughing greeted Jean as soon as she stepped inside. *What an awful place to have to be while you're sick,* she thought again. It was spotlessly clean but so bare and ugly, and there were not enough nurses to answer calls quickly. She headed for the nurses' desk for instructions.

For the next three hours, she filled water pitchers, emptied bedpans, changed soiled beds, and held the heads of vomiting children. She helped a nurse sponge a baby to bring down its fever, and then rigged up a steam tent for an elderly woman who was racked with bronchitis. She ran with a message from a nurse to a doctor and back again.

From time to time she had glimpsed Tom through a doorway, helping on the men's ward. She'd managed to avoid him all week, and the less she had to do with him, the better. In time her attraction to him would wane, but in the meantime, it was a stupid embarrassment.

Just before going home, she stopped in the doorway to the children's ward and peeked in to see if they were all sleeping and covered.

"All done for the night?" came Tom's voice from behind her.

She swung around, almost bumping into him. In a white lab coat, he stood leaning against the door casing with one hand, so close she had to retreat a step to look up at him.

"I didn't hear you coming!"

"Every time I've seen you, you've looked the other way," he corrected. Tipping his head to one side, he peered down at her. "Are you angry at me for some reason?"

"No. Of course not. I've just been busy." He was blocking the door, and she couldn't get away. She stepped forward to suggest that she wanted to leave, but he didn't move. Instead, he just stood staring at her, his head to one side. He reached with one finger and pushed back the strand of her hair that kept slipping across her forehead and tucked it behind her ear. His touch was electrifying.

She stared into his dark eyes. For an endless moment, his

look was tender, loving. He seemed about to kiss her . . . or she was about to kiss him.

In panic she cried, "No!" and pushed on his chest with both hands.

He stepped back. "I beg your pardon," he said sardonically. "Ladies first." He gracefully bowed her through the door. She whisked past him. He walked away without a backward glance.

With burning cheeks she snatched her coat from its peg and walked out the door.

Had she been mistaken in thinking he was going to kiss her? If she were wrong, she had been childishly insulting. She tried to recall the details of that moment, but the memory was already garbled, blended with her memory of Dave pushing her hair back and tipping her face up to his. She broke into sobs.

★

Because of the hospital's tremendous need, Jean worked there the next night. She decided to treat Tom as if nothing had happened, but she did not see him. Nor did she see him the next night or the next. She heard that he and other firefighters had fought a serious chimney fire that threatened one of the blocks.

Saturday morning Jean awoke with a shaking chill, a painful sore throat, and barking cough. "Oh, Mary," she groaned. "Stay away from me. I've got the plague."

Mary ignored her. She climbed out of bed and came over to feel Jean's forehead. "Ouch, kid. I think you better see a doctor. I'll run over and ask the nurses what to do."

Jean felt too ill to argue.

After a while, a nurse came in with Mary. She sent Mary off to breakfast and then looked at Jean's throat and took her temperature. After peering at the thermometer she said, "If I help you dress, do you think you could walk over to the hospital?"

"Yes, but why can't I just stay here?"

"If you leave now, your roommate may be spared. You've got a bad case of flu if I ever saw one."

"But I have papers to grade," Jean argued, unwilling to admit she had more than a bad cold. "And I have to teach Monday."

"Believe me, you won't feel like teaching on Monday," said the nurse. "This is going to get worse before it gets better."

## CHAPTER 11

The isolation ward was one long, open room with screens between beds. By the sound of the coughing, every bed must be occupied.

Jean felt a little foolish climbing into a hospital bed. Before afternoon, however, she was glad to be there. Despite aspirin, her fever soared and her whole body ached. When she walked to the bathroom, she was so lightheaded, she had to lean on the wall to keep from falling, and nothing eased her cough.

It was so painful to swallow, the nurses' aides had to urge her to drink. She began to doze, to slip in and out of unpleasant dreams.

"Jean," someone called.

She opened her eyes to find the Japanese doctor standing beside her bed. "I'd like to try a new medicine on you. It can't help flu, but you've got a nasty bacterial infection in your throat." He handed her a large white pill and a glass of water.

While writing on Jean's chart, he said to the Japanese nurse, "Give her one every four hours, and draw blood in the morning. We'll need to monitor it."

The pill stuck halfway to Jean's stomach; she gulped the rest of the water and finally got it down. "What is this stuff?" she asked.

"It's called sulfa," the doctor said. "It's been a godsend on the battlefield for preventing infection in wounds, but we're just beginning to discover what it can do for throats like yours and for pneumonia."

"Have I got pneumonia?"

"You've got the beginnings. We're hoping the sulfa will stop it. You try to rest now, but you must force yourself to drink all the fluids the nurses bring you. I've prescribed a different cough syrup that may ease your cough without stopping you from clearing your lungs."

He left. The nurse filled her glass again. "Try to drink this."

Jean obeyed and then dropped her head back to her pillow. The room rocked crazily around her. She closed her eyes, wishing she were home in Salem in her own bed.

She was so tired—

It was a hot summer day. Her back ached from lying too long in the hammock in the backyard. She tried to climb out, to change her position, but the hammock wrapped around her and pulled tighter. "Grandmother!"

"It's all right, Jean. Just rest, while I straighten your covers," said her grandmother. "Here. It's time for another pill."

Jean awoke enough to see she was in the hospital at Tulelake. They must have called her grandmother. Good. She'd know what to do for this aching and coughing. Jean relaxed.

Several times she awoke to see through a blur that Grandmother was still sitting beside the bed, offering her a drink, smoothing her covers. *I'll never make fun of her nursing ways again.*

Jean awoke, coughing, choking, gagging. She struggled to sit up. Someone held a basin under her chin. Everything looked so fuzzy. She spit out and laid her head down again, panting.

Grandmother urged her to swallow another pill. The room faded away.

Dave was sitting beside her on the top step of the front porch. She snuggled against him, leaning her head against his shoulder. "I always knew you'd come home."

He held her close and told her he'd never leave again. And then suddenly he picked up her left hand and cried out, "You're not wearing my ring! It was a mistake to think I could come back to the life I left." He leaped to his feet and ran down the steps.

"No! No—"

She awoke coughing.

A strange voice said, "We'll have to stop the sulfa. Her hemoglobin is dropping."

The puzzling words reminded Jean of the Red Queen and White Queen, talking nonsense in *Alice in Wonderland*.

Jean struggled to go back home . . . to find Dave and tell him his ring was safe . . . safe . . . somewhere. *Dave! Dave—*

Grandmother put a cool cloth on her forehead. It felt good, but she must find Dave—

Shells whistled . . . bombs thundered. Out of the spinning dark, Dave caught her hand and she wrapped her arms around him. He held her close.

A strange man's voice cut through the roar of the war—"She's young and strong. She should be throwing this off."

Grandmother said, "We will keep trying."

Jean wondered who they were talking about and why they were suddenly there with her and Dave.

"We've got to wake her," came another man's voice.

Someone gripped her shoulder.

Her back was aching. She opened her eyes. Above her floated two Japanese faces. She closed her eyes. *Dave, don't leave me here!*

"Jean, look at me. It's Tom. Open your eyes and look at me."

Tom? Tulelake. Hospital. She didn't want to see Tom! She searched for a way back into her dreams. If only she could touch Dave once more—

"Jean, you've got to wake up." Strong hands lifted her by the shoulders and propped a pillow behind her.

"Here, dear, drink this." A woman's voice . . . not her grandmother.

Jean opened her eyes and found Helen's Aunt Tatsu holding a glass of water to her lips. She took a sip and then drifted back into blessed drowsiness.

Strong hands shook her. "Jean! Wake up!"

She tried to flee deeper into sleep.

Hands jerked her upright and stuffed another pillow behind

her. Tom said, "Open your eyes. I know you can hear me." He shook her.

"Tom, be gentle," cautioned Aunt Tatsu.

"No. That hasn't worked. Jean, do you care about anyone besides yourself? Shall we call in several tired nurses and doctors to pamper you?"

*How dare he?* Jean's eyes flew open. She squinted and focused on him. "Go away," she rasped.

"Not until you try to stay awake and drink and eat and cooperate with your nurses," he said firmly. To implement his words, he pulled a chair over beside the bed and sat down.

"How dare you accuse me of wanting to be pampered?" she croaked. The effort set her coughing.

"Oh, Tom, now see what you've done," said Aunt Tatsu, jumping up and putting an arm around Jean's shoulders.

"She's got to cough to clear her lungs," he said. The two of them held her upright until she quit.

"Get out," Jean whispered at Tom.

Tom frowned at her. "Only if you promise to cooperate."

"You can't order me around." Her words came out in a squeaky whisper, which made her angrier.

He laughed.

She clamped her teeth against the urge to cough and glared in silent rage.

"Now you look more like yourself," he said, still chuckling. "Maybe I can trust you to stay awake after all." He rose to his feet and strolled away.

She leaned back on her pillows, panting from the exertion and glowering after him.

Aunt Tatsu asked, "Could you drink a little tea?"

She sounded just like Grandmother. Had Grandmother ever been here? Jean nodded. "Tea does sound good," she whispered.

After tea, a nurse brought her bouillon and some clear fruit-flavored gelatin.

While Aunt Tatsu helped her lie down again, Jean asked, "Did I talk in my sleep?"

The older woman shook her head. "No. You were very quiet. Too quiet. We were worried about you."

"Thanks for coming. Have you been here long?"

"For a while."

"I'm really tired and sleepy."

"Then you sleep. Now that you've taken nourishment, you can rest again."

"May I call you Aunt Tatsu?"

"Yes, if you like."

"I had an Aunt Esther once. She got cancer and died, but the person you remind me of most is my mother. She died too." Jean realized she was rambling. She closed her eyes and soon fell into a dreamless sleep.

When she awoke, she was ravenous. Winter sunlight slanted across the bed from the window. Aunt Tatsu was dozing in the chair beside her bed. Jean turned to look at the sky, streaked with high clouds.

"Jean?" called Aunt Tatsu. "You're awake."

Jean turned back to her. "Yes. How long have I been sick?"

"Five days. It's Thursday."

She had missed the whole week of school? "Poor Helen."

"She's doing all right. A couple of mothers are assisting her."

Later, while Jean ate a poached egg on milk toast, Aunt Tatsu admitted that she and three of her Issei friends had taken turns sitting with Jean. "You were too sick to leave alone, and there aren't enough nurses."

Around them, beyond the screens surrounding the bed, a chorus of coughs reminded Jean she was one of many. "You mean you and the others have been with me all week?" she asked in amazement. "I don't know how to thank you."

Tatsu politely brushed away her thanks. "It's just something we can do. You don't raise a family without learning how to do some nursing."

"Yes, but . . . I'm not family."

"You know what Jesus said about being a neighbor?"

Jean remembered from Sunday school. "The good Samaritan story."

Tatsu nodded. "The one who needs me is my neighbor and my family."

"I wish you truly were my aunt," Jean said soberly.

Tatsu chuckled. "But if what Jesus said is true, I am."

Jean laughed with her. "Thanks!" She finished her meal and leaned back, savoring the wholesome comfort of feeling full after being very hungry.

"Tom will be glad to hear you're on the mend," said Tatsu.

"I doubt that. He thought I was playing games to get attention."

"He only said that to strike some sparks, to wake you up. My dear, you were slipping away. The doctor thought you were dying. And Tom just set his mind to do something about it. I think he may have saved your life."

Jean sat speechless for a moment. "I was that sick?"

Tatsu nodded. "No one could rouse you. The doctor had done all he could. I thought Tom was too harsh, but now I see why. You have been on the mend ever since."

"I had a lot of dreams. I really didn't want to wake up," Jean admitted. "Will Tom be at the hospital tonight?"

"I'm sure he will. Helen wants him to bring get well cards the children have made for you. She isn't allowed in the contagious ward. Same for your teacher friends. They've been turned away all week."

Tatsu excused herself for supper, and Jean lay down to rest. Next thing Jean knew, she opened her eyes and Tom was at her bedside.

"Mailman. Express delivery from Miss Thornton's second-grade class." He laid a stack of folded newsprint papers on the top of her covers.

She picked up one. "Oh, how cute!" She glanced from the greeting to him. Lacking the energy to deny the stir of gladness she felt at the sight of his smiling face, she gave in to the pleasure. It was so good to see him.

Tom, in his white lab coat, was obviously taking time from work. He ignored the chair, but lingered. "Helen said to tell you the kids all bought extra defense savings stamps in hopes it would make you feel proud of your class."

"I'll write them a note of thanks as soon as I can. In the meantime, will you tell them I am very proud of them?"

"Sure. You look better after the scare you gave us."

"Aunt Tatsu told me. I didn't know I was that sick." She

wanted to thank him for his part in trying to help her, but she sensed he would not want to talk about it.

"How do you feel?" he asked in a professional manner.

She smiled. "You sound like one of the doctors. Are you sure you haven't missed your calling?"

He smiled back. "Quite sure. I've about decided I must have signed on at the hospital to prove to myself I was not cut out to be a physician."

"Well, I'm glad you were here to help me." As she had guessed, he didn't want to talk about that.

A shadow of discomfort crossed his face. "I hoped you wouldn't remember. Well, I've got to get back to work, and you need to rest. Enjoy your get-well cards."

"I will, and thanks."

His back was already turned. He waved a hand without looking back.

*Strange man. So distant and cool now, yet so caring. I shouldn't have reported anything he said to Uncle Al. I'm positive he'd never be involved in a hostile act against our country.* Her next thought was even more chilling. *Maybe I've misunderstood all the men I've reported on.*

The more she recalled and reconsidered, the more she felt she was right. It was as if her illness had cleared away some kind of mental fog. Remembering things Tom had said, she realized that even his most aggressive remarks could be taken two ways. As soon as she could, she would write to Uncle Al and tell him.

★

Next morning, Jean asked the doctor how soon she could leave the hospital.

"Maybe in a couple of days," he said. "Even then, you'll have to stay indoors for a few days. We don't want a relapse."

"That's the understatement of the year," Jean said with a laugh that made her cough.

Aunt Tatsu came after lunch. "Is there anything I can bring you?" she asked. "We have some notions in our co-op stores."

"If you have a magazine you're through with, I wouldn't mind. No matter if it's old. I haven't looked at anything but the newspaper for weeks."

After Aunt Tatsu left, Jean lapsed into boredom. From time to time she walked about the isolation ward, wrapped in her warm robe and slippers, but there was nothing to see or do and she felt in the way of the busy nurses and aides. She hoped Tom would come again but tried to prepare herself for the fact that he probably wouldn't. Exhausted, she climbed into bed and slept until suppertime.

Soon after her tray was removed, Tom arrived. He laid her box of stationery on the bed. "Mary thought you'd like this, now that you are recuperating, and Aunt Tatsu sent this." He laid a copy of *McCall's* magazine beside the stationery. Then he dropped a book beside it. "And I thought you might like a really good read." It was a collection of humorous American essays. "When you grow a little stronger, I'll bring you a heavier tome."

She picked up the book eagerly. "It's been so long since I read anything for fun."

He shook his head in exaggerated concern. "Not good. No wonder you got sick."

She laughed. "You think reading for fun can keep one well?"

"I think nourishing our minds and souls is as important to health as good food is. Our culture is slipping away from age-old truths that every good mother used to know."

"You put stock in old wives' tales then?" she teased.

"Not all of them. But there's a lot of old truth that needs to be looked at again. I guess that's one reason I decided to change my major. That and the fact that I could never stand to lose a patient. I was lucky enough to learn that before I entered medical school." He paused, remembering.

"Are you going to tell me?" she asked lightly.

"Yeah." He remained standing, as if he must be ready to go if summoned. "There was this kid. I was volunteering at the city hospital like I am now. He was sixteen, recovering from an accident that left him with only one leg. I spent a lot of time with him. He started counting on me when things were rough. And then I came one day and his bed was empty. Just like that, a blood clot took him. Losing him laid me so low, I knew I'd never survive as a physician. A doctor has to be able to live above his losses."

"But you see patients die here. Why do you volunteer?"

"It's different when it's not my responsibility. Not easy, but different . . . and you've seen how badly they need help."

"Yes. I don't like hospital work either, but I wanted to help."

"When you're released, you must not come back," he said abruptly. "You'll be susceptible to pneumonia for some time. You've got to protect yourself. The doctors will tell you that, of course," he finished almost apologetically and fell silent.

"I wish I could get out of here tomorrow," she remarked.

"You'll be released as soon as possible, but not a minute sooner than is good for you, so you might as well relax and enjoy a rest," said Tom.

"Because enjoying will get me well quicker," she supplied, mimicking his matter-of-fact tone.

"Exactly," he said without an answering smile. "See you later." He left.

With her stationery at hand, she ought to write to Uncle Al, but she would have to wait until she could carry it to the post office herself. She picked up the book from Tom.

Every time she talked to him, she felt more certain she had utterly misjudged him. How could she have been so wrong? It was as if she'd been blind. *I can't believe I've given such misleading information.*

*The war is the reason,* said a little voice inside her head. Losing Dave and the threat of war coming to the West Coast. It was like a voice from the past, totally unrelated to the reality of today.

She had been removed from the war for several days, and she didn't want to get back into it, but she must. *Oh, Dave, how could I forget you . . . and Rodge . . . and Pearl Harbor?*

She tried to see Dave's face in her mind as she always had to comfort herself. She couldn't call up a perfect image! His face, so dear, was fading from her memory. *I must see his photo,* she thought in panic, but she couldn't, not until she could go back to the apartment.

Feeling trapped, Jean sought distraction by writing to her grandmother, taking care to play down the seriousness of her illness. Then she wrote a note to Caroline, hoping the letter would be forwarded if she had left home to live near the base where Rudy was still in training.

Finally, tired and unhappy, she picked up the book Tom had left. She couldn't keep her mind on it. Soon she fell into a troubled sleep.

★

Jean was not released the next day. Tom stopped to say that Aunt Tatsu wouldn't be in to visit because now Uncle Shuji had come down with the flu. Tom lingered no longer than it took him to deliver the message.

The next evening Tom said Uncle Shuji had been admitted to the hospital. He too had pneumonia but was responding well to treatment.

By Sunday Jean's cough was loose and less frequent. Her strength was returning rapidly. She hoped to be released, but the doctor said no.

Outside the wind roared across the frozen earth. Jean paced most of the day, refusing to be served anything she could get for herself. The weight of all she wanted to do when she got out pressed her spirits down. She finally climbed into bed, hoping she could sleep and forget about everything. She couldn't.

When Tom came in after supper, he took one look at her face and said, "Are you worse?"

She shook her head. "I'm just frustrated. I want out! How is Uncle Shuji?"

He came over and sat in the chair by her bed. "Pretty well. They're not sure it is pneumonia." He changed the subject back to her. "You'll probably get out tomorrow. My mother always said she could tell when we were well—we got cranky."

Jean smiled in spite of herself. "That's what Grandmother always said too."

"So you might as well relax and—"

"Enjoy myself," she finished with a chuckle. It felt good to laugh . . . and so good to be with him. She was too tired to worry about the consequences. Might as well forget for a while and just enjoy the presence of this attractive man who had saved her life.

Impulsively she asked, "If you could be anywhere you wished tonight, where would you choose?"

He responded instantly, "Paulina Lake in central Oregon. Ever been there?"

"No. What's it like?"

"Like heaven on earth. It's part of a volcanic crater. The water is turquoise blue. The shore is like a landscaped garden with great slabs of cream-colored rock and short shrubs that look as if God had just pruned them. Pine trees stand around, sheltering everything and whispering in the breeze."

"And are there fish?"

"Rainbow beauties, but I mostly remember the peace. Sometimes when I can't sleep, I think about it instead of counting sheep." He smiled lazily. "What about you? Where would you like to be tonight?"

She had been so caught up in his description, she'd forgotten about her own dream place. She thought back to Uncle Al's farm. "I used to visit my uncle's farm on a high hill south of Salem. From the old apple tree in his orchard I could see all the way to Mount Hood and Mount Jefferson. He built me a tree house there, where I felt snug and peaceful." She was about to add that that's where she'd like to be, but she realized in a flash of surprise, she was happier right now, here with Tom.

*No, that's not true. I need to get back to the real world.* She stiffened and said somberly, "It was silly of me to bring up childhood dreams. Those days are gone forever; the war has changed everything."

Tom raised his chin and looked at her with lowered lids. "I disagree. We'll need every dream we can cling to, to get through this war and not be destroyed." He stood up. "Dreams are necessary for us as internees, and they're just as important for all of you who are on the other side of the fence."

For Jean his words drew a proper line between them. She was careful not to cross it again. Their conversation dwindled to small talk.

After a bit, he excused himself and went to work, and she fruitlessly pursued sleep. The fence between them was far higher than he could ever guess, for he had saved her life, but she had betrayed him.

# CHAPTER 12

To Jean, staying indoors in the apartment offered little improvement over hospitalization. Cold seeped in through the walls and floor. The coal stove was like a campfire, making her too hot on one side while cold on the other. To combat the persistent chill that iced her feet and crept up her legs, she put on pajamas under slacks and wore two pairs of socks.

She wrote a careful letter to Uncle Al, telling him everything she could think of to exonerate Tom. She added that she now felt none of the men she had listed were likely to be any danger to the war effort. Sealing the letter, she decided to take it directly to the post office. If she were quick, she could be back before Mary came in from school.

She found she couldn't walk fast. Her legs felt heavy and tired. She did the best she could, but she arrived back home breathing hard and coughing.

Before Mary came home, Helen knocked at the door. At Jean's invitation, she came in and laid some papers on Jean's desk. "The children sent you welcome-home notes. These papers are all corrected. I just wanted you to see how well they are doing."

"Thanks. I needed this." Jean reached eagerly for the top paper and scanned the childish scrawl. "They're such good kids," she said. Laying the papers aside, however, she turned to Helen. "How's it going? They give you enough help?"

"Teaching by myself kept me hopping for a couple of days. Now two teaching assistants help with paperwork and our reading time. The three of us don't do as well as you and I did though."

Jean sensed that Helen's guard was down. During her absence, Helen's cautious armistice had disappeared and in its place was a hint of friendship. Jean welcomed the change. "That's kind of you to say, but I know you could do it alone," she corrected. "How is Uncle Shuji? I was getting daily reports from Tom while I was in the hospital."

Helen's warm brown eyes looked away. "They say he has lung cancer."

"Oh no," groaned Jean.

"They've known from the first day, but Tom didn't want you to know while you were so sick."

"Is he . . . how long do they think he has?" she asked painfully.

Helen shook her head sadly. "Not long. It was a hemorrhage that sent him to the hospital. One more could be the last. He was able to hide earlier symptoms from all of us because he'd had a smoker's cough for years, and we never wondered why it didn't go away when he quit smoking."

"I wish there was something I could do for Aunt Tatsu; she's done so much for me," mourned Jean.

"She knows you aren't strong enough to sit with him. My mother and father and her friends all go, and Tom and I do what we can. But she won't stay away long enough to really rest."

"I don't blame her. Oh, Helen, it's so unfair!" she cried. "He's one of the kindest, most talented men I've ever met. And your aunt is one of the most loving."

Helen nodded and said with resignation, "Not much in life is fair."

A sorrowful silence fell between them until Helen broke it. "I need to go eat early so I can sit with Uncle Shuji while the others eat."

"Give him my love, please. And tell Aunt Tatsu . . . I'll be praying for them."

Helen nodded again. "See you tomorrow."

As soon as she left, Jean sat at her desk, bowed her head, and tried to pray. She said all the proper words, but she felt

God was a million miles away. She tried to recapture her Christmas feeling, that God loved each person in an intimate, fatherly way, but she couldn't.

Nevertheless, she pleaded for comfort for Uncle Shuji and Aunt Tatsu.

★

The day Jean returned to her classroom, Uncle Shuji died.

Jean attended his funeral the following Sunday afternoon at the Union Church. The barrack was filled to overflowing. There were no flowers, but after the minister's message, many people stood to offer eulogies.

A young man sang "Beyond the Sunset," and Tom read one of Uncle Shuji's poems, which reminded Jean of Walt Whitman's poetry, a love song to America.

When Tom finished, he said, "Shuji Kagawa wrote his last poems for you who are here in Tulelake colony. He wanted to encourage you. I've obtained permission from the *Tulean Dispatch* to make a booklet of them, using their mimeograph machine. The booklet should be available next week at the churches and in the co-op stores. Proceeds from the sale will fund a writing contest for our high-school students. Shuji Kagawa's poems have been published in many prestigious Japanese magazines, but he believed this last mimeographed publication would be his most important."

Pallbearers carried Uncle Shuji's body in its wooden coffin out to the barren patch of ground that had been designated for burials. Jean, the only Caucasian in the procession, walked with the family. She hadn't noticed the cemetery until now. When they reached the place, she was shocked to see so many graves, both large and small; the camp had existed for less than nine months.

She looked around sorrowfully. To be buried in a place like this during an imprisonment, however necessary . . . no memorial stones, no plantings or decorations, just stakes with names marking the mounds. *Uncle Shuji deserves better,* she mourned. Then she added angrily, *They all deserve better.*

Jean tied her woolen bandanna tighter under her chin as they gathered around the frozen grave hole. How had the men been able to hack it open?

The minister said the last words and the coffin was lowered. Mr. Kagawa dropped a handful of frozen soil onto it. Jean wept for the family and then walked away, leaving them with their closer friends. In a few minutes, however, Tom and Helen caught up with her and accompanied her back into the project. It was too cold to linger at the grave.

Tears kept trickling down Jean's cheeks. She brushed them away with the back of her hand.

Tom said, "He died very peacefully. He wanted us to be happy for him. He believed he left the world a slightly better place than he found it."

"I knew him for such a short time. I feel cheated," said Jean.

"He would have considered that the highest of compliments," said Tom.

"He liked you too," added Helen. "He would be pleased that you came to his funeral."

"It was beautiful to hear everyone's stories about him. That kind of memorial can't be bought."

"Yeah," said Tom. "His life and his writing are both fine memorials. He was an honorable Japanese man and also an ardent American patriot. He hoped his last poems would inspire fresh love for the country that mistakenly imprisoned him.

"I don't know how much you know about U.S. laws and the Japanese, but he and the others who immigrated here have not been allowed to become citizens. He had hoped to see the day when Japanese immigrants would be treated like others and he could become naturalized. When he realized he'd never make it, he never gave up that hope for others.

"He insisted the American dream would come true someday for us, as it has for European immigrants. He believed that fair-minded Americans will recognize the injustice of this internment some day and make sure that it never happens again. All of his last poems are songs of praise for the America he envisioned and believed in."

"I wish he had shown me some of those poems," said Jean.

"He would not have wanted to embarrass you," explained Helen.

"Embarrass me? What do you mean?"

"He would have thought that drawing your attention to the American dream now, while we are interned, would embarrass you," said Helen.

"Oh." Too late Jean realized she should have thought of that.

Tom came to her rescue, offering an excuse for her lack of sensitivity. "You've lived in a different world, being born to Caucasian parents in your native country."

Bewildered, she said, "I guess so, but such careful courtesy is mind-boggling. You see how dense I am. If he had let me read those poems, I would only have thought about the American dream and not about the internment. It's wartime. Things can't be normal right now for any of us."

"Maybe so," said Tom. "But things are more normal for some people than for others. By canceling out our civil rights, the government deprives us of any way to prove our loyalty." He was impassioned but not angry.

Jean glanced up at his profile. Was his anger gone? Had he changed while watching Uncle Shuji die, or was it a temporary mellowing because of the funeral?

He kept his dark eyes fixed on the frozen road ahead, giving her no clue beyond the even tone of his voice. "There's a rumor going around; I think there's something to it. We may be allowed to enlist. As soon as I can, I will. Like Uncle Shuji, I believe America is worth dying for, even though it has temporarily failed us."

"You mean you'll be released from here to go into the service?" asked Jean.

He nodded, still gazing ahead. "There's talk about a registration of all Japanese in the internment camps. It sounds as if those of us who want to may be released to join the army."

"Tom, you never said a word about this to Mother and Father," Helen accused.

"Well, it's still a rumor, and you know how wild rumors can be around here, and you shouldn't pass this on," he cautioned, "because I haven't been able to verify it, but I do trust the person who told me. He has a family friend in congress who's sympathetic to our situation."

Jean pursued his first statement. "So if you can, you'll join up. Have you wanted to enlist all along?"

"Sure, but there was no way. The men who planned this internment wouldn't listen to any of us. Now that our armed forces are beginning to push the Japs back in the South Pacific and Burma and Alaska, and there hasn't been a single act of sabotage attempted by anyone of Japanese ancestry, I think some of the hysteria is fading. I think the people who put us here may regain their reason." Jean was startled to hear him use the word *Japs,* and with the same connotation any American soldier would. They were his enemy.

Their walk brought them to Jean's apartment. They stopped. She looked up at him with awakened understanding. "I hope the rumor is true," she said.

She felt as if her country had betrayed her, just as it had betrayed him. She hoped he would be granted a way back to self-respect, but she believed she might never escape her secret shame.

"Going to church tonight?" asked Helen.

Jean shook her head. "I'm pretty tired."

Tom studied her face with his physician's look. "You're too pale. You shouldn't have come to the cemetery, but we all appreciate it, especially Aunt Tatsu. You should climb into bed with a hot-water bottle on your feet and take a nap," he advised.

She smiled weakly and nodded. With a wave good-bye, she climbed the steps and went inside.

She wasn't chilled at all from the weather. Her chill came from the inside. She had betrayed Tom and Helen and all their family. She had acted out of prejudice just as much as those who had planned the internment. She had willingly fallen for every word of it, even before Uncle Al had asked her to become a fact finder. Just like the others, she had used expediency as her excuse. One couldn't tell German aliens and Italian aliens from the rest of the Caucasians, but at least the Japanese threat could be contained.

Mary was out somewhere, probably at Ann's apartment. The coal stove still gave off some heat. Jean shoveled in more coal and then slumped into her upholstered chair. She stared out the window at Castle Rock. Beyond it stood Mount Shasta in the distance, with its head in the clouds. Gazing at its peaceful white sides, she thought, *I'll never feel clean again. I'd like to walk out there and never come back.*

More than anything in the world, Jean wished she had never come to Tulelake to spy. She went to her dresser and pulled out Dave's picture. *They killed him,* she reminded herself. *I had to do something.* She studied his honest eyes. They gave her no comfort, for if he knew the Kagawas, even he would condemn her for betraying them.

All of her reasons for being a fact finder melted before a single truth: She had misjudged a whole group of people because she had believed stereotypes. She had expected Japanese people to have many characteristics in common. Among other things, she had expected them to be inscrutable, devious, and treacherous. And in blindness to her own prejudice, she had become inscrutable, devious, and treacherous.

She sat staring at Dave's picture until the light outside began to fade. Mary was still gone. Unable to bear her thoughts, she decided to go to church after all. With the hot plate, she made herself a cup of tea, ate an apple, and left a note for Mary.

By the time she reached the chapel, it was dark outside and the service had begun. Someone beckoned her to a seat. She flashed them a smile of thanks, sat down, and joined the singing, all the while looking for Tom and Helen. They were nowhere in sight. Maybe the family wanted to be alone tonight.

The pastor's sermon gave Jean no solace. She wondered why she had come and began to count the minutes until she could leave. When the closing hymn ended, she headed for the door, hoping to get out without having to talk to anyone. Beside the door, with a beaming smile, stood Pastor Ichiba. She could not avoid his outstretched hand. As his fingers closed warmly on hers, she wondered if he could see how trapped she felt.

"We are so glad to see you well again," he said. "You look troubled," he continued without hesitation. "Was the funeral difficult for you?"

"Yes and no," she answered as directly as he had inquired. "Uncle Shuji's life was an inspiration, but to have him die here . . ." She shook her head in sorrow.

"He would tell you that where one dies or how one dies is of little consequence. What is important is who one is. Shuji's blessing was that he never grew deaf to the voice of Christ."

Jean stopped wishing she could get away from Pastor Ichiba. She asked urgently, "How does one hear the voice of Christ?"

He said, "My answer to that may sound like a paradox. I think one must obey Christ in order to hear him. Shuji said that in the beginning of his faith, he obeyed what he learned about Christ from the Bible. And then one day, he could almost hear the Lord speaking in his mind, guiding him and encouraging him. He said the secret after that was not to say no to the Lord."

"And the war did not change that for Uncle Shuji?" She knew the answer as she asked.

"He kept his attention on Christ, who does not change, come war or peace."

"You mean war should not change us either? But war demands action that would be unconscionable at other times. Doesn't it?"

"Not for Shuji," said Pastor Ichiba.

Others were leaving the building. They nodded in a friendly manner to Jean and Pastor Ichiba but did not interrupt them.

"Do you hear Christ inside yourself?" persisted Jean.

"Yes. I have been so blessed."

Jean said, almost to herself, "With the war and all, I've felt God had bigger things to think about than me."

"In wartime, most of all, we must not grow deaf to his voice. He accomplishes big things through the small people who listen."

Jean nodded uncomfortably. She could not take in any more. Excusing herself as politely as she could, she left.

On the cold walk home, she looked up into the blackness pierced by numberless stars and wondered how anyone could possibly hear from the God who had set them in motion.

## CHAPTER 13

Monday morning before walking to school, Jean went to one of the pay phones near the soldiers' quarters and called her uncle's office. Her breath made a fog as she spoke to his secretary.

"Your uncle is in England," Miss Landry said. "I expect him back later this week. I'll tell him you called."

"Thanks. It's urgent."

Disappointed, Jean ran back to her apartment and wrote a brief note. "February 1, 1943: Dear Uncle Al, I can no longer participate in any way in this undercover business. I'm positive that everything I wrote about Tom Kagawa was biased and totally misrepresented him. I was utterly wrong. I presumed a lot about the other men too. I really need to talk to you, but I write this, in case you don't get my phone message. Count me out of everything. All my efforts now will go toward clearing the names of the people I mistakenly incriminated."

She reread what she had written and underlined a few words for emphasis. Sealing it, she carried it to the post office on the way to school.

The week passed slowly as Jean waited to hear from her uncle. Finally on Thursday, she and Helen bundled up after school and joined some of their pupils, ice skating on the artificial pond the men had created in a fire break when they couldn't keep the children from making their own rinks between the barracks. The fire department considered ice between the buildings a hazard for the firefighters.

Many parents had managed to acquire skates for the children from mail order or friends back home or hand-me-downs. The skates didn't always fit well, but with wobbly ankles the children scooted around the smooth surface, giggling and whooping. When Jean lost her footing and took a tumble, a dozen small hands reached down to help her up.

She waved them back with a laugh. "I'm afraid I'll fall on you."

Helen came to a swirling stop beside her and gave her a steady hand. "I thought you could skate," she teased.

"I never said that. I said I had tried. We had an ice skating rink in Salem, but somehow it's something I never had time for." She struggled to her feet and stood carefully.

"You should have said so. Here, hold my hand." Helen started off with Jean in tow. Jean plodded along with stiff, chopping steps.

"Relax. Bend your knees a little more. Lean the direction your foot is going."

"That's exactly how I fell down!" Jean exclaimed, but she tried again. With Helen holding her, she began to get the feel of it.

After a few times around the man-made pond, Helen said, "You don't need me anymore." Away she glided, avoiding the children, who were now skittering around like water bugs.

Soon mothers came and called the children to supper. Helen skated to Jean's side. "I have to go now. How about meeting me back here about eight o'clock, when the kids are indoors? Look at the moon! We can skate in the moonlight." Her eyes sparkled with anticipation.

Jean glanced at the full moon, well above the horizon, just beginning to shine in the waning daylight. "Oh, I'd love to, now that I can stand up. I'll bring Mary too."

"See you then."

★

Mary jumped at the chance to skate in the moonlight. The two of them ate quickly, hurried through their pupils' papers, and dressed for action. Jean pulled on navy blue wool slacks, matching cable-knit sweater, and topped it with her Navy-style pea jacket. For once she could make good use of the red mittens, muffler, and knit cap her grandmother had sent for Christmas. Mary dressed all in red.

Walking the project streets in the moonlight, Jean giggled at Mary's description of the last time she'd skated in New York.

Mary elaborated. "In the town where I grew up, my mother tied skates on my feet as soon as I could walk, gave me a push out the back door, and said, 'Stay in the yard.' In the winter she had whole days of peace and quiet when my sisters and brothers all got big enough to be pushed out the back door."

"I never know how much to believe you."

"I never say a word I don't mean," said Mary in an injured tone. "Golly, look at that moon. Can't wait to get my skates on. It'll be like flying."

"I just hope I can keep from falling and learn how to stop. The moonlight is magical—makes you forget there's a war on . . . even here."

When they arrived, the pond was full of adult skaters sedately circling in the same direction. A few twirled in the center. Mary was away and flying on the ice before Jean was ready to stand up. At last Jean cautiously entered the skating traffic, wondering if she would be able to find Helen. She promptly slipped and caught herself. *If I fall, at least Helen will be able to spot me.*

She talked herself into relaxing. Soon she was moving easier, changing speed and direction without mishap. She even stopped abruptly without falling over someone who tumbled in front of her.

On her second time around, Helen glided to her side. "I almost didn't recognize you. You can skate!" she exclaimed. "Come on." She caught Jean's hand and led her away from the crowd. "Hold both my hands and turn your feet as I do."

It wasn't difficult to see Helen's movements in the bright moonlight, and she was a good steady prop until Jean got the hang of it. Soon they were skating as partners, turning this way and that. Helen finally brought them to a halt beside a group of skaters standing at the edge.

"Can you believe it, Tom? Jean just learned to skate today, and she's already doing partners with me."

Tom separated himself from the group and grabbed Jean's mittened hands. "Great. Let's go." They glided away, facing each other.

"You're not going to overdo and get too tired are you?" said Tom. It was more of an order than a question.

"I'm feeling better than I have in long time. Haven't coughed all day."

"You still need to be careful."

"I will."

Tom was a better leader than Helen. At least she felt safer in his strong grip. She watched his feet and matched his moves, turning, leaning, dipping, swaying. After a bit, she could follow without watching his feet. She looked up. He smiled approvingly. They flew around the ice. Time stopped. The war and her worries faded. They were one in a private world of motion, grace, and beauty.

He slowed and pointed upward. "Look. There's a rainbow around the moon."

She caught her breath. A full circle of soft colors glowed around the bright orb. "How can it do that when the sky is clear?"

"Ice crystals," said Tom. They skated slowly, watching it for a few minutes, then Tom swirled her on faster again. "It won't go away. You can look later."

He led her to one end of the ice to a private little lagoon that curved away from the other skaters and gave them space to practice alone. He showed her how to change directions with movements that were like dancing. As she picked up the steps, he led her through them faster. Finally, he spun her in a tight circle turn to stop.

She almost made it, then skidded and wobbled. Laughing, he tightened his grip on her hands and tried to help her straighten up. She slammed into him. He wrapped his arms around her, holding her in a tight hug. For a frozen second he seemed like the only stable thing in the world. Slowly, he eased his hold on her and gazed down at her with a look that hit her like an explosion. She should push away, but she only wanted to move closer. He gently pulled her close again and kissed her. With an incredible longing, she kissed him back.

He released her. Keeping hold of her hands, he eased her away.

"Please excuse me for taking unfair advantage. You're so beautiful in the moonlight," he said in a low voice. He pushed her a little farther from him but still held her hands. "And you did throw yourself at me," he accused laughingly.

She laughed and retorted, "I did? *You* threw me at you! You should have known I could never manage that kind of a stop."

"Okay. Come on. Let me help you back to Helen." He dropped one of her hands and skated beside her as if she were a child in tow, leading her back onto the crowded portion of the ice and finally to Helen.

Jean skated with others and alone, but not again with Tom. She was relieved and at the same time frustrated. She needed a spell of quiet to get used to this new feeling. She felt like a rainbow had burst open in her heart. She wanted to dance and sing and laugh and be in Tom's arms forever.

She loved him. She knew with every instinct and every ounce of reason she possessed it was not just a physical attraction. She loved him as she had never expected to love another man. And although he'd made a joke of it, she knew he was just as surely drawn to her.

The rainbow ring stayed around the moon, lighting the way home for Jean and Mary. Walking after skating, they felt earthbound, inches shorter, and lead-footed. Mary was too tired to marvel about the rainbow any longer. She said she could hardly wait to climb into bed, while Jean felt just the opposite. The excitement of new love would likely keep her awake the whole night.

★

All the next day Jean alternated between joy and a gripping terror that she might not be able to undo the damage she had done by reporting Tom to Uncle Al. She could hardly concentrate on teaching. Fortunately, Helen had grown used to managing without her and, at Jean's suggestion, unquestioningly slipped into taking charge.

*Will Uncle Al never call?* Jean fussed to herself, forgetting he probably would not call during the day because he knew her classroom was a mile and a half from a telephone.

When school was out, Helen asked, "Why don't you have supper at my mess hall tonight? We can skate afterward again without the kids." They had brought their skates to school, so they could go out with the children.

Jean couldn't say no; she might see Tom.

At suppertime, skates in hand, Jean followed Helen into the project mess hall. They had no more than sat down with their food when Tom, Fuj, and Yosh came and sat across from them.

Jean's pulse raced at the sight of Tom.

He smiled and said, "Did Helen tell you about the registration?"

Jean glanced at Helen.

Helen shrugged. "I forgot."

"So there is to be one?" Jean asked.

Tom nodded. "We'll all have to register. The women too. Everyone over seventeen, but they want the men registered first."

Fuj didn't look as pleased as Tom. He said, "We're supposed to swear allegiance to the United States and say we're willing to fight for our country. It's an insult after we tried to enlist months ago and they put us here."

Yosh added, "And why should everyone have to register? Our fathers can't serve in the military. For that matter, how many of the women and girls can? The whole thing's crazy."

"But the army is forming an all-Japanese combat team. Recruiters will be here Saturday," said Tom. "I for one am going to forget my pride and sign up."

"But that's tomorrow!" Jean exclaimed.

"Yep. I aim to be first in line," said Tom.

*Oh, no,* she cried to herself. *Must I lose you too?* Aloud she said in as cheerful a voice as she could muster, "So you're really getting what you wanted."

"Right. Like Uncle Shuji said, people are getting over the panic and coming to their senses."

"You mean they've finally realized they're wasting manpower in these camps," grumbled Yosh. "I'm not so sure I'm going to sign anything. Tad sure isn't."

At the mention of Tad, the exuberance left Tom's face. "Tad has let some other men turn him into a hothead."

"You have no right to say that," said Fuj, "when you haven't been listening to them. They make a lot of sense. America has never wanted us. After the war, if you make it back, you'll have nothing here to come home to."

Helen exclaimed, "Fuj, you don't know that! You admitted life was pretty good for you in Long Beach. It can be good again."

Fuj's voice softened when he turned his eyes to her. "I'd like to believe that, Helen, but I don't see any hope."

"The future will be what we make of it," insisted Helen. "As long as we're willing to work, we can have a good life again."

"What if Japan should win?" Yosh broke in harshly.

"What?" cried Helen.

"Where will we be," he pressed, "if Japan wins and occupies the U.S.? Will we be treated worse if we have fought against Japan while being children of Japanese citizens?"

"That is not a viable question," Tom said. "I'm an American, and I'd die for the United States before I'd serve any other country."

Yosh frowned. "I used to feel that way, but now I don't know." He glanced at Jean. "I suppose that sounds like traitor's talk to you."

She shook her head. "I don't know what to think. I suppose I would have some big questions, too, if I were in your shoes."

In a friendlier tone, Fuj said, "Jean the diplomat. For her sake, why don't we talk about something else?"

"Sure," said Tom, keeping his eyes on her face.

The men, however, obviously couldn't think about anything else. For that matter, neither could Jean. After a few minutes of discussion about the weather, Jean stood up. "Helen, I just remembered I promised to call my grandmother tonight," she fabricated. "I'll have to skip the skating."

They were all swift to say good-bye. Except maybe Tom.

★

When she arrived at the apartment out of breath, Mary handed her a note. "You're supposed to return this call. It came through at suppertime."

"Oh, it's Uncle Al."

"I hope there's nothing wrong," said Mary.

"No. No, I'm sure not. I was expecting him to call some time this week. Thanks. I'll go now and see if I can get a turn to use the pay phone."

"Want me to come along?"

"Oh, no thanks!"

Mary nodded and smirked. "Maybe it's not Uncle Al? I wouldn't have eavesdropped," she chided.

Jean laughed and left.

By some good fortune no one else was making calls. She dialed, gave the operator the number, and then waited for her to place the long-distance call to Uncle Al's apartment. He answered on the second ring.

"Jeanie, I thought you'd never call back. What are you doing out this late after being so sick?"

"I just had supper at a project mess hall. Anyway, I'm fine now."

"I wanted to tell you I was able to locate Giselle and Claude through my connections in England. They . . . Claude is working in the French Underground."

"Oh, I'm so glad they're alive, but working in the Underground? That's awfully dangerous!"

"Yes. I sent a message asking him to try to get Giselle and the girls out."

"I hope he can."

"Knowing Giselle, I doubt she will leave Claude. But I had to ask. . . . You sure you're over the effects of your illness?"

"I'm good as new. Uncle Al, did you get my letter dated the first of February?"

"I have it in my hand. I was going to talk about that next. I'm afraid you've become too emotionally involved with those people. At any rate, I wanted to assure you that you don't need to gather any more information. Have you heard about the registration?"

"Yes. Just tonight the men in the mess hall were talking about it."

"Registration of the Japanese will end the need for any more fact-finding. As for removing Mr. Kagawa from your report, or anyone else for that matter, it's too late. The file is out of my hands. I'll be out there soon to interview the men you mentioned, so I may need your help, secretly of course, if there's any difficulty identifying all of them. Other than that, your work is finished."

"Uncle Al," she cried. "You've got to keep Tom Kagawa out of the questioning. Surely you can."

"No, I can't. In this war, we're in a near-death struggle. We dare not ignore your earlier suspicions."

"But he's innocent. Don't you understand? I made a mistake!" Her heart was pounding so fast she could hardly get her breath.

"Jeanie, you're overwrought. I'm sorry I put you through this, but let go of it now. You've done your part, and Dave would be proud of you. Now please get yourself off to bed and get a good rest."

At the mention of Dave, Jean's voice failed her.

"I'll be seeing you soon," her uncle said. "Jeanie . . . You there?"

She choked out, "Good-bye."

## CHAPTER 14

The registration, which had given Tom hope for freedom to enlist, created a climate of anger and fear throughout the Tulelake camp. Jean could see the worry on the internees' faces and hear the frustration in their voices.

Helen was so upset that Jean went to the administration building after school and asked for a copy of the forms the Japanese people were being asked to sign. One of the secretaries gave her a surprised look but handed her the papers. She took them back to her apartment for a careful read.

Absently, she tossed her coat on her bed and sank into her chair. According to Helen, questions 27 and 28 were the most disturbing. She located question 27. "Are you willing to serve in the armed forces of the United States in combat duty wherever ordered?"

Jean frowned. Everyone seventeen and older must register. Nothing exempted anyone above that age. Sixty-year-old men who had never been allowed U.S. citizenship could easily assume they would be drafted if they said yes. And what about mothers, wives, and daughters, old or young? No wonder people were confused and frightened.

Furthermore, this added to a persistent fear among the Isseis. They were enemy aliens. If they said no to question 27, they would be suspected of disloyalty to the United States and subject to more rigorous imprisonment. Who could consent to this kind of jeopardy?

Jean shook her head over the stupidity of asking everyone

to answer the same question with no qualifications or explanations.

Then she read question 28. "Will you swear unqualified allegiance to the United States of America and faithfully defend the United States from any and all attack by foreign or domestic forces; and forswear any form of allegiance or obedience to the Japanese emperor and to any other government power or organization?"

This question, according to Helen, was as threatening as the other, for if an Issei man—loyal to the U.S. or not—were to say yes, he would lose his Japanese citizenship and become a stateless person. And again, as with question 27, if he answered no, he would be in danger of separation from his family and imprisonment.

Jean laid the paper on her desk and stared out the window at the rows of black barracks stretching as far as she could see. How many innocent people would be too frightened or too angry to sign the loyalty oath? What would happen to them if they didn't? No wonder Helen was angry.

Jean had not seen Tom since the forms had been made public.

If Helen was so angry, what about him, with his strong sense of justice? What would his answers be?

Mary came in pink-cheeked from the cold, said, "Hi," and dropped her papers on her desk.

"Hi," Jean answered.

At her automatic response Mary turned and asked, "Have a bad day?"

"No." Jean picked up the registration form and handed it to her. "Have you read this?"

Mary glanced at the heading. "No, but I heard that school is going to close so teachers can help with the process. They say the registration is supposed to get all the paperwork out of the way so people can leave easily when they find work on the outside."

"Well, whoever wrote questions 27 and 28 had no understanding of the Japanese people and what it will do to them."

Mary turned the paper over and read. With a sigh, she handed it back to Jean. "Maybe so. What does Helen say?"

"That hardly anyone is willing to say yes to either question."

"Surely question 27 doesn't mean everyone saying yes would be liable for the draft."

"If you were them, would you take the chance?"

Mary pondered and shook her head. "It's hard to imagine. I guess I feel that anyone who can't say yes should go back to Japan, and they probably would be happier there, so what's the worry?"

"But what if they don't want to return to Japan? And yet they don't dare renounce the only citizenship they have."

"You sure have become an advocate for these people . . . which is all right, but it seems to me you've changed an awful lot since last September."

Mary's observation roused a prickle of apprehension in Jean's mind. Answering honestly could reveal her feelings about Tom and possibly much more that must be kept secret. But she ignored the fear and said simply, "I've learned a lot."

Mary's eyes narrowed with suspicion. Without warning, she asked, "What goes on at that Japanese church?"

"Same as goes on in any church," said Jean, ignoring for the moment the fact that Mary had not attended a Protestant service.

"You must be making some friends," Mary persisted.

"Yes. At least I hope I have." Jean couldn't keep the softness from her voice as she thought of Tom.

Mary peered at her and then shrugged and sighed. "I warned you, and you wouldn't listen. You're in love with one of them, aren't you. Is it Tom?"

Jean felt her face betray her secret with a furious blush, but she said nothing.

Mary proceeded as if she had answered. "I guess I can't blame you. He's a nice guy and attractive, but you can't be serious!"

Jean burst out, "I didn't mean to. I didn't want to!"

"Does he know?"

"No."

"He's not slow. If you ever look at him the way you looked

when I mentioned his name, he's bound to guess. What do you plan to do now?"

"Do?" Jean echoed blankly. "I don't plan to do anything." She had not allowed herself to think beyond the immediate task of clearing him of her unjust accusations.

"How does Tom feel about these sticky registration questions? Is he going to say yes to both of them?"

"Last time I saw him, he thought the registration would be a good thing because it would clear the way for him to enlist and also ease the process for work release permits for everyone else. Now that so many people are confused and frightened by the registration, I don't know how he feels."

"What if he refuses to say yes to those questions? People who say no will probably be sent to Japan."

An expanding whirlpool of dread sucked at Jean.

★

Schools closed for the registration on February 9. Jean and the other teachers attended a briefing in the administration building on how the forms must be completed and how to answer the internees' questions.

To encourage cooperation and understanding, the *Tulean Dispatch* printed a speech given by army personnel who had arrived to oversee the registration and accept enlistments. In the lead article, the officer in charge urged residents to register promptly because such a response would prove their innocence and loyalty to the United States. On February 10, registration began by calling people in according to their block numbers. Men were to report to the administration recreation hall. Women were asked to report to the visitors' building.

Jean, at her desk in the recreation hall, spent the day trying to assure the older men that answering yes to question 27 would not mean they'd have to leave their families and go into the army. Still, they fearfully refused to give any answer.

The next day the *Tulean Dispatch* announced that question 28 had been revised for aliens. It now simply asked, "Will you swear to abide by the laws of the United States and to take no action that would in any way interfere with the war effort of the United States?" Or aliens could give a qualified answer to the original version, rather than just yes or no. This should have been reassuring, but Jean could not see much lessening of anxiety among the Isseis who talked with her.

Some of the young men came to register, eager to show their loyalty and also to enlist, but others refused the summons entirely. She watched for Tom but never saw him.

When the long day ended, Jean lingered to straighten her desk and was the last teacher to leave the building. Alone, she headed for her nearby apartment, exhausted from the stress of explaining the same things over and over—sometimes to the same men.

According to Uncle Al, her fact-finding information had helped in the preparation of this registration. What a fiasco. Yet how could she blame others, after what she had done? She strode homeward, head down, through the fast-falling darkness. As she crossed the fire break between the administration building and the teachers' apartments, angry shouts drew her attention. Behind her a gang of men were yelling. In the last bit of daylight, she saw one take a swing at another.

She froze in her steps. The scene reminded her of the brawl she had witnessed at Willamette University. She didn't know what to do. Surely someone nearby—or the military police—would stop the fight.

Ahead of her a man came running from the project. She didn't know whether he aimed to get into the fight or to quell it. When he reached her, he skidded to a halt. "Jean! What in blazes are you doing here?" It was Tom.

The sudden sight of him set her heart racing. "I'm going home," she said, feeling her answer was as obvious as his question. "I've been helping with the registration."

"You shouldn't be out after dark by yourself!"

Jean gestured toward the fracas. "What's happening?" she asked with an embarrassing catch in her voice.

"A gang has been trying to force people to say no to the questions about serving in the military and swearing allegiance to the United States. Last night they beat up some guys with baseball bats."

"Can't they be stopped? Where are the military police?"

"It would be better if we could handle them without the military. Run home and stay inside, and don't tell anyone about this. Please. Maybe I can quiet the situation before the MPs hear the noise."

She hesitated, fearing for him. "You should stay out of it—"

He grabbed her by the shoulders and gave her a push. His grip was fierce, even through the thick fabric of her winter coat. "Go!"

She ran, heart pounding now from fear, as if she were a child fleeing monsters in the dark. Panting, she threw open the door of her apartment, stumbled inside, and leaned against the wall. Tom could be hurt. Why would that gang listen to him? He shouldn't even be associating with men who could be arrested.

★

The registration progressed far more slowly than anticipated, and during that time Jean did not go to the Union Christian Church. Somehow she couldn't face the people, especially Pastor Ichiba.

Violence at night grew worse, and the gang members had not been identified. In the *Tulean Dispatch,* Project Leader Harvey Coverly published a warning that anyone who willfully obstructed recruitment processes would be subject to a fine of "not more than $10,000 or not more than 20 years imprisonment." In the paper the next day, an army major added that people could say yes or no to the troubling questions, but they could not refuse to be registered without breaking federal law and suffering the consequences.

Threats and explanations didn't stop the gang's efforts to intimidate internees who wished to cooperate with the registration. Nevertheless, gradually more and more men came in. In the end, registration kept schools closed for more than two weeks. By March 10, most of the Niseis had registered, and the Isseis were being pressured to come in so the registration could be completed.

At last Jean could return to her classroom. She had not seen Tom since the night he'd ordered her home. He had not come to her area for registration, but surely he'd registered. Hadn't he? The sudden question sent a shiver of apprehension up her spine. When Uncle Al came, if Tom had not registered, nothing she could say or do would save him from imprisonment.

*Maybe Uncle Al won't come after all,* she thought. *Maybe the registration is all there will be.*

At school on Monday, before the children arrived, Jean asked Helen as casually as she could manage, "Did Tom enlist as he planned?"

Helen paused in her sorting of the children's papers and gave her a troubled look. "For a while, when the registration turned out to be one more act of suspicion against us, Tom was going to say no to both questions 27 and 28 on principle, but his honest desire to enlist got the better of him. He finally answered yes-yes and enlisted the same day."

She pursed her lips and frowned. "But now something seems to be holding up the process. He thought he'd be called up in a couple of weeks. Others are receiving their notices to report, but he hasn't heard a word. He's pretty down about the whole thing."

Jean's stomach tightened into a knot of nausea. Had her fact-finding discredited his own oath of allegiance? "Well, he surely will hear soon," she said quickly, hoping she didn't look as distraught as she felt.

At lunchtime Jean asked Helen to stay with the children while she made a phone call. She ran to the pay phone by the military barracks and gave the operator Uncle Al's phone number.

His secretary answered on the second ring. Upon hearing Jean's voice, she exclaimed, "I thought he would be there by now! He flew to San Francisco yesterday and was taking the train to Tulelake. Is there anything I can do for you?"

"No. No thanks. It's nothing that can't wait until I see him. . . . Good-bye."

She jogged to get back to school by classtime. All afternoon she couldn't keep her mind off the fear of what Uncle Al's arrival might bring. Despite her growing panic, she completed the day without any raised eyebrows from Helen.

★

Uncle Al appeared at suppertime. The sight of him inside

the door of the mess hall unnerved her. She scrambled to her feet and ran to greet him.

"Uncle Al, what a nice surprise!" In a low voice, she added, "We need to talk. Can you take me out to dinner now . . . outside the camp?"

He gave her a fatherly hug. "Sorry, I'm tied up. The FBI agent and the colonel who came with me insist on going over some of the material tonight. I just wanted to say hello and let you know I'm here."

"The FBI! I didn't know they would be involved."

"As I told you before, this is more far-reaching than you can know." He patted her shoulder. "Now don't look like that. No one will know about your part. All anyone else will ever know is that I'm just here to visit my altruistic niece for a moment. You're looking well, Jeanie. I'm relieved. I was as worried as your grandmother about sending you here."

"I'm fine," she answered stiffly. "Uncle Al, please let me talk to the other investigators who came with you. I've learned a lot more since I stopped reporting to you."

"No, Jeanie. Surely you can see that such an act could reveal your part in this. I won't let you do that. In fact, I forbid you. Now go finish your dinner," he glanced at the tables and concluded, "such as it is. I'll take you out to a nice restaurant tomorrow night." He patted her shoulder and left.

Jean stared after him in frustration and then returned to her seat beside Mary.

"Who was that?" asked Mary.

"My uncle."

"He looks important. What's he doing here?"

"He's a senator," Jean muttered. "He's here on some kind of investigation."

Mary's eyes widened. "You never told me you had a senator for an uncle."

"I didn't think it was important."

"Do you have any more interesting relatives that you don't think are important?" Mary teased.

Jean couldn't manage the expected laugh. She shook her head. "I'm sorry, Mary. He brought me bad news . . . something I can't discuss."

Mary sobered instantly. "That's tough, kid. If there's anything I can do, let me know."

Jean nodded. "Sure."

★

That night in the *Tulean Dispatch,* which Jean now read regularly, she was relieved to see that thirteen gang members had been arrested and removed to Alturas County jail. The gang seemed to be composed of men born to U.S. citizenship but educated in Japan. It was hoped the arrests would put an end to the violence in the camp. And maybe it would modify Uncle Al's witch-hunt.

Jean barely slept that night. When she finally dozed off, it was only a couple of hours until daylight.

★

By the time Jean met Uncle Al the next evening at the main entrance to the administration building, her ears were ringing from stress and lack of sleep.

He had no more than greeted her when Tom Kagawa rounded the corner of the building and nearly collided with them.

Drawing back, Tom apologized. "Oh, I'm sorry." And then, seeing her, he said, "Jean!" He looked from her to Uncle Al and back again. "Please excuse my clumsiness and my interruption."

"You're not interrupting anything," said Jean. She glanced at her uncle. Where were his manners?

He came through. "You're certainly excused."

The two men stood eyeing each other cautiously. Neither spoke.

Jean said nervously, "Tom, I'd like you to meet my uncle, Senator Al Moore."

"Your uncle? Senator Moore is your . . . uncle?"

Before she could respond, Uncle Al said, "Mr. Kagawa and I have met. In fact, we spent a couple of hours this afternoon talking."

"You've already questioned Tom?" she exploded. And then she heard herself as Tom was hearing her.

"Already?" he asked in a dead tone. "What do you know about Senator Moore's business here?"

## CHAPTER 15

Before Jean could answer Tom's question, Uncle Al said firmly, "She doesn't know as much about it as you do, Mr. Kagawa."

Tom's eyes never left Jean's face. He seemed not to hear Uncle Al. "Did you know Senator Moore was coming here?"

"Yes. He told me on the phone."

"And he didn't say why?"

"Not exactly—"

"Do you know now what he's doing here?"

"See here, young man. My niece doesn't have to answer any of your questions," warned Uncle Al.

"Nor do I have to answer any more of yours," Tom responded in a tightly controlled voice.

"I want to answer," Jean broke in. "He's my friend, Uncle Al." She turned to Tom and said, "Yes, I know what he's doing, and I don't like it."

"Tad pointed out to me that every man called in today was someone you had known. I nearly decked him for the suggestion. Now I wonder." His tone was not wondering; it was accusing.

Jean longed to reach out and touch his hand—to create some kind of a bridge between them, if only a physical touch. "Tom, please believe me. I've been trying to convince Uncle Al that questioning you and the others is all wrong. . . ."

Tom's jaw tightened. "So where did he get our names for his little special investigation?"

"I . . ." Jean floundered. There was no answer she could give but more lies.

Uncle Al took charge. "Mr. Kagawa, you will not intimidate my niece. Stay away from her or your troubles will be worse." He took Jean by the arm and pulled her with him as he walked away.

She gave Tom a final beseeching look. For an unguarded instant his face twisted with pain, and then a shield of icy anger hardened his features. He turned his back and strode into the administration building.

Not releasing his hold, her uncle led her to the military sedan parked on the roadside. An army sergeant hopped out and opened the back door for Jean. She stepped up onto the running board and climbed in. Her uncle walked around to the other side, let himself in, and slammed the heavy door.

"You have no right to order Tom to stay away from me," she fumed, not caring what the driver thought. "He is a kind person, and he's innocent."

The sergeant put the car in gear and headed for the highway.

"You did not hear Kagawa's tirade this afternoon," Uncle Al said. "We started in a civilized, humane manner, and he tried to turn our interrogation against us as if we were on trial. I could easily imagine him acting as the classic rabble-rouser if given the opportunity. Now, let's forget about him and have a quiet dinner in that little cafe up the road. They're preparing a special spaghetti sauce just for us."

At the thought of spaghetti, Jean wanted to retch. Her stomach was in her throat, and the world tilted crazily every time she turned her head. "Uncle Al, I don't feel well. I've got to go home."

"Come on, Jeanie. Getting out of the camp will do you good. This whole situation has been too hard on you."

"No. I need to lie down. Please take me back." Her voice quavered out of control. She leaned back in the seat and closed her eyes.

Uncle Al ordered the driver to turn back to her apartment and solicitously helped her to the door. When Mary greeted them, he told her to get Jean into bed and see if she needed a doctor.

Before Mary could answer, Jean said, "Thanks, Uncle Al.

I'll be all right after a good night's rest. I scarcely slept last night." Her voice was still shaky and so were her knees, and she made no effort to appear any better than she felt.

He gave her a troubled look, patted her on the shoulder, and departed.

"Come on, kid. You look awful," said Mary, guiding her to her bed with an arm around her shoulders. "Your uncle's pretty bossy, but I think he's right about you. Climb into bed, and I'll fill my hot water bottle for your feet."

Mary also made her a cup of cocoa on the electric plate and watched until she finished drinking it. "Are you gonna get pneumonia again?" she asked anxiously.

Jean shook her head. "No, I'm just tired. I feel better, lying here." She snuggled deeper under the plump comforter her grandmother had sent and tucked her feet under the hot water bottle. "Mary, may I ask you something in confidence?"

"Sure," said Mary, sitting on the edge of Jean's bed to listen.

Jean stared at the ceiling and searched for words. "If you loved someone, and then something turned up that made it look as if the one you loved had lied about you . . . and those lies ruined your reputation . . . and jeopardized your future . . . could you ever forgive a person who did such a thing?"

Mary considered for a respectful length of time and, although a puzzled frown lingered on her brow, she said, "I think I could, if I learned the evidence was circumstantial, as you suggest."

"What if the evidence was partly true? What could the guilty person do to be forgivable?"

"Apologize . . . tell everyone the whole truth. Maybe find a way to undo the damage. . . . I don't get it, Jean. Has someone done this to you?"

"I can't tell you. That's why I had to say 'in confidence.' But you do think forgiveness is possible when there's been a terrible betrayal?"

"Anything is possible. I want to believe forgiveness is always possible."

"Me too. Thanks, Mary." At last Jean felt sleepy. She let her eyes close.

★

At school the next morning, as soon as Jean arrived she asked Helen if she would teach by herself for a while. "Maybe all morning," she said.

"I can. But why? Are you ill again?"

"No. I'm going to walk in on that interrogation committee. I'm going to stand up for Tom and the other men they've been questioning."

Helen asked bluntly, "Why should they listen to you?"

"Didn't Tom tell you that Senator Moore is my uncle?"

Helen's mouth fell open. "No. Do you think you can influence Senator Moore?"

"I've been trying to, but frankly, I haven't gotten anywhere. I hope the others can be more objective about the value of my judgment."

"According to Tom, your uncle and the others twisted everything he said."

Jean huffed a disgusted sigh. "I'm not going to let them get away with that," she vowed. "Somehow I'm going to make them listen to the truth."

Helen broke into a pleased smile. "More power to you. I'll hold down the fort until you get back."

Guilt swept over Jean. She had been betraying Helen, too, lying to her and using her. The only difference was that Helen's reputation would not be hurt. Or would it? If Tom were branded a traitor, could it reflect on his sister?

Helen was still smiling hopefully when Jean waved goodbye and stepped out into the cutting March wind.

On the way to the administration building, Jean rehearsed what to say. Reaching her destination in record time, she silently bypassed the reception area where only one woman was bent over a filing cabinet.

*Good,* she thought. *It's still early enough to catch the investigators before they call in any more men.* She tiptoed down a hall to the office Uncle Al had described as the interrogation room. The door was closed. Men's voices murmured indistinctly on the other side.

She rapped once, swung the door open, and entered.

The three men, looking like a panel of judges, were seated

behind a long table, facing the door with open notebooks lying in front of them. Uncle Al was to her left, a graying army colonel in the middle, and a pudgy man with a boyish, scrubbed appearance on her right.

Uncle Al stumbled to his feet, his face registering alarm. "Jeanie, are you all right?"

She stepped confidently to the table. "I'm fine, Uncle Al. A good night's sleep was all I needed." She turned and smiled at the other men. "Are you going to introduce me?" she asked, carefully avoiding her uncle's look of sudden understanding and consternation.

"Yes. . . . Gentlemen, my niece, Jean Thornton, who, as I told you, is teaching second-grade children here in the project. Jean, Colonel Johnson and Mr. Miller from the FBI."

The two men stood, nodded, and smiled congenially.

Jean returned their smiles and their nods. "Colonel Johnson. Mr. Miller. I'm happy to meet you. I hope you'll pardon me, marching in here unannounced like this. I have a good reason."

At that, they gave polite nods again. Mr. Miller's slight bow would have done credit to a Japanese man.

*Now's the time,* Jean told herself. She took a deep breath. "I hoped I could talk to you before you began your day, and I want to emphasize that my uncle did not know I was coming. It was all my idea."

They smiled and waved her to the chair in front of the table. "May I get you a cup of coffee?" said boyish-faced Mr. Miller.

"Thanks, but no," Jean responded warmly, still avoiding her uncle's silent glare of warning as she sat down.

The other two men tugged at the creases in their trouser legs and sat down carefully, as if at a formal tea. Uncle Al stayed on his feet, towering above everyone with arms folded.

Ignoring him, Jean focused on the colonel and the FBI agent. She leaned forward, resting her fingertips on the edge of the table in what she hoped was an innocent, nonaggressive gesture. "Uncle Al told me why you're here," she explained, "and I felt I could give you some pertinent information because I've become acquainted with many of the families here." She paused, respectfully looking from one to the other.

Colonel Johnson, in an easygoing manner, said, "Go ahead, please."

"I've been attending the Union Christian Church in the project. Did you know, sir, that more that one third of the people here are Christians?"

"Uh . . . er . . . no." He glanced at Uncle Al. "Did you know that?"

"That never came up, Bill. But I did know that what we're concerned about is only a handful of possible hotheads out of 15,000 nonthreatening people."

"Well," said Jean, "I'm here to tell you that the hotheads have already been jailed in Alturas County jail. The men you're questioning are loyal Americans. They're passionate for justice, not for treason. I met and came to know many of them while dining with my Japanese assistant teacher. In the six months I've been here, I've heard more statements of love for America and belief in our ideals than I heard in Salem the past six years. These people accept the internment as a patriotic duty because the country they love has asked this of them. I suspect not many Caucasians would respond that way."

Uncle Al unfolded his arms and slapped his palms down on the table as he leaned toward her. Enunciating each word sharply, he said, "Jean, we know all this, and truly we are remembering this fact as we question the men on our list. If you saw their behavior yesterday, you might revise your belief that the troublemakers are gone."

Jean faced her uncle head-on. "Tom Kagawa is my teaching assistant's brother. During the registration last month, he pledged his loyalty to the United States and enlisted immediately in the army. His one wish is to serve his country. I know him to be a law-abiding, good American and a sincere Christian."

Colonel Johnson cleared his throat and said in a fatherly tone, "Young lady, your description of Mr. Kagawa is at odds with his behavior here."

Jean restrained the flare of anger his paternal attitude aroused. "He gets angry over injustice," she said calmly, "but that doesn't mean he wants to commit treason. He truly wants to serve our country. I've come to know him well enough to vouch for that."

Mr. Miller straightened his papers with hands that looked better suited to handling a logger's saw and said, "Miss Thornton, I think I can speak for all of us. We want to be fair."

"Thank you, Mr. Miller. In view of that, why have you twisted Mr. Kagawa's words to turn them against him?"

"Now see here, Jeanie," Uncle Al sputtered. "Being my niece does not give you the right to accuse or insult this committee."

"I don't mean to insult anyone, Uncle Al, but Mr. Kagawa is a totally loyal American. I can't stand by and do nothing when I see him so misjudged."

Colonel Johnson and Mr. Miller, as if by a silent agreement, stood up.

With lips that smiled and eyes that contradicted his friendly voice, the colonel said, "We will hold all of your recommendations under advisement, Miss Thornton. We'll talk with Mr. Kagawa again, keeping in mind what you've said. We do realize that internment can make a spirited man fighting mad. We just have to be sure where that anger will be directed."

Uncomfortable with them towering over her, Jean rose to her feet. By their stances and expressions, she knew she would lose ground if she said more. Taking leave of them, she said, "Thank you for listening."

Uncle Al came from behind the table and followed her to the door.

"Trust them," he muttered in a do-as-I-say manner. "They are fair-minded men."

Unable to respond to such an assessment from the man who had persuaded her to spy, Jean said nothing.

As he let her out, he added under his breath, "Don't ever ignore my orders again."

She lifted her chin and looked him squarely in the eyes. "I can't promise that."

★

Jean made it back to school by recess time and joined Helen outdoors with the children, playing Mother-May-I. Helen gave her a questioning smile, to which Jean could only throw up her hands in an "I don't know" gesture.

As the day passed, however, she whispered to Helen, in bits and pieces, what had happened. At the end of the day Helen volunteered, "Tom will be glad to know what you did, whether you've been able to make a difference or not. And I'm glad too." She hesitated. "You know, at the beginning of the year I thought we never could be friends, but I was wrong. Only a friend would do what you did today. Thanks."

"Oh, Helen." Jean flushed uncomfortably. "Well, thanks." She struggled to concentrate on Helen's offer of friendship while she longed to run and hide in utter shame.

An hour later, while Jean was correcting papers in her apartment, someone pounded on the door. She supposed it was Mary with her hands full and trotted to answer.

It was Helen, crying. "They've taken Tom to jail," she sobbed.

"Oh no," groaned Jean. "When . . . how?" She pulled Helen inside and led her to a chair.

Helen choked out, "Two MPs came right after I got home. They handcuffed him like a criminal, right in front of Mother and Father and Peter. At least Margie wasn't home yet. . . ." she cried, too distraught to stay logical. Pulling herself together, she went on, "They took him away in an army car. Can you talk to your uncle again? My brother isn't a traitor . . . he isn't!" She covered her face with her hands and sobbed.

Tears welled up in Jean's eyes, but she was too frightened to give way to them. Kneeling by Helen, she awkwardly put an arm around her. When Helen began to quiet, Jean said, "Will you be all right if I leave you? I want to run and find my uncle. Maybe somehow . . ."

Helen uncovered her tear-streaked face and rubbed her eyes with both hands. "Yes. Hurry." She stood up. "I'll go back to my family and wait with them."

Jean snatched up her coat and dashed for the door.

At the administration building, the interrogation room was open and empty. Jean darted to the front desk and called to the nearest clerk, "Do you know where Senator Moore is?"

"He may have left the building, but did you look in the coffee room?"

"No. Thanks." Jean rushed to the room where a portable electric plate kept coffee and tea water hot all day. Sure enough, Uncle Al stood near the pot, his back to the door, nursing a cup of the bitter brew and chatting with an office employee.

Jean reached her uncle's side before he saw her. Her arrival stopped the two men's conversation. "Excuse me," she said without hesitation. "Uncle Al, may I talk to you as soon as you're finished here? I'll wait over there." She gestured toward a card table at the other side of the small room.

Uncle Al's shoulders rose in a silent sigh, but he said, "Certainly."

Waiting at the table, Jean fidgeted until he finally joined her. He placed a cup of coffee in front of her and then sat down with his own. "I suppose you've heard about Mr. Kagawa," he began in a weary tone.

"Yes. You've made a horrible mistake," she exclaimed. "His family is heartbroken. I told you the truth about him. Why didn't you see to it that justice was done?" she demanded, forgetting her normally respectful attitude toward him.

"Mr. Kagawa put himself where he is. We gave him every benefit of the doubt, and he blew his last chance. He talked himself right into jail."

Jean winced. "He's in jail already?"

"He soon will be. The MPs will hold him here at Tulelake until morning."

"Can't you still do something to get him released?"

"No. It was Johnson's and Miller's decision, but from what I observed, I felt their judgment was right on target."

Jean closed her eyes and drew in deep breath. *I've got to stay calm.* Opening her eyes, she said with fresh determination, "I want to talk to Tom."

Uncle Al shook his head warningly. "Jeanie, I ordered you to stay out of this investigation, and I meant it."

"Uncle Al, you can't even begin to understand what this is doing to his family. For their sake I must see him and take his message back to them. Please. . . . It's my fault they're going through this. Don't you understand how that makes me feel?"

She could tell from the way his eyes avoided hers that she finally had gotten through his defenses. Bowing his head, he talked to his coffee cup. "I'm sorry I ever asked you to do this. I should have known what it would do to you. Okay. I'll get you in to talk to him." He met her gaze again and commanded, "But you must never let your conscience lead you to confess about your fact-finding assignment. Can I trust you to stay mum?"

"Of course," she promised. "I couldn't bear to have him know what I've done."

"Well, I'm catching the northbound train in an hour. Let's get this over with." He stood up and led her through the building and out to a nearby barrack. As they approached the tar-papered building, Jean noticed soldiers guarding the doors and even watching the barred windows. Uncle Al walked to one end of the prison barrack and into its tiny office. He introduced himself and said, "My niece, Miss Thornton, wishes to visit one of the prisoners—Mr. Kagawa."

The sergeant at the desk said, "Yes, sir, Senator Moore." A corporal wearing a ring of keys on his belt stepped forward and opened a door that led down a hallway lighted by a single bare bulb. He stood back to let them precede him.

"Just take her," said Uncle Al. "I'll wait here."

Halfway down a narrow passage, the corporal unlocked a thick door into a tiny room. Tom stood staring out of a single barred window with his back to them. He did not acknowledge their presence.

The guard, keeping his eyes on Tom, said, "I'll wait here." He stationed himself in the open doorway.

"Tom," Jean ventured. Her voice failed her.

He stiffened. A perceptible stillness fell over him, reminding Jean of a fawn she'd once stumbled upon in the woods.

Longing engulfed her—to run to him, to throw her arms around him, and hold him close. . . .

Slowly he swung around and faced her. The hollows under his high cheekbones seemed deeper. "What are you doing here?"

"I had to talk to you, to tell you how sorry I am . . . and that I'm going fight to get you out of this. It's all so wrong," she ended lamely.

"How do you know? Maybe if I get out of here I'll go blow up the Shasta Dam or mine the bay at San Francisco."

"Is that how you talked to my uncle?" she asked anxiously.

"Your uncle. Senator Moore." He sneered as he said the name. "He's a living lie. He wouldn't know the truth if it seized him by the throat and yelled in his face."

"Tom. Please. I may be able to get him—the committee—to change their minds. If that doesn't work, there are other ways to fight for your rights. I'll find a good lawyer—"

"Bah! The law serves only those with the power to bend it or buy it. The law put us in Tulelake, and the law will put me in prison." Suddenly the fight went out of him. He leaned back against the wall and looked down at her with tired eyes. "Go back to your own kind, Jean. Your laws are not for me."

"That's not true," she insisted. "Remember Uncle Shuji's dream of America. He believed justice would come. . . ."

Tom ran his fingers through his rumpled hair. "Why did you come here?" He shook his head in resignation. "There's nothing you can do to help, so why?" Before she could speak, he began to frown. Straightening, he leaned toward her, defensive as a trapped animal. "Unless, maybe you've got a guilty conscience. Maybe Tad was right. Maybe we do have you to thank for this whole farce of an investigation." He glared into her eyes as if to read her mind.

She wanted to scream, *No, no.* She clamped her mouth shut. *I can't lie to him, never again.*

Still staring at her, Tom exploded. "Tad was right, wasn't he? That's why you ate in the project mess halls and kept coming to the Union Christian Church. You were spying on us." He moved toward her, arms stiffly at his sides. "Get out of here. If I have any luck left, I'll never have to look at your face again!"

She backed toward the door, not afraid of him as much as she was afraid for him. The soldier darted to her side and said, "Best you leave now, Miss Thornton."

She lingered for one last word. "Tom, one way or another, I'm going to clear your name."

He raised his chin disdainfully and turned back to the window.

Jean outpaced her escort down the hall and marched through the tiny office and on outside without a glance at her uncle.

"Jeanie, wait," he called.

She glanced back and ground out, "You could have stopped this, and you know it!"

She ran for her apartment.

Half an hour later Jean heard the whistle and chug of the northbound train. Her uncle had not pursued her and now he was gone. She would apologize to him, but not today.

Unable to face Tom's family with no good news, she enlisted Jimmy Duggan to carry a note to Helen and begged off going with Mary and Jimmy to a party at Ann's apartment.

That night Jean watched the starry sky through the small-paned window above her bed. Was Tom looking at the stars through his barred window? They had thrilled to a rainbow around the moon. Would they ever share anything beautiful again?

# CHAPTER 16

Jean slept fitfully and woke up tired. It was Saturday, a day usually spent on personal chores.

She whisked through cleaning the apartment with Mary. As she wiped the eternal gritty dust from the window sills, Mary asked a few questions about Uncle Al and the interrogation and then settled on the subject of Tom.

"So it's not a passing fancy. You really love that guy," Mary observed sympathetically.

"Yes. I never thought I could." She stopped. "I don't mean that the way it sounds. I meant . . . Well, I never told you about my fiancé Dave. He was killed at Pearl Harbor. I just couldn't bear to talk about him."

"Dave!" Mary echoed. "Not Rodge?"

"No. Rodge was Dave's best friend. He shared my grief over Dave, and then he began to think he loved me, and I didn't want him to. Then when he was missing, it was almost like losing Dave all over again. Does that make sense?"

"Whew! I guess you are the proverbial 'still water running deep.' You've knocked the pins out from under me. Can you tell me about Dave now?"

Jean dipped a cloth in the vinegar water she had mixed for wiping the window glass and stretched to rub the highest panes first. The action gave her time to consider what to say about Dave. She explored her memories of him: his tender smile, his gentle caring ways, his touch, his kiss, the dreams they'd shared. "Yes," she said slowly. "I can tell you. The hole in my heart is still there. It just doesn't hurt so much. Now I can remember and be glad for his love."

Mary sat down on the edge of her bed, uncharacteristically quiet. Her eyes brightened with sympathetic tears.

"Would you like to see Dave's picture?" Jean offered softly.

"Yeah. Sure," said Mary, wiping her eyes.

Jean went to her dresser drawer and pulled out her grandmother's Bible. From under the envelope containing her engagement ring, she lifted Dave's oil painted portrait photo that showed the deep blue of his eyes and the red gleam of his chestnut hair. Handing the print in its cardboard folder to Mary, she began to tell her about the first time she saw Dave. Some time later she finished with their wedding plans and his death at Pearl Harbor. "I didn't believe I could ever love another man. I was going to be an old maid schoolteacher, and now . . . I guess I still will be an old maid schoolteacher."

"If you're permanently stuck on Tom, you will," said Mary.

Mary agreed much too readily to suit Jean. She rubbed and rubbed the window glass with a clean dry towel and then dried her hands. Whether it would be helpful to the Kagawas or not, she had to visit them today.

Mary handed her Dave's photo.

Jean tenderly carried it to her dresser and laid it on the Bible, saying, "I've got to go run some errands." She put on her coat and tied her white wool bandanna under her chin. "See you later."

"Sure. 'Bye," said Mary, still subdued.

★

Jean walked straight to the Kagawa apartment. Helen answered her knock and quietly invited her in.

Mrs. Kagawa rose from a chair near the stove to greet her.

Peter called in a subdued voice, "Hi, Miss Thornton."

He didn't run to her. Instead, he pushed his toy car through the small world he had built of homemade blocks on the floor near his mother's chair.

"Did you get my note last night?" Jean asked Helen.

"Yes." Her lips barely moved with the word. Her eyes were puffy, but her face remained a carefully controlled mask.

"I'm so sorry I wasn't able to help. My uncle was the only

one still here, and even if I could have influenced him, the other two had their minds made up," Jean said to the two women.

"Thank you for trying," said Tom's mother. Her eyes, too, were swollen.

"I just want you to know I'm not quitting. I'm going to fight to clear Tom's name, and I'm not going to give up until everyone knows he's innocent."

"You are so kind, but you must not put yourself out for us," said Mrs. Kagawa. "You might get into trouble too."

"Don't worry about me. Just try to believe that Tom's name will be cleared. Really," Jean urged.

"We will try," murmured Mrs. Kagawa.

"What do you think you can do?" said Helen in a hopeless tone.

"I'm going to write to the attorney general and to the ACLU."

A flicker of interest crossed Helen's face. "Maybe you could get some help too from the JACL—the Japanese American Citizens League," she suggested.

Mrs. Kagawa said in a worried voice, "No, Helen. There's not much they can do for something like this."

"Well, if you can give me an address, I'll ask," said Jean.

Helen pulled a box from under her cot and rummaged through some papers. "Here." She handed Jean a typed page with an address underlined.

Helen and her mother sat silently.

"Well, I need to go," said Jean, feeling as if she were intruding on their grief, especially since she couldn't reveal how deeply she shared their feelings.

They made no effort to detain her. Instead, they walked her to the door. Mrs. Kagawa said, "We are praying for Tom and that justice will be done. Will you pray too?"

"Of course I will. . . . I am," stammered Jean.

They parted as painfully as they had greeted each other. Jean didn't know if their discomfort was the result of their grief and fear or a subliminal response to her agonizing guilt, which made her uneasy and awkward.

As she walked back toward the schoolroom to pick up

papers she had forgotten the night before, she noticed a number of familiar faces among the passing mothers, children, young men, and the elders, but none of the adults greeted her. She began to watch for eye contact. No one would look at her. *What's wrong?* she wondered. *They can't know what I've done.*

*No, it's just my guilty conscience again,* she chided herself. *I'm imagining things.*

And yet before she reached the school barrack, she was shaking. People were acting differently. No one had met her eyes. They must think she had done something wrong or they wouldn't behave this way.

She couldn't get to her school fast enough. She fled into her unheated classroom and collapsed onto the chair at her desk. Her heart was thumping in panic. Raising her hands to her face, she cried instinctively, "Oh, God! What can I do?"

Gradually her pulse slowed and the familiar room, smelling of bare boards, coal dust, and paste, penetrated her distress. The warmth of the children's love seemed to reach out to her from their tables and neatly stacked chairs. When she calmed down, she thought, *Pastor Ichiba . . . maybe he can help. Yes. I'll tell him what I've done and ask him what to do.*

★

She knocked lightly on the door of Pastor Ichiba's apartment. Mrs. Ichiba opened to her. Her round face, with its frame of thick white hair done in a bun on the top of her head, always reminded Jean of Mrs. Santa Claus. Mrs. Ichiba beamed with a smile that crinkled her eyes shut. "Ah, Miss Thornton. Do come in."

"Thank you, but I was hoping I might talk to Pastor Ichiba . . ." She hesitated to say, "in private," for their small apartment allowed no privacy. "Is he at the church?" Jean asked hopefully.

"He is right here, but he will be glad to walk to the church, if you wish to talk. Come in, come in."

"Thank you." Jean stepped inside. Pastor Ichiba was already fumbling into the sleeves of his coat.

After greeting her he made no effort to converse, and she was glad. She didn't know how she was going to have the courage to confess what she'd done and wasn't sure how he would take it, even if, as a pastor, he was used to hearing about all kinds of sins.

They walked silently to the nearby church. Leading her into the chapel hall, Pastor Ichiba quickly laid and lighted a fire in one of the stoves. "It is not good to sit in the cold, when one's heart is aching," he observed.

Jean bit her lip to keep it from trembling. Would he feel so kindly toward her when he learned the truth?

When the stove began to radiate a little heat, he pulled two chairs into the warmth and gave Jean a little bow as he indicated the one for her.

"Now, Miss Thornton, you wanted to talk to me?" His eyes were attentive, his smile gentle.

"Yes. I have to tell someone and you're the only one . . . I felt I could trust. Oh, Pastor Ichiba, I've done something so horrible. . . ." She covered her face and sobbed.

Without a word he waited, but in his silence Jean felt patience and acceptance. When she could, she began to talk, keeping her face averted. Giving no thought as to whether she might be harming Uncle Al, she told him everything, except her love for Tom.

He kept her talking with only one-syllable comments—the Japanese *hai,* yes, and an occasional, "I see."

At last she could think of nothing more to say. "I am so sorry and so ashamed," she concluded. Peeking at his face, she found his expression as accepting and kind as ever, with none of the loathing she felt for herself.

He said gently, "Miss Thornton . . . may I call you Jean?"

"Please do."

"Jean, your greatest pain is from Christ himself weeping inside you. You betrayed him when you betrayed the person he meant you to be. And when you betrayed Tom and Helen and the others, you betrayed Christ again. Do you see how this can be?"

"I don't know," she admitted.

"As you told me what you had done, did you recognize your first fateful step in the wrong direction?" he probed.

"I . . . hated the idea of lying, but I did it anyway because of the war."

"Go back farther in your memory," he urged gently.

"I lied to Grandmother—and earlier to my mother and my father."

"And what did you tell yourself at those times?"

"That lying could make things better—easier—so it was okay. But I knew, I always knew lying was wrong." She looked at him in amazement. "My first mistake was to lie to myself!"

Pastor Ichiba smiled. "You have wisely found the beginning of all deception. Now you need to forgive yourself. The beginning of forgiving yourself is to ask Christ to forgive you," said Pastor. "When this is done, you then may see how to make restitution."

"I need to think about this," Jean admitted.

He smiled and rose to his feet. "If you want to talk again, I will be glad to listen," he said.

Jean stood up. "Thank you. I will. Pastor, one more thing—what I told you about my Uncle Al . . . well, he was worried that someone might find out, and I promised—"

"Do not worry. It is as if you had never mentioned it."

"Thank you." Jean drew her coat on and yet, still lingered. "Pastor, I need to ask—will you forgive me?"

"I forgave you as soon as your words reached my own deceiving heart," he said simply.

She nodded. "I think I knew you did, but I needed to hear you say so. But what do you mean—about your own deceiving heart?"

"Not one of us lives beyond babyhood innocence without lying to ourselves. You are not alone. May I pray for you before you leave?"

"Yes, please," she said. Uncertain of the procedure, she bowed her head and closed her eyes as they stood there.

He spoke as if he were talking to a third person right beside them. "Lord, please comfort Jean as only you can comfort, and we both thank you."

His prayer was so brief and so unlike any praying Jean had ever heard that she opened her eyes with a start.

Pastor Ichiba reached out and touched her forehead lightly with his fingertips. "Now, go in peace."

"Thank you," she whispered. After his touch, there was no

specific feeling she could name, and yet she felt different. Yes—she was calmer and she felt safe. It was as natural as the change in her breathing, and yet somehow it was beyond natural. How could his prayer give her peace?

★

Jean's walk back to her apartment was much different from her earlier race to her classroom. People who knew her still avoided looking at her, but she felt as if she were inside a bubble of peace. She was sorry but not frightened by their obvious distrust. She felt certain that somehow she would be able to make amends for her part in hurting anyone in the project.

In the apartment she found a note from Mary saying she was helping Ann make a new skirt.

Jean put more coal in the stove and then picked up Dave's portrait. She kissed the image of his smile. "I love you, Davy, and I always will," she whispered.

Lifting a watercolor of the Willamette Valley out of its frame, she tucked his photo in its place and hung his smiling face on the wall above her bed. Her spying days were over forever.

Then, instead of packing her grandmother's Bible back into the bottom of the drawer, she sat down and read about Christ.

After a while she raised her eyes and looked out the window. Aloud she said, "Please forgive me, Lord Jesus." As she uttered the words, by an indefinable inner recognition, she knew that he did. She was free to try to undo the damage her spying had caused.

★

Monday morning a cold rain was falling, which probably would turn to ice at nightfall. Helen came into the classroom, pale and panting, and collapsed onto her chair as soon as she hung up her wet coat.

Jean called from her desk in concern, "Do you feel well enough to teach?"

"Once I get going I'll be okay," said Helen. "I saw Tom this morning."

"You did!" Jean laid down her pencil to listen.

Helen nodded. "Dad and I went. Now Tom's on his way to

the county jail in Portland, which they've told him is the most secure in our part of Oregon."

"Oh. . . . How is he taking it?"

Leaning her elbows on her table and her chin on her hands, Helen gave a long sigh. "I don't know. I've seen him angry, and I've seen him depressed, but I've never seen him the way he is now. It almost scares me."

"What do you mean?" cried Jean. "Do you think he's suicidal?"

"He's . . . he's cold and bitter, and yet at the same time, he's like a coal mine on fire—burning up on the inside until there's nothing but a hole where the coal used to be." Helen dropped her face to both hands and shook her head. "I don't think he's suicidal, but will there be anything left of my brother when this is over?"

"Oh, Helen," mourned Jean.

The first children began to arrive. Both women greeted them and helped the girls out of their galoshes and boys out of their boots. In minutes the room was filled with chatter and the odor of wet wool steaming beside the coal stove as the children spread their coats to dry.

Jean rang her handbell for class to begin. After the flag salute and one verse of "America the Beautiful," she asked them to move their chairs into a circle near the stove. "We'll do our reading there until the room warms up."

The children were inattentive from the start of reading. Several of them whispered and argued until Jean, in exasperation, asked the worst culprits to come to the front of the class and tell everyone what they were talking about. Heads down, a boy and a girl came forward.

"Now, Kenji," said Jean. "Will you tell the class what is so important that you and Gracie can't stop arguing about it?"

He bit his lip and dragged one toe nervously across the floor. Chin down, he said, "I just told Gracie her big brother is a liar."

"Then I think you should apologize to her," chided Jean.

"But teacher, her brother said something bad about you," Kenji argued.

Jean's heart literally skipped a beat. *This can't be happening.*

"We need to talk about this," she said carefully. "Gracie, what did you say that made Kenji think such a thing?"

"My brother said his friends were put in jail because you told the FBI they were dangerous. Did you do that, Miss Thornton?" Gracie asked, anxiously peering up at her from under her straight black bangs.

"Oh, Gracie. Please tell your brother I went to tell the FBI that those young men were not dangerous."

Helen stepped forward. "This is true, boys and girls. Remember last Friday morning when Miss Thornton was gone until recess time? She went to help the men who had been arrested."

Kenji jeered at Gracie, "See? I told you our teacher wouldn't do anything like your brother said."

"Shh," Jean shushed them. "That's all right, Gracie. You only said what you heard. Kenji, thank you, but please, let's not have any arguments over what other people say. In our classroom we're like a family. Let's help each other. If you hear anything that worries you, come tell Miss Kagawa or me, and let us help you understand." Jean stood up. "Now I think it's warm enough to take your chairs back to your tables, and we'll work on our writing."

The rest of the day went smoothly. Jean hoped she had soothed the effect of the rumors upon her pupils.

On Tuesday afternoon, however, the principal summoned Jean to her office. A red spot on each cheek and red blotches on Mrs. Smith's neck signaled a problem. She motioned Jean to sit in the chair in front of her desk. Jean obeyed. The older woman's stern demeanor made her feel more like a pupil than a teacher.

Mrs. Smith said, "Do you remember your indoctrination last September, when we spent several hours discussing ways to earn and keep the trust of the Japanese parents in this project?"

"Yes, I remember."

"Then why have six different fathers come to me today to complain about their children's teacher? You, Miss Thornton. They are calling you a spy!" Tapping her desk with her pencil to emphasize each word, she said, "What have you done to earn this notoriety?"

"Maybe they misunderstood what I did," Jean said. "I talked to that interrogation committee last week. One of them, Senator Moore, is my uncle. I tried to persuade the committee that the men they were questioning are innocent, law-abiding citizens."

"When did you do that?" Mrs. Smith asked sharply.

Jean straightened on her chair and admitted, "I left Helen in charge of the class Friday morning—just until recess time."

"You did this without my permission and obviously did not succeed in your mission of mercy," Mrs. Smith stated flatly.

Jean nodded, miserable again for failing.

Mrs. Smith huffed in irritation and sat tapping with her pencil for endless seconds. Finally she said, "I think we should ask the parents of your pupils to come to your classroom tomorrow evening and let you talk to them all at the same time. It will be your task to squelch these unpleasant rumors and renew their confidence in their children's teacher and, indirectly, in our whole staff."

Jean's heart lurched and lodged someplace just below her throat. She knew of no way to defuse rumors that were closer to the truth than anything she could say.

## CHAPTER 17

The next night as the mothers arrived for the meeting, so did many fathers and brothers. Mrs. Smith greeted them at the door.

Jean regretted her principal's insistence on conducting the meeting in her classroom where no comfortable seating could be arranged. How could anyone feel charitable under these conditions? She also regretted her own success in persuading Helen to stay home. Wanting to spare her the stress of such a meeting, Jean had overlooked how helpful Helen's remarks could have been.

When everyone found a place to sit, with the men on tabletops and the women on the children's chairs, the room grew ominously quiet. Mrs. Smith spoke first, apologizing on behalf of all the teachers for causing concern to the parents. She then introduced Jean with a warm commendation on how well her pupils were performing in state tests.

Extending her hand toward Jean she said, "Now Miss Thornton will clear up the unfortunate rumors that may have upset you these past few days."

With the worst stage fright she'd ever experienced, Jean stepped forward. "Ladies and gentlemen, thank you for coming out tonight. Some of you are here for the first time, and I want to welcome you to your children's classroom." Suddenly, the familiar room and the memory of her pupils' cheerful smiles and hopeful eyes helped her find words.

"When I came here last fall—just out of college—I worried about how to communicate with your children and inspire them to learn. In a very short time, they began to teach me. By their behavior, they showed me a new meaning for family loyalty, respect for those in authority, cooperation for the common good, the value of learning, faith in the future, and love for our country. I didn't need to inspire them. You, their parents, already had done that."

Jean paused and glanced over her audience. She couldn't read their faces, but she felt less threatened. Clearing her throat, she continued. "If I ever become a truly good teacher, your children and you will deserve the credit. You have taught them well. I love each one of them, and I think they love me too. We're like a family here in this room during the school day.

"It saddened me Monday to learn that some of them were troubled by rumors about me. We talked about it, and I hope I relieved their anxiety." She then told them what she had told the children.

"I failed to change the minds of the investigators, and I'm so sorry." She paused to steady her voice. "I feel as bad as if the accused men were my brothers." Her voice quavered again.

She cleared her throat. "I've watched your courage as you endure the internment. I know how hard you've worked to protect your children and make the best of this cruel situation. I want to thank you for the privilege of teaching your children, and I hope you will trust me to continue.

"Even if you don't, I will keep fighting to clear the names of the men who have been unjustly arrested. I guess in closing I just want to say I'm sorry and ashamed that our country has violated your rights, and I pray that some day the United States will formally apologize. Thank you for your kind attention." She gave them a little bow and turned to Mrs. Smith.

The principal stepped forward. "Do you have any questions you'd like to ask Miss Thornton?"

A stocky man in blue overalls and bristling black hair stood up slowly. "I would like to say that I am glad we have a teacher like Miss Thornton."

"I agree," said another man.

"I think she's doing a good job," said the softer voice of a woman.

"I think we should each do our part to stop this rumor business," said the man in the overalls. "Please raise your hands if you agree."

The audience sprouted a crop of waving arms.

"Anyone opposed?" There were none.

"Miss Thornton, you mentioned fighting for the release of the six men jailed," called a young man, who must have been a student's big brother. "What can you do?"

"I'm writing to the ACLU and the attorney general. From their responses, I'll decide what to do next. I won't let go of this," said Jean.

The young man nodded. No one else asked any questions.

Mrs. Smith came to Jean's side and took over. "We teachers want to thank you for your cooperation, understanding, and support. We'll do our best for your children. Please feel free to linger and visit, if you wish."

Several parents came to shake Jean's hand and to commend her. It made her feel terrible. She was as much of a lie as her uncle.

After the crowd thinned, the young man who had asked what she planned to do to free the men sauntered over to her. He looked vaguely familiar.

He said, "You probably won't be able to help those guys. A couple of them were agitators, and we all knew it. But Tom Kagawa—he had to be caught in a frame-up. I heard him repeatedly try to talk the others into signing the loyalty oath. He believed the government would give us a fair chance if we could wait patiently for the war panic to die down."

"You saw Tom doing this?"

"Sure. A lot of us did. I didn't agree with him, but I respected him. His biggest mistake may have been in spending so much time with those of us who aren't so trusting of the government."

"Would you be willing to testify in Tom's defense?"

He gave her a look of mixed emotion. "Yeah, but why would anyone listen to me?"

Jean's mind leaped to new possibilities. If she could get a hearing with the right people, there could be more than one man willing to testify. She persisted. "But you will testify, if I can get people in power to listen?"

He nodded in an offhand manner and volunteered, "My name is Jiro Shiogo. I'll be around because I answered no to question 27." He had refused to serve in the military.

"Thanks," said Jean with growing excitement. "I'll let you know."

He nodded again and strolled away.

The room emptied rapidly. After the last parent departed, Mrs. Smith commended Jean and also left.

With this ordeal over, Jean felt little relief. The big task of clearing the men's names lay ahead.

That night she sat up late, shielding her desk lamp so as not to bother Mary, and labored over the composition of her letters to the attorney general and the ACLU. She did not write to the Japanese American Citizen's League because Helen had revealed that the JACL had stood for careful cooperation with the government since the beginning of the internment. It seemed to Jean that, as a voice for Japanese Americans, the JACL might not be pleased that Tom had given the government an excuse for suspicion. Also, from as much as she could understand, the JACL did not have political or legal power.

Next morning she mailed the letters on her way to school. Until she received answers, there was nothing else she could do.

★

A week later an office clerk from the administration building came to Jean's classroom with a message that she was to call Senator Moore at his Washington office immediately. "He said it was an emergency," said the young Japanese woman who brought the message.

Jean's first thought was of Grandmother. Leaving Helen in charge, she bundled up against the March wind and ran. She banged the door open at the administration building and asked, "Is there a phone I can use for a collect call to Senator Moore in Washington?"

"Right here," answered the receptionist. She stood up to give Jean space.

Jean spun the dial, spoke to the operator, and the call went through swiftly.

Uncle Al came on as if he had been sitting by the phone. "Jeanie, I just got a call from the attorney general, who happens to be a friend of mine," he rumbled. "How dare you break your promise to me?"

"I didn't promise," she denied, keeping her voice low. "Uncle Al, is this the emergency? When I got your message I was afraid something had happened to Grandmother."

"Your grandmother's fine, but I'm not. You stop this dangerous nonsense right now. Don't you realize you could be charged with treason if any of these men prove to be guilty of collaboration with the enemy? And if you were, I couldn't help you! Jeanie, don't you know there's a death penalty for treason during wartime? One American citizen has already been executed for assisting an escaped German POW."

"These men are not POWs! They're American citizens. They're not guilty of anything more than speaking their minds."

"At a time like this, under certain conditions, even speech can be judged an act of treason."

"Then I'll just have to take my chances—"

"Stop talking nonsense," he snapped. "Who else have you contacted about releasing Mr. Kagawa?"

"That's none of your business," she declared.

"You can bet your life it's my business. My career's on the line, as well as your own safety. I don't know what's gotten into you, but I managed to stop action from the attorney general. I persuaded him you're still a schoolgirl and just became emotionally involved with those people."

His voice dropped, but his tone grew ominous. "If you keep on with this crusade, you could endanger national security or, at the very least, destroy my reputation. Others are involved who can't be wasting time on court appearances to defend me or my committee's decisions." He paused. "You must not trigger any investigation."

Jean didn't respond.

He continued, trying to press his point with reasoning. "In a war innocent people get hurt. If there is any injustice, it will ultimately be corrected, but right now we're in a battle for our very survival."

Jean considered whether she might affect the war effort in

unanticipated ways. She decided. "I haven't said or done anything that should be a problem."

"In the wrong hands, the information you possess could hurt the very people you want to help. Believe me. If you back off, the situation will not get out of hand, but if you don't . . ."

*He knows how to get to me. I'll have to be careful not to involve more Japanese people.* "Uncle Al, I can't let innocent men be put in jail and say nothing. But I will be more discreet."

"Discreet!" he yelled. "You stop this nonsense right now!"

Jean flinched and held the receiver away from her ear. "Good-bye, Uncle Al." She hung up.

That night after thinking about his warning, Jean wrote a second time to the ACLU and withdrew her complaint about Senator Moore's investigation and her request for legal help. She would have to find some other avenue of action.

★

Sunday morning, for the first time in weeks, Jean attended the Union Christian Church service. She sat beside Tom's family. His absence created a gaping empty spot in their midst.

A missionary, Dr. Langston, who had recently arrived from Japan on the neutral Swedish ship *Gripsholm* in a prisoner exchange, answered questions about his treatment in Japan and gave a short homily.

While listening to him, Jean's thoughts strayed to Tom. Would any clergyman visit the jail to bring him hope? She imagined him staring out of a barred window in a gray concrete jail, surrounded by criminals. *Oh, God, he's there because of me. Please help him.*

Dr. Langston captured her attention again with a story from his own imprisonment in Japan. He had despaired of being released, but some unknown person had negotiated his freedom. He would never be able to thank that person but hoped he could help other prisoners in the same way.

Afterward, Jean stood in the long line of people wanting to speak to Dr. Langston. When her turn came to shake the missionary's hand, Pastor Ichiba introduced her as one of the colony's schoolteachers.

She went through the necessary pleasantries and then

asked, "If I wait until the others leave, could I speak to you in private, Dr. Langston?"

His warm grip on her hand tightened. "Certainly, but please wait right here where I can see you."

She took a chair not far from him. It seemed as if everyone in the congregation wanted to shake his hand, but he greeted each one with intense concern and interest. An unusual man, Jean decided. Spare in frame, he had to be up in years. A fringe of white hair encircled his shining bald head, but his movements were that of a vigorous younger man.

At last the people left, and Dr. Langston came and sat beside her. "Now, how may I help you, Miss . . . ?"

"Thornton," she supplied. "Please call me Jean." She told him about Tom, his arrest, his innocence, and her determination to free not only him, but the others if possible. "From what you said, I knew you'd understand their plight and my urgency. Is there any way you can help?"

He looked crestfallen. "My dear, I don't see how. I've been out of the country for several years, and I've never dealt with any political or legal process. Missionaries try to avoid those things," he admitted somewhat sadly.

"I see," she said, trying not to give in to disappointment. "Well, if you should think of anything or meet anyone who could help, please let me know."

Jean walked home from church frustrated. What could she do? Tom despised her and rightly so. She hated what she had done and the cover-up she still must maintain. She angrily kicked at a small rock underfoot and sent it tumbling to the edge of the roadway.

Rounding a corner into the next fire break, she noticed a cluster of men arguing. Even as she curiously searched the group for a familiar face, one man smashed his fist into the face of another, decking him. Instantly the rest of the men leaped at each other, yelling.

*Another fight. And I was so sure all violent people had been jailed.* These men were drawing blood. Suddenly she saw a raised baseball bat. It crashed down. She whirled and ran for Pastor Ichiba's nearby apartment.

# CHAPTER 18

Breathlessly Jean pounded on Pastor Ichiba's door until he appeared. "Please come quick! There's a terrible fight! They've got clubs!" She pointed down the road.

He rushed down the steps in his shirt sleeves and also pointed. "Run to that barrack over there, second door down, and ask for Reverend Matsumoto. He's a Buddhist priest. He will help us." He took off jogging toward the fight. Behind him Dr. Langston loped to catch up.

The Reverend Matsumoto had just come home from his church services. A younger man still in his prime, he sprinted to the scene. Jean followed, unsure of whether she should go home or wait to see if she could help in any way. Other people, hearing the commotion, ventured out their doors to peer down the road.

By the time Jean reached the scene, the Reverend Matsumoto had pulled several of the men out of the ruckus and they were standing back, watching with clenched fists. Pastor Ichiba called out several others by name. Slowly they stood up and backed away from the battle. At last the commanding presence of the three older men seeped to the center of the melee of angry bodies. Raised fists lowered, the mob broke apart, and men became individuals again. Those on the ground staggered to their feet, dirty, bruised, and bleeding. One man cradled his arm as if it were broken.

Mr. Matsumoto demanded, "Is this the way you honor your parents? How shall we show the world we are peaceful people when we attack each other?"

Pastor Ichiba added, "Will you make the lies about us into the truth?"

Dr. Langston kept his counsel to himself.

Jean froze where she had stopped, unable to walk away and let it be their problem.

Pastor Ichiba said, "We cannot settle differences with baseball bats. Give that to me," he ordered, reaching out a waiting hand. The bat was passed to him.

"Are there more?" asked Rev. Matsumoto. Two more bats exchanged hands. "Now every one of you will come to my apartment and talk this through peaceably. Pastor Ichiba, you and your guest please join us."

"Certainly," said Pastor Ichiba. By this time a curious crowd had gathered. He turned to them and said, "Everything will be all right. Please go back to your homes." He turned to Jean and quietly asked, "Will you stop at the hospital and ask them to send transportation? I think at least one man needs help."

"Yes." His request galvanized her to action again. As she moved past the men who had been fighting, one recognizable face came into focus—Jiro Shiogo, who had agreed to testify for Tom.

She stopped beside him. "Jiro," she asked in a low tone, "what happened?"

He frowned. "Stay out of our business," he warned. "I saw you running to the old pastor's place."

"I didn't want anyone to get hurt—"

"You're just like Tom," he hissed angrily. "Not smart enough to face reality. These religious guys are selling our rights down the river with their pacifist ideas and pie-in-the-sky promises. The only way we'll ever get what we want is to fight for it, and there are a lot of Niseis around here who need to learn that lesson."

Jean retreated a step. "I'm sorry you feel that way. . . ." she stammered, confused by his change to overt dislike.

"Sure you are," he accused sarcastically. "Forget about my testifying for Tom Kagawa or any other idiot who thinks America will ever give us respect."

The bitterness on his face hit her like a physical blow. She wheeled and ran for the hospital.

★

Jean missed lunch in the mess hall. At the apartment, Mary sat thumbing through the latest *Saturday Evening Post.* Her radio filled the room with a soothing Sunday afternoon symphony.

"Any good news on the radio?" Jean asked.

Mary shook her head. "About the same. The Russians are trying to keep the Germans out of Kharkov. In Africa, Montgomery has made Rommel retreat a little. Lowell Thomas said that Stalin has deliberately refused to tell the Russian people about our lend-lease aid, which is helping the Red Army. Can you beat that?"

"Stalin is a strange ally, all right." Jean threw her coat across her bed and curled up in her overstuffed chair.

"How come you missed lunch?" asked Mary.

"The church had an interesting guest speaker. I talked to him for a few minutes, and then on the way home I got involved with a fight."

Mary dropped her magazine. "You what?"

"I wasn't in the fight. I ran and reported it, and then I hung around until it was broken up."

Mary scooped up the magazine from the floor and said, "You won't give up, will you? You can't leave these people to their own problems. You could have been hurt."

"No. I was perfectly safe." She gave Mary a quick rundown of her race for help and then her sprint to the hospital. "So you see, I was involved but not involved. I'm starving. Have you got any of those cookies left?"

Mary fetched her package from home and also produced a can of evaporated milk and a can of cocoa. Being an expert cocoa maker, she mixed the milk and some of the cocoa and set it on the hot plate. "I only have a little cubed sugar. We can add it to our cups. That'll make it go farther."

Jean munched a chewy oatmeal and raisin cookie, still thinking about the Japanese men fighting each other. "Mary, prejudice isn't limited to judging people by skin colors and ethnic backgrounds."

"You noticed that, huh?"

Jean stayed serious. "I thought I understood all the variations, but it shocked me to see Japanese fighting against Japanese when they were all in the same boat. It was a clash of ideas and attitudes, but I think a subtle prejudice lay underneath the animosity too."

"We do the same thing," said Mary. "Any time someone gets in our way, we start stereotyping—mental shorthand—so we don't have to think."

"Right. You know, if there were only one thing I could accomplish during my lifetime, I'd want to wipe out prejudice. It's so blind and hurtful. I'm going to start with me," she concluded soberly.

"Good place," agreed Mary with a wicked grin. "I think this cocoa's hot now." She poured two steaming mugs full and handed one to Jean. "One or two, mademoiselle?" she asked in an uppity tone, proffering the sugar cube package.

"Two, please." Jean was still too distracted to play games. "Now that Jiro says he won't testify for Tom and Uncle Al is so upset—insisting I may hurt more than help—I need to think of some surefire way to free Tom that won't make waves in the wrong direction."

"Why don't you get the president to pardon him? No one could argue with a presidential order."

Jean blinked. "Mary," she said slowly, "I think you've got something." Her mug of cocoa sloshed over and dripped on her lap. Uncaring, she set it on the floor beside her chair and jumped up. "You angel!" She gave Mary a big hug, let her go, and spun around the room like a ballerina. "Why didn't you think of this sooner?"

Mary sat dumbfounded. "You can't be serious. You can't reach President Roosevelt. Even if there wasn't a war on, you couldn't. Even if you could, he's the one that signed the order to round up the Japanese people and put them here. Jean! I was only kidding!"

Jean stopped whirling, carefully picked up her mug of cocoa, and sat down. "You forget my uncle is a senator who talks to the president regularly. All I have to do is make Uncle Al see how safe this would be."

"But you said he was mad at you the last time you talked to him."

"He was, but I know Uncle Al. He loves me like a father. If he can, he just might do it." She looked at her watch. "It's 5:30 P.M. in Washington. I think I'll call his apartment and see if he's there."

A few minutes later, outside the soldier's quarters, Jean waited for a buck private to finish using the pay phone, glad there was no line of men waiting. At last he stepped out of the booth and she stepped in.

Pulling the door snugly shut, she laid out all of her change in organized piles and dialed. On the instructions of the operator, she dropped in half of her supply of silver coins.

Uncle Al's phone rang five or six times. She was about to give up when the receiver clicked. "Senator Moore speaking," came his voice.

"Uncle Al! It's me, Jeanie."

"Hello. How are you?"

"I'm fine. I'm sorry I hung up on you the other day. I thought about what you said, and I don't want to cause any trouble. I thought you'd like to know—"

"I'm glad you've come to your senses and glad we're speaking again." He sounded like his old self.

"I'm not trying to set up any investigations or anything."

"That's very sensible."

"I do have something I'd like to ask you."

"Yes?"

"It occurred to me that one person I could talk to without exposing any secrets, who could clear Tom's name with a word, would be President Roosevelt. He already knows all that I've done. Would that be okay?"

He didn't answer.

She held her breath and waited.

"You can't be serious," he said flatly.

"Please, Uncle Al. If you could get me in to talk to him, I know I could convince him that jailing Tom is a mistake. I just didn't know enough about the Japanese people in the beginning to report accurately."

"I'm not going to go into this again, Jeanie," he warned.

"Why are you so stuck on the case of this one man? If he weren't a Jap, I'd think you were in love with him."

Jean cringed at the contempt in his voice, but she said levelly, "Uncle Al, I don't want to hear you ever call these people Japs again."

"Jeanie, what's come over you?" He was on the edge of yelling again. "They even call themselves Japs."

"They humble themselves in a lot of ways they shouldn't have to."

"Look, I'll not stand for any argument about this. I told you how dangerous it would be to interfere now. Forget your rescue scheme. And I want you out of that place at the end of the school year. Until then, you behave like a professional and concentrate on your teaching."

"But Uncle Al—"

"Your three minutes are up," broke in the operator. "Please deposit one dollar if you wish to continue."

Two soldiers stood waiting outside the folding doors of the phone booth.

"Okay, Uncle Al," she said stiffly. "Good-bye."

"Good-bye."

★

The next day after school, Jean walked straight to Pastor Ichiba's. She was at her wit's end, thinking of Tom in jail, seeing Helen so distressed, and knowing how badly the rest of the family felt. Some people were beginning to shun the Kagawa family as if Tom were a traitor. They feared for their own sons who had associated with him.

Once again Pastor Ichiba walked to the church with Jean so they could talk in private. The building seemed more welcoming because the stove was still warm from some earlier meeting.

Jean told Pastor Ichiba everything she had tried. "I don't know what to do next. I hoped you might have an idea," she explained.

"I have no knowledge that would help you. I can only counsel on spiritual matters. Tell me, have you been able to do the things you described without dissimulation?"

"Not exactly. I simply can't tell the whole truth. Perhaps I'll never be able to tell anyone but you."

"I understand, but this is very dangerous for you. You may find yourself becoming entrapped in deceit again."

"I know. I'm doing the best I can. I'm reading the Bible every day and praying."

"All God asks is that we do the best we can and trust him to empower our efforts," he assured her. "You look tired. You must pace yourself for a long race." He asked her to read the ninety-first Psalm every night before going to bed and invited her to call on him again whenever she wished.

With that they parted. Disappointed, Jean trudged home, arriving just in time for supper.

That evening Mary tried to cheer her up and then finally retreated to her homework. Jean leaned over her own papers, but she wasn't working on them. She couldn't get her mind off Tom. She wanted to write to him, to encourage him with reports of what she was trying to do, but she feared her letters might just trigger more rage and resentment.

Longing for him, for at least some contact with him, crashed in on her. The old lethargy she'd felt after Dave's death crept over her. There was no hope for Tom . . . no hope for her. She wished she'd never been born. She climbed into bed without a glance at her grandmother's Bible or Dave's smiling image above her bed.

★

Before dawn Jean awoke in her warm bed to a startling thought. *I should tell Helen I'm in love with Tom.* She immediately rejected the idea, threw off her covers, and got up.

All day long, however, at odd moments the thought returned, only more specifically. *If I told Helen how I feel about Tom, maybe she could help me communicate with him.* She pushed the idea away.

At the end of the class day as they were straightening the room for tomorrow, the thought intruded again. Jean laid down the green construction paper she was cutting in halves for an art project and said, "Helen, I need to talk to you."

A few feet away, Helen looked up from sweeping and asked, "What about?"

"About Tom. I'm in love with him," Jean blurted.

Helen's eyes widened.

Jean blushed, and then she went lightheaded. She slumped into her chair at her desk and pressed her fist against her lips.

Helen laid aside the broom and pulled her chair over to Jean's desk. "In a way, I'm not surprised," she admitted. "And in another way, I'm shocked. How long have you felt this way? Does Tom know?"

"How long? I'm not sure. Maybe since the first day I saw him. Does he know? No! And I don't want him to."

Helen's face brightened. "Your love for him might give him hope."

"No! I can't throw myself at him! You know that."

Helen became more circumspect. "Yes. I guess I got a little excited. He'd run like a scared jackrabbit."

"I'd like to write to him. I think knowing about my efforts to free him might encourage him, and I want to hear from him, too, to know what he's thinking and feeling. But right now I'm afraid a letter from me would make him angrier."

"He's not angry at you. He's angry about being questioned and put in jail."

"No. It's me, too, and he has good reason. But wouldn't he feel better if he believed I was fighting for him?"

Helen pursed her lips. "Yes. I should think he would."

"Will you help me write to him?"

"I don't understand. Just go ahead and write to him. He will be glad to hear from you."

"But he thinks it's my fault he's in jail," admitted Jean.

Helen frowned in disbelief. "That's crazy. He's not stupid."

Jean sighed. She'd known from the moment she started, she'd have to tell the whole truth, yet it was so painful. "Helen, I'd like to tell you some things no one else knows, except Pastor Ichiba. You may hate me when I'm done, but I hope you'll still believe I truly love Tom and that I'll never give up trying to clear his name."

# CHAPTER 19

Jean felt she was laying down her life and her reputation for Tom by telling his sister the whole truth. In anger, Helen could expose her duplicity to everyone and maybe even cause the kind of trouble Uncle Al had feared.

And yet there was the chance that if this one person close to Tom knew the truth and could forgive her, maybe someday Tom also could forgive her. It was a risk she had to take.

"I think I'd better start by telling you about Dave, the man I was going to marry," said Jean. She talked rapidly at first but slowed when she reached Pearl Harbor Day. With difficulty she tried to describe what Dave's death had done to her. She watched for Helen's reaction as she mentioned the time at Willamette when men, some who were her friends, had attacked the Japanese students.

Helen's face remained sympathetic.

Jean struggled on to her agreement to spy for Uncle Al.

Helen's eyes narrowed, her mouth tightened, her body grew tense—but she listened without interrupting.

Jean admitted using Helen to get into project mess halls and meet internees. She admitted sending negative reports to Uncle Al.

Helen burst out. "You scum! You slimy cheat! You're the traitor!"

"Yes, I know," admitted Jean miserably, "but please hear the rest."

Her instant admission of guilt seemed to help. Helen's nostrils quivered with outrage, but she kept her mouth shut.

Jean continued, describing her loss of Rodge, and then the realization she had made a terrible mistake. She detailed her growing love for Tom and her efforts to stop her uncle and her final decision to try to talk to President Roosevelt.

Anger and disgust tightened Helen's features. When Jean concluded with a description of the last time she saw Tom, Helen jumped up and exploded. "No wonder he hates the sight of you. So do I!"

She picked up her things and stamped toward the door.

"Helen. Please, please forgive me," pleaded Jean.

"I'd rather spit on you!" cried Helen. She slammed the door behind her.

Drained and defeated, Jean put her head down on her desk. She had gambled and lost. She didn't know what to expect of Helen now.

After a while she straightened. She might as well head for home. As she gathered her papers, her glance fell on the bonsai tree on the front of her desk. What had Tom said to the children? Habits can bend and shape us?

*Well, at least I broke free from deception with Helen,* she thought with a wry smile.

★

The next day Helen assisted as well as ever, but she spoke to Jean only when Jean asked her a question. The day passed painfully and slowly. Jean wondered how she could get through many days like this.

The following day passed as miserably until a few minutes before dismissal time, when Pastor Ichiba appeared at the door. He asked to speak with her after class. Surprised, Jean invited him in and gave him her chair, while Helen finished teaching the children a new song.

As soon as the children marched out the door, Helen greeted Pastor Ichiba and excused herself. Ignoring cleanup chores, she left too.

Jean turned to Pastor Ichiba with a tired smile. "I'm glad you came to visit," she said, determined to forget Helen and concentrate on his kind face.

"I have news that may interest you," he said. "Dr. Langston is going to speak before a congressional committee on his experience in Japan. He also plans to speak on the Japanese situation here in the United States."

Jean wondered why he had made a special trip to tell her this. Then a hopeful idea dawned. "He's going to Washington, D.C.?"

Pastor smiled placidly. "Yes. The problem is that his wife, who has always served as his personal secretary, is too frail for this trip."

Jean held her breath.

Pastor Ichiba said, "He took the opportunity to ask Helen Kagawa to go with him, feeling she might be given a chance to speak about her own experience during the war relocation."

Jean let out her breath in disappointment. *So that's why Helen ran out on the chores,* thought Jean. *Since we're not speaking, she had to ask Pastor to tell me she's leaving.* "I see," she said aloud.

He held up his hand. "Not yet," he said with a twinkle in his eyes. "There is more. Helen has refused to go. She insists that you should be the one. I tried to tell her you could not leave your teaching position, but she seemed confident that you would find a way."

Jean's mouth fell open. "She did? Oh, I can! I'll work it out!"

"I don't know what you two have concocted, but I wish you the best," he said, rising to his feet. "May I tell Dr. Langston you will accompany him three days hence?"

"Oh, yes!"

"His mission board will pay your railway fare and room and board. You will need to meet him in San Francisco and leave from there. I will obtain the times and the itinerary for you."

"Oh, Pastor Ichiba! You don't how much this means to me."

He smiled and bowed. "I'm sure you will do your best for all of us."

★

"Mary, Mary!" Jean shouted from the apartment door. "I'm going to Washington, D.C. Nothing can stop me now." She grabbed her roommate, who was standing at the mirror applying fresh lipstick, and spun her around.

Mary broke loose and cried, "You what?"

"I get to go to Washington with Dr. Langston and talk to a congressional committee and maybe see the president. Helen and Pastor Ichiba worked it all out."

"But your class. . . You can't just leave."

"I'll resign if I have to. Helen's a great teacher. She can finish the year without me."

"Hoo-ee," said Mary. "I'm sorry I ever mentioned the president. How soon would you leave?"

"I've got only a day or two to pack and then catch the bus for San Francisco. I'll start packing tonight. And I'll write to Tom and tell him what I'm doing."

"If I were you, I wouldn't get his hopes up yet," cautioned Mary.

Jean paused. "You may be right."

Mary shook her head in disbelief. "I thought I was the impulsive one here. By the way, I heard from the Red Cross today. They said they can put us in any number of wartime positions overseas after just a few weeks of training. Are you interested?"

"Sure," said Jean offhandedly. "That may be just the thing when school's out. I wonder how cold it is in Washington, D.C., this time of year."

★

Helen came into the classroom the next morning as cool and distant as she had been when she left the day before.

Jean tried to break the ice. "I really appreciate what you've done. A trip to Washington would be exciting for you."

"Let's get one thing straight. I don't want your thanks because I didn't do it for you. I did it for Tom."

"Still, I'm grateful. I'll do the best I can for him and the others too. I really will try to talk to the president."

"Fat chance. But at least you'll be in the same city."

"Helen, I am so very sorry for what I've done," Jean offered softly. "I hope someday we can be friends again."

Helen shrugged. "Just do your best for Tom."

Jean gave up trying to make peace and concentrated on the tasks at hand. "Will you hold the fort this morning while I talk to Mrs. Smith about taking time off?"

"Sure."

★

As Jean had guessed, Mrs. Smith refused to give her a leave of absence.

"Then I resign," Jean said.

"You can't do that. It will be a permanent mark on your record."

"Okay," Jean readily agreed. "Today's my last day. Helen is teaching very capably right now. She'll do fine until you can decide what to do in my absence. Are there any papers I should sign?"

"They will be at the administration building reception desk at 3:30 this afternoon," said Mrs. Smith in icy tones.

★

Shortly after noon recess, a young woman from the administration building brought Jean a message. Her grandmother had called and asked Jean to call her immediately after school. If she did so, Jean would have to tell about her resignation without revealing her work for Uncle Al. *Will the deceptions never end?* she thought wearily.

She went to her coat hanging on the wall and tucked the note in an outer pocket.

Jean decided not to tell the children she was leaving for good. Helen agreed. At the end of the day, they said good-bye, thinking she was only taking a short trip. She pasted on a smile. They were her children. She had so wanted to see them through the year—to fulfill her commitment to give them skills and confidence for their uncertain future. She helped them with buttons and boots and hugged each boy and girl one last time.

When they were gone, Helen said, "I've already prepared the worksheets for tomorrow. I'll sweep while you clean out your desk."

"Thanks. I don't have many personal things. You'll need all the rest." Jean put her few possessions in a paper bag, and straightened the remaining tools of the teacher's trade: good scissors, an eighteen-inch straight edge, a paper punch, glue, a first aid kit, three rubber stamps with a purple ink pad, and a box of gold stars.

She carefully cleaned her desktop, even dusting under the

bonsai tree. She gently wiped the prickly needles with her dust cloth. The tiny wild pine stood trapped in its shallow dish with bound branches sprouting new growth. Tom had said it would grow more and more beautiful because of the restraints.

Helen, sweeping nearby, volunteered, "Tom did a good job on the tree."

Jean responded, "Yes, it's thriving, even though it's a prisoner. I wonder if Tom will grow in jail as well as his tree is growing here."

"You should wonder," grunted Helen bitterly. She began to sweep furiously and only muttered when Jean called goodbye to her.

On the way home Jean pulled a crumpled note from her coat pocket by accident while reaching for her handkerchief. It was the note to call Grandmother. Jean passed her apartment and went on to the phone booth, hoping Grandmother was at home so she wouldn't have to try again later.

Grandmother answered with uncharacteristic excitement. "Jeanie, I knew you'd want to know right away! Rodger is alive! He was among a few prisoners the Marines rescued when they occupied a small island near where his ship went down."

Jean slumped against the wall of the booth. "Rodger . . . alive? Oh, are they sure?"

"Absolutely. He'll be coming home soon."

"Oh, that's wonderful!" Jean cried.

★

Back in the apartment, after Jean finally tired of talking about the good news that Rodge was alive, Mary asked, "How did your grandmother feel about you rushing off to Washington with a strange man?"

"He's not a 'strange man,'" laughed Jean. "Actually, I think she was pleased after I explained who he is. She agreed not to tell Uncle Al. I want to surprise him, if I see him at all. I aim to get an appointment with the president before Uncle Al can stop me."

"You're expecting the impossible. I hope you won't be too disappointed," worried Mary. She dipped her comb into a glass of water, moistened a tress of hair, and rolled it deftly onto a metal curler. "I hate sleeping on these, but the wind and rain destroyed my hairdo today," she complained.

"Me too," said Jean, running her fingers through her shoulder-length bob. "Maybe I'll wear my hair up while I travel. It won't need to be set so often."

"I'm sure going to miss you. I hate being alone here."

"I'll miss you too. I've never had a such a good friend as you."

"Thanks. Let's do go into the Red Cross together. Maybe somehow we'll end up at the same place."

"Okay. As soon as I get back from Washington, I'll apply."

"I'll wait and we can apply at the same time." Mary stopped rolling her thick dark hair and picked up the hand mirror to check for any missed strands. "That's so great about Rodge," she said thoughtfully. "Do you think he's still in love with you?"

"Maybe. I don't know if he received my last letter."

"Are you going to tell him about Tom?"

"There's no hope for me with Tom. I don't intend to tell anyone how I feel about him."

"That's smart," agreed Mary as she wrapped a hair net over her lumpy curlers.

Jean's eyes came to rest on the bonsai tree the Kagawas had given her for Christmas. As difficult as wartime travel was, she wouldn't be back to Tulelake and the little tree would not survive shipping. "Mary, would you mind packing my things and shipping them to Salem for me?"

"Be glad to." Mary's eyes followed her gaze to the little tree. "What should I do with the bonsai?"

Jean considered. "I'll take it to Mrs. Kagawa. I'll have time for that."

★

In the morning after breakfast, Jean and Mary said goodbye quietly as they'd planned, keeping the news of her resignation from the other teachers until after her departure. With the bonsai tree in her hand, Jean felt strange walking through the project to the Kagawa apartment instead of going to school. Halfway there it suddenly struck her that Helen could have told her family the truth about Jean's spy mission. Jean hesitated. Maybe she should have Mary deliver the tree later. Then she decided if she were Helen, she wouldn't have burdened her already grieving parents with such unpleasant news. Wanting to reassure the Kagawas of her intentions and hopes, Jean took a chance and walked on.

When she reached her destination, Mrs. Kagawa was the only one home. Her face showed only a friendly welcome—Helen had not told her.

Relieved, Jean held out the potted tree. "I'm leaving this afternoon, and I want the tree to have a good home. I hope we will meet again, but I won't be coming back to Tulelake."

Mrs. Kagawa's sad eyes brightened at the sight of the tree. "I will take good care of it, and who knows? Maybe someday I can return it to you. Helen told us what you want to do. We are so grateful. Please come in. Let me make you a cup of tea."

"Thank you, but I really must hurry on. I have a lot to do before leaving."

"I understand. We shall be praying for you."

"Thanks. I won't give up, Mrs. Kagawa, not until Tom's name is cleared." Jean backed away filled with all that she could not say.

Mrs. Kagawa smiled and nodded as if she understood.

Next Jean walked to the Ichiba apartment. She accepted Mrs. Ichiba's smiling invitation to come in but politely refused tea and a chair.

Pastor Ichiba gave her an envelope with written instructions for meeting Dr. Langston in San Francisco. He also gave her a small envelope fattened with dollar bills. "The people at church want to help with your expenses. A teacher's pay cannot go very far."

She tried to give it back. "I can't accept this," said Jean. "They have so little, and I can afford the trip."

He refused to take the envelope. "If you allow them to be of service, you will relieve their suffering. You will give them a feeling of some power over their fate."

"But I may fail. I may not do them any good at all," worried Jean.

"That you are trying is all they expect. Please respect them by accepting their gift."

Jean's fingers tightened on the envelope of bills that represented hours of work at sixteen dollars per month wages. Carefully, she placed it in her purse. "Please give them my deepest thanks."

"I shall indeed. You go with our prayers and blessings."

★

Before school was out that day, Jean climbed aboard a bus bound for San Francisco with one small suitcase. Settling into one of the few empty seats, she leaned back and closed her eyes to avoid talking.

As the miles disappeared under the whining tires, she welcomed a growing optimism. To have Rodger alive lifted her spirits. One seeming miracle made another more possible. Somehow she felt she would be able to undo the damage and hurt she'd caused Tom.

As far as she could tell, Helen hadn't told anyone about Jean's role behind the recent arrests. Maybe she never would if Jean succeeded in obtaining Tom's freedom.

# CHAPTER 20

Dr. Langston turned out to be a fascinating traveling companion. His stories about his life in Japan before the war entranced Jean. In a courtly way, he watched over her comfort on the crowded train.

Cross-country travel by rail during wartime was challenging. Pullman cars with sleeping facilities were in short supply, and with the military having priority, Dr. Langston only obtained second-class seats. When the train stopped long enough, Jean jumped off and bought sandwiches at food stands. In some towns, local people met trains and offered home-cooked food through USO canteens. Soldiers, who had adopted Dr. Langston and Jean, brought them these treats.

After a couple of nights of trying to sleep hunched in a seat and with no way to really bathe, Jean felt rumpled and frowzy, but Dr. Langston looked impeccable and seemed untouched by the discomfort. People from nearby seats gravitated to his humor and warmth. Soldiers and sailors laid aside their card games and leaned over the backs of seats to trade jokes with him and to chat with Jean. Most of the servicemen were on their way to the Atlantic theater of war.

By the fifth day, when the train steamed into Washington, D.C., Jean's aching back and unkempt feeling faded as she peered out the window for her first view of the nation's capital. The servicemen around her fell silent, occupied with their own thoughts.

She and Dr. Langston had acquired friends from a dozen

different states. The pain of war drew them together in a brief but warm camaraderie.

When the train pulled to a stop, three of the men carried Jean's and Dr. Langston's suitcases to the station platform. Intentionally, no one used the word good-bye when they parted.

"Watch out for wolves," Jerry, a sailor, warned Jean.

"Yeah, don't fall for any lines from the army or the marines," added his buddy Tony.

"Buzz off, you swabs, and stop trying to interfere with the morale of the army. Whatever you do, Jean, don't trust a sailor," said Private First Class Nelson.

Jean laughed. "Thanks for the advice. You take care of yourselves."

Dr. Langston shook hands with them and returned a couple of bear hugs. "God bless you," he said to each one. As he watched them disappearing in the crowd, he said, "God forbid that they should die so young."

To a passerby his words would have sounded like a simple heartfelt statement. Jean knew he was praying. The boys, as Dr. Langston called the servicemen, made her feel good about being an American. They were caring and committed, taking on a painful responsibility without complaint.

Union Station arched high over their heads like a cathedral. Most of the hundreds of people, shoulder to shoulder, were men in uniform.

As she and Dr. Langston moved through the milling crowd, Jean noticed many black servicemen with their families. She suddenly realized she'd seen no faces of color among the people who had ridden in their train car. Soon she saw signs above drinking fountains and on rest room doors that designated "Whites Only" or "Coloreds Only."

She was embarrassed to have to obey the signs when she used the rest room. *Tom probably would say this is the real world,* she thought. In Salem there had been one or two restaurants that displayed window signs saying, "We cater to whites only," and then after Pearl Harbor, two or three cafes had hung signs saying, "No Japs allowed." These had been on the perimeter of Jean's life, in places she didn't frequent. Her first glimpse of legal segregation made her angry and ashamed.

While Dr. Langston acquired the assistance of a red cap, a black man whose job was to help travelers through the station, Jean considered her strong feelings against segregation. She realized she might not be so angry if she hadn't lived in the internment camp. In fact, if she were to be totally honest, she might not have been embarrassed.

As they moved among the mass of travelers toward the white columns that marked the route to taxicabs, Jean glanced up at a giant painting suspended in the open arch above. It pictured soldiers from the Revolutionary War, labeled 1778, and soldiers of 1943 above a slogan, "Americans always fight for liberty." The porter was able to get them a cab that already had two people in it. He apologized but said they were fortunate. The city had become so crowded since the war, it was even difficult to get a seat on city buses.

As soon as they checked into the hotel, Dr. Langston excused himself to rest, leaving Jean free for the remainder of the afternoon. She washed her face, put on fresh lipstick, brushed her hair onto the top her head again, and pinned it expertly into swirls and curls. In a few short minutes she returned to the lobby.

"Excuse me," she said to the desk clerk, a young man with thick glasses that explained why he was not in military service. "Can you tell me how a person would go about getting an appointment to see the president?"

He stared at her through the magnifying lenses and then grinned. "You're kidding, right?"

"No. I really want to know."

He scratched his chin. "I suppose you'd have to call some secretary at the White House and ask how. Or do you know any senators? Sometimes a senator or congressman can arrange an appointment for people from their states."

"Well, thanks," she said. "Ah, would you have any change for the phone?"

"Sure."

She handed him some of the dollar bills from her envelope. Scooping up the change he laid out, she took it to the long bank of phone booths and found one that contained a complete phone book. Perching on the built-in stool, she searched the book and began making calls. After forty-five minutes of dogged persistence, she actually reached a White House secretary. In courteous Bostonian tones a woman said no one could see the president privately. "You understand, Miss Thornton," said the woman, pronouncing her r's as ah's, "that although he cares about individual problems, he relies on others to take action for their constituents. I recommend that you talk to your state senator, and let him carry the ball for you."

"Thank you. I'll try," said Jean, knowing that was a dead end. She couldn't ask any of the congressmen or the other Oregon senator without Uncle Al's getting wind of her efforts. She gave up and returned to her room for a much-needed bath and rest.

★

The next morning twenty men, an even mix of congressmen, senators, and army officers, met in a thickly carpeted room in a government office building to question Dr. Langston about his experience in wartime Japan. They gathered comfortably around an immense table under a bright chandelier. Heavy blackout curtains were pulled back from the windows, but still seemed to darken the sides of the room.

Jean sat near the middle on one side of the table between the chairman, Mr. Ames, and Dr. Langston. She would take notes for Dr. Langston and keep his papers in order.

At the last minute, after everyone else was seated, Senator Al Moore walked in. He returned Jean's look of surprise with a raised eyebrow and a suspicious glare.

Dr. Langston answered a variety of questions, ranging from how he had been treated in Japan to observations of military interest. He said that Japanese fighters he'd seen had not been able to match the speed of an American bomber that flew over Tokyo. He could not identify the models of the planes in either case. He and Mrs. Langston had been treated respectfully, considering the fact that they were imprisoned. Food had been poor.

"What about American-born Japanese? Did you know any?" asked Senator Moore.

"Yes. The Japanese government was pressuring them to renounce their U.S. citizenship. Most of them refused."

"What happened to the ones who refused?" Senator Moore pursued.

"Some were treated with suspicion, but for some reason, others were treated as well as Japanese citizens."

"I understand you've visited our internment camps for Japanese people here. How did our treatment of aliens compare with your treatment in Japan?" asked Senator Moore.

"Excuse me, senator," said Mr. Ames. "I've been asked that we delay discussion of our internment camps until tomorrow's meeting. One interested guest cannot be here today."

Uncle Al nodded. "Certainly."

"We'll adjourn then until tomorrow, same time."

In a few scant seconds, Uncle Al reached Jean and leaned over her shoulder. "What are you doing here?"

She smiled up at him. "As you can see, I'm assisting Dr. Langston."

Dr. Langston chimed in, "And doing a bang-up job of it, Senator Moore. You know my secretary?"

Uncle Al actually fumbled for words. "Know her? She's my niece." He swiftly recovered his aplomb and stretched out his hand. "I'm pleased to meet you, Dr. Langston, after hearing about you for so long." He turned back to Jean. "He wouldn't have told you, but he's one of our foremost authorities on the Japanese culture. He's authored several books that our government uses in military training."

"No, he didn't mention that, but I've received a crash course while traveling with him," said Jean.

"I wish you had let me know you were coming, Jeanie, so I could show you around. As it is, I'm up to my neck with meetings and appointments. I'm really sorry. I can't even take you out to dinner tonight."

"Well, I wanted to surprise you. I planned to pop in on you after Dr. Langston's meetings were over. As for dinner, our hotel has a good dining room. Anyway, with the city blacked out, there's not much to see at night."

"Right. You'll enjoy the Washington Monument someday when it's lighted again. Right now it's only got a tiny light on top to warn planes away. Well, I must go. A pleasure to have met you, Dr. Langston. I'll be back tomorrow. Jeanie, will you walk with me to the door?"

"Okay." *Here it comes. He knows very well why I didn't tell him I was coming.*

They were scarcely out of earshot when he leaned close and ordered, "Jeanie, don't try to see the president, and you must not discuss the Tulelake investigation with anyone. One of the men you reported on has already been found guilty."

Jean felt as if he'd hit her in the solar plexus. "Of treason? Who?"

"Not treason. At this point he's just been determined to be a danger to national security and will stay in prison for the duration." Almost as an afterthought, he added, "It was not your Mr. Kagawa."

Jean let out her breath in relief. "Imprisonment of any of those men is ridiculous."

He leaned closer and ground out, "You don't know that. Now give up this wild mission of mercy. It is too dangerous."

Jean straightened and squared her shoulders. "I've come a long way Uncle Al. I resigned my job to do this. I will not go home without trying to obtain a full pardon for Tom."

"Tom!" he exploded. Several men turned to look at him. He lowered his voice. "Kagawa is a harebrained hothead. Don't you get any further involved with that Jap. I won't have it."

"Uncle Al, I'm not a child to be ordered around. Good-bye." She turned and marched back to Dr. Langston. Gathering her notes and Dr. Langston's papers, she placed them in his briefcase while he talked with an army officer. When she looked up again Uncle Al was gone.

★

The afternoon sun was warm and the sky blue. While Dr. Langston rested in his hotel room, Jean put on her saddle shoes for walking and headed for the White House. She didn't know what good it would do, but she couldn't just sit in her room doing nothing.

Crowds filled the sidewalks, and every kind of bus and

trolley imaginable rolled through the streets. Some must have been resurrected from a long retirement. Trolleys, with clerestory windows above, especially looked like vehicles from the Gay Nineties as they clattered and clanged their way down Pennsylvania Avenue. She climbed onto one for a ride to the White House. She had to stand all the way, but still she glimpsed the city as it passed by. Here and there on tops of buildings she saw the long barrels of antiaircraft guns aimed at the sky. Beside some historical memorials sandbags formed bulwarks around more antiaircraft guns. Soldiers stood guard, ready for action.

When she neared the White House, she hopped off and walked until she could see the entrance. Army guards with bayonets against their shoulders marched back and forth barring the way. She lingered, looking and wondering who in all of Washington would be sympathetic, or at least fair-minded enough, to listen and help her get in to talk to the president.

"Excuse me, Miss . . . Thornton, isn't it?"

She turned to find a middle-aged man, one of the men who had been in the morning's meeting, standing at her elbow. She brightened. "Yes. You were listening to Dr. Langston this morning, weren't you?"

He acknowledged yes with a dip of his head. "I'm Congressman Jones, Illinois. I understand you're Senator Moore's niece."

"Yes."

Smiling in a friendly manner, he said, "Has he been showing you the town?"

"Well, no. I didn't tell him I was coming. I wanted to surprise him, so he doesn't have much time for me in his schedule." Suddenly she got an inspiration. "Are you going into the White House?"

"As a matter of fact, I am." He glanced at his watch. "I have an appointment in a few minutes."

"I've been so wishing I could meet the president. Uncle Al says it isn't possible, but is there a way?"

"He's right, but . . . say, can you be here at nine sharp tomorrow morning?"

"Right here on this corner?"

"Yes. I'll be back for another meeting with the president. If I can get permission, you could go in as my secretary. Mind, you couldn't do more than shake his hand and maybe not that, but you'd have a story to tell your grandchildren."

"Oh, I'd be ever so grateful, if you could . . . if I could . . ."

He smiled, evidently pleased. "I'll call you at your hotel this evening to let you know."

Giving him the name of her hotel, Jean could scarcely control her excitement. As he strode away, she called, "Mr. Jones, would you please not tell my uncle—not even that I asked? He might misunderstand and be upset . . ." She stopped, not wanting to fabricate.

He waved his hand in a half-salute and said, "I understand."

She could only hope that he really did.

She returned to the hotel exhilarated, and before Dr. Langston was ready to go down for dinner, Congressman Jones called to tell her to meet him as planned. "I'll be walking or I'd pick you up. Walking is one of my personal quirks. Saves on gas and good for my health. Sure you can meet me by nine?"

"Oh, yes. Thank you!"

At dinner Jean explained to Dr. Langston about her unusual opportunity to see the president. "I won't be going with you to breakfast. Instead, I'll see you at your meeting."

He was happy for her, but concerned. "I wish I could go with you. Will you have a chance to talk to the president about your friend Tom, do you think?"

"Maybe, or at least to ask for another appointment later."

"My prayers will go with you."

The next morning Jean walked with Congressman Jones to the executive office building in the west wing of the White House. He led her down a wide hall and into a spacious oval-shaped office. Through the windows she could see a garden and beyond it the White House proper.

The office contained a desk of dark wood, on which stood a tall brass lamp and a large bouquet of spring flowers in front of a large blotter pad, a telephone, a calendar, an ashtray, and a few neatly arranged papers. Behind the polished desk stood a large high-backed chair upholstered in a plush fabric that made it look like a piece of living-room furniture, except that this chair swiveled. No one needed to tell her. It was the president's chair, thickly cushioned to ease his back and paralyzed legs. Seeing where the president sat gave Jean a feeling of being in the presence of the disabled man, whom she felt no one could call crippled.

Around the room sat half a dozen other men. Jean immediately began to calculate her chances of being able to say anything at all to the president, and her hopes began to dim.

Mr. Jones took a chair where Jean could sit beside him, opened his briefcase, and handed her a stenographer's pad. "Try to catch the gist of things and write briefly in English, none of that shorthand stuff. Simply give speakers' names and key words. It's not critical, or I'd have to have my regular secretary, but whatever you do will be a help."

After a few minutes, the men around Jean began to shift their feet and to talk in undertones. She whispered to Congressman Jones, "Is something wrong?"

He looked at his own watch. "The president is normally seated and waiting for us, and today he's fifteen minutes late." He began to tap his fingers nervously on his open sheaf of papers.

At last a door opened and a man stepped into the room. Everyone stood up. The man came in alone and stood in front of the executive desk. Raising his hand in both greeting and a gesture for silence, he said, "Good morning, gentlemen."

"That's Harry Hopkins," whispered Mr. Jones, "the president's good friend and assistant."

Mr. Hopkins said, "You can probably guess why I'm here, instead of the president. He awoke indisposed this morning—nothing serious—and until the last minute, he planned to be here anyway, but the doctor prevailed, insisting that he remain in bed for the morning. You'll be rescheduled, but please leave me your briefs for him to consider before your next appointment."

Reluctantly the other men rose, presented papers to Mr.

Hopkins, and left muttering among themselves. Mr. Jones waited until last and urged Jean forward with him.

"Harry, this is Miss Thornton from Oregon. She's Senator Moore's niece and was hoping to meet the president. Maybe she can at least go home and tell folks she shook your hand."

Jean would rather have remained anonymous and quietly disappeared. What if Mr. Hopkins told Uncle Al she'd been here? All she could do under the circumstances, however, was smile and accept Mr. Hopkins's extended hand and pray he would swiftly forget her.

"Al's niece? You tell him to bring you along next time he comes over."

*Oh, no. At this rate, he's not likely to forget me.* "He won't have time. I'll be returning to Oregon late this afternoon," she said, wanting to pull her hand from his and run.

He let go. "Too bad. Next time then." With a good-bye, he left by the same door he'd entered.

Congressman Jones looked at his watch again. "I have to go to my office this morning. Can you find your way alone to your meeting with Dr. Langston?"

"Yes, I'm learning my way around. Thanks for getting me into the president's office even if I didn't get to see the president. It was very kind of you."

"My pleasure. Sorry our plans didn't pan out. You really must come back to D.C. for another visit and have your uncle show you around."

"I will indeed." At the corner of Pennsylvania Avenue, Jean said good-bye to the Congressman who liked to walk.

Jean arrived at Dr. Langston's meeting a few minutes late. Everyone was seated, including Uncle Al. He gave her a searing look, as if he suspected where she'd been.

Jean turned her attention to Dr. Langston, who handed her his papers already sorted in the order he wished, and the notebook she had been keeping for him.

The chairman opened the meeting and asked Dr. Langston to begin his report on the Japanese in America. While Dr. Langston spoke Jean could simply listen; he only wanted notes on what others said. Listening, she let her eyes move from face to face down the table. She almost gasped aloud when she came to the face of a woman, the only other woman at the table—Eleanor Roosevelt! Jean had long admired this controversial woman. She even loved the political jokes about Mrs. Roosevelt's travels that made her seem omnipresent. After all, she was President Roosevelt's legs and eyes and ears and good at the job.

Mrs. Roosevelt caught Jean's eyes on her and gave her a warm smile, nodding as if they already knew each other.

Dr. Langston paused for questions, and Jean set to her task of taking notes, swiftly recording the give and take. Apparently several men had strong feelings about the necessity of the internment; two others questioned the legality of the act. It was grueling work to keep up with the fast exchange.

Mrs. Roosevelt asked many piercing questions. Jean struggled to catch them all: Is the food nourishing and properly prepared? Are the hospitals adequately staffed? What is the infant mortality rate compared with normal towns in America? What is the death rate among the older people? What do the adults do in the work programs? What is being done to keep up the morale of the young people? What is being done to prepare the adults for war work outside the camps?

Dr. Langston did his best to answer with facts project leaders had given him.

The first lady's intensely sympathetic stand on behalf of the Japanese internees was quite the opposite of her husband's public pronouncements. *Why didn't I think of it before?* thought Jean. *She's the one I should talk to.*

Mrs. Roosevelt's questions put some of the men on the defensive, but they were cautious about arguing with her. Finally she asked, "Dr. Langston, what has the internment camp done to the family life of the internees?"

He replied, "My secretary, Miss Jean Thornton, has been teaching grade-school children at Tulelake camp in northern California. Perhaps you'd like to address that question to her."

"Certainly. Miss Thornton, you must have been in position to see firsthand the effects on the children and on families in general."

Jean's heart hammered in panic at suddenly being the center of attention, but here was her chance to say something on behalf of the internees. "Yes, Mrs. Roosevelt, I was in a good position."

"Please stand up, Miss Thornton, so everyone can hear you clearly," Mrs. Roosevelt invited, smiling. "These men do not all have ears as good as mine," she added lightly. The men laughed with her and at themselves.

Jean laughed too. It was the little break she needed to get her wits about her. She stood up and waited. When the chuckles died down, she said, "I went to Tulelake last August. From the beginning, my second-grade pupils were somewhat withdrawn and fearful. The young adults—college age and up—were frustrated and angry. The teens at first seemed like teens anywhere. In a few short months, however, juvenile delinquency became a serious problem.

"Families in the internment camps have lost their bearings. Parents are no longer respected or listened to because to their children they seem to be impotent victims. There are activities for all ages to help morale, but not much families can do together. They're crammed into tiny rooms in tar-paper barracks with no privacy and scarcely enough floor space for beds." She paused for a breath.

One congressman burst out in exasperation, "There's a war on, Miss Thornton. In any other country, they'd be in real prisons."

"I'm sorry, sir, but I disagree," Jean snapped back. "These people are not guilty of any crime or espionage. Two-thirds of them are American citizens. As the Portland *Oregonian* newspaper said recently, their only crime is the fact that they have Japanese ancestors. And furthermore, sir, this is not any other country. This is the United States of America. We have a bill of rights and a Constitution that make the internment without a trial unconstitutional as well as immoral!"

Mrs. Roosevelt flashed her a huge smile of approval and started clapping. Several men joined her. The rest sat looking glum. Uncle Al didn't crack a smile, but then he, too, began to applaud, albeit halfheartedly.

"Thank you, Miss Thornton," Mrs. Roosevelt said. "You have answered my question admirably. Dr. Langston, have you visited all of the internment camps?"

Jean sat down and started writing again.

Dr. Langston replied, "Yes, I visited all ten. You see, of the 110,000 internees, one-third are Christians. As a Christian missionary, I visited the church services in each camp."

"Would you say conditions for family life in the other nine camps paralleled those at Tulelake?"

"Yes. Parents mentioned these problems in every camp."

"Thank you, Dr. Langston. Your turn, gentlemen," she concluded, relinquishing the floor.

The questioning continued, but no one asked anything more of Jean. She'd had her chance, but had not been able to say anything to help Tom. She tensely scribbled notes until the end of the session.

When Mrs. Roosevelt rose to leave, Jean jumped to her feet to follow. Several men crowded around Dr. Langston, however, blocking her way. By the time she broke through them, the first lady, surrounded by her escorts, which Jean now recognized as secret service agents, walked out the door.

Jean started to run after them, but Uncle Al was suddenly beside her, gripping her arm. "Forget it," he said.

She tugged to break his hold. His fingers tightened. "Don't make a scene, Jeanie. You're in my territory now. The wrong impression will do more harm to your cause than good."

"Let go of me!" she hissed.

"Where were you this morning?" he demanded.

"I'm not going to tell you."

"Al, I hear this is your niece. She's quite a persuasive speaker."

Uncle Al turned to the man standing at his side. "Jim, I'd like you to meet Jean. I was just congratulating her myself."

Jean was forced to play her uncle's game. It was too late to pursue Mrs. Roosevelt. While she greeted the man politely and answered his friendly questions, Uncle Al let go of her arm.

After that useless interchange, she went back to Dr. Langston's side and stayed there. She must talk with Mrs. Roosevelt. If she had to, she'd stay in Washington after Dr. Langston left. She had enough money for a few days.

Uncle Al lingered until the last man left and insisted on

driving them to their hotel. "I still bring my car to work, and you'll never be able to find a taxi in time to make your train. The city has grown so fast our transportation can't keep up. Neither can a lot of other services."

Dr. Langston thanked him profusely. "I confess that Washington traffic intimidates me. And taxi drivers seem to intentionally ignore white-haired old men."

"They do that to everyone nowadays. When does your train leave?"

*Oh, no,* thought Jean. *He's going to make sure I leave.*

Dr. Langston said, "In just a couple of hours. We checked out this morning and deposited our luggage at the hotel desk."

"That gives you time for a bite to eat, if I drive you. I'll take you to my favorite Italian restaurant."

"I thought your schedule was full," said Jean.

"I had a cancellation. It leaves me just enough time to see you off," he said cheerfully.

"Then lead the way, Senator Moore," said Dr. Langston. "I shall be eternally grateful."

Uncle Al ordered his car to be brought to the entrance of the building. He drove, expertly dodging through traffic to a small basement restaurant. The buttery fragrance of garlic bread wafted by when they entered.

Uncle Al regaled them with stories of Washington. Jean set herself to appear interested while she mentally plotted how she could escape him without making a scene. Uncle Al had proved he could thwart her if he knew what she was doing. She must make him believe she had given up and was going home peaceably. She put on a show of relaxed enjoyment, praising the spaghetti and talking eagerly about going home to search for a new war job.

The lunch and picking up the luggage filled more time than Jean had expected. Nevertheless, at Union Station Uncle Al took time to park the car and escort them all the way to the boarding platform. He carried their suitcases to their seats and stowed them, and then he performed an agonizingly long good-bye. Gregarious Dr. Langston ate up every word the senator had to say. "All 'board!" came a conductor's call from outside their car. Uncle Al fled, shouting final words of advice all the way to the door.

By the time he disappeared, the train shuddered and started to roll. Jean could hear the heavy chuff-chuff of the steam engine. She leaped to her feet and said to Dr. Langston, "I can't explain, but I can't go with you. Don't worry. I have money. And I have Uncle Al." She ran through the car into the next one. A conductor was standing by the closed door. She cried, "Help! I've got to get off."

He threw the door open, steadied her as she stepped down to the lower step, and helped as she jumped from the slow-moving train. She made it, but with only her purse. Her carry-on suitcase remained with Dr. Langston.

When she was safely on the platform, she searched for a glimpse of Uncle Al. Fortunately, she was a good distance from where he had jumped off, and with so many people on the platform, she couldn't see him. To be sure she wouldn't bump into him, she rushed into the closest "whites only" rest room. She redid her whole upswept hairdo, her lipstick, and even filed her nails. The attendant began to stare at her suspiciously.

Watchfully Jean returned to the huge central room, headed for the bank of phone booths, and called the hotel where she had stayed, hoping for a room. They were full. She spent a disastrously large amount of money calling and calling. No one in Washington had rooms available on demand.

When she explained her plight to one man, he said, "Lady, don't you know there's a war on? Give it up and bed down on a bench in the railroad station. Ordinary people come and go all night. The police and MPs make sure it's safe."

In the end that's what she did. It was too late to go out on the streets to look for anything. She bought a sandwich in the station and then sat beside a family that looked permanently settled in on a hard bench. It was going to be a long night.

# CHAPTER 21

Jean dozed a little just before morning. With blackout covers closing out exterior light, she only knew when morning came after looking at her watch.

She stretched painfully. She had a crick in her neck, and her head ached. The family beside her still dozed. She stood up quietly and headed for the rest room.

Thank goodness she'd had the forethought to put the hotel soap, her toothbrush and paste, and her deodorant in her purse. She wet her face, rubbed on soap with her hands, and splashed with cold water. For convenience, the rest room wasn't a whole lot different from the shower room at Tulelake. The roller towel would not pull down. Patting her face with toilet tissue sufficed. With fresh lipstick and her hair smoothly brushed into a pile on the top of her head again, she ventured out to a coffee counter.

She ordered coffee and toast, which came with margarine and no jelly. Resigned, she carried it to a small table where someone had left their early edition of the *Washington Post.* She picked up the paper and read as she drank the weak excuse for coffee and nibbled at her bland toast.

On page three a small article jumped out at her. Mrs. Roosevelt was scheduled to speak at the dedication of the children's wing of a hospital in Tyler, West Virginia, today at 11 A.M. Tyler was just across the Potomac River, on the outskirts of Arlington. Surely buses ran there if she couldn't get a seat on a train.

Jean tore out the article with the name and address of the

hospital, finished her coffee, and strode to the information desk.

The uniformed woman there said, "Take the bus. It's cheaper and you can probably get right to the door of the hospital by transferring." She gave Jean directions to the correct bus stop.

For the next two hours Jean transferred from one crowded bus to another because she had boarded the wrong one at her first transfer point. When she finally climbed onto the right bus, it zigzagged all over Arlington, making stops every few blocks. Just as she despaired of ever reaching the hospital in Tyler on time, the driver called out the name of the hospital. "Right over there, miss," he said, pointing to the corner of a large brick building beyond tall hardwood trees that were lacy with the first baby leaves of spring.

Jean walked at least two blocks down one side of the hospital to reach the main entrance. Going straight to the matronly receptionist, she asked how to get to the dedication ceremony.

The woman told her and then asked, "Excuse me for asking, but do you have a ticket?"

"A ticket? Must I have a ticket?" Jean asked in dismay.

The lady smiled sympathetically, "I'm afraid you must. The dedication is also a fund-raiser put on by the hospital auxiliary. I heard that seating was all sold out last week."

"Oh, no," groaned Jean. "I have to see Mrs. Roosevelt. I've come by bus from Union Station in Washington, D.C."

"That's too bad. Are you visiting the capital for the first time?"

"Yes. I'm a schoolteacher from Oregon."

"My, you are a long way from home. My daughter's a teacher too," she confided. The phone rang and she answered it.

Jean lingered, uncertain of what to do next. She wasn't about to give up when Mrs. Roosevelt would soon be in this very building.

The receptionist came back and said in a low voice, "If you just want to be able to tell your pupils back home that you saw the first lady in person, there may be a way." She picked up a scrap of paper and began to draw a simple map of the hospital. She made an "X." "This is where you are. If you go down this hall, out to the parking lot, around this corner, and back in this door, you'll find a small lobby and a waiting room for parents. Here, across the hall is where Mrs. Roosevelt will speak. If you were to sit in the parents' waiting room—this is the door she will come through from the street—you'd get a glimpse of her as she comes in."

"Oh, thank you!"

"You're welcome. Mind you, though, please don't mention me if you should get chased out."

Jean promised, scooped up the map, and headed for the parents' waiting room. When she found the cozy room, she chose a chair near the door and swiftly wrote a note on the back of a picture postcard she'd purchased at Union Station. "Dear Mrs. Roosevelt, please may I talk to you privately about an unjustly jailed Japanese American man? Jean Thornton." She thought for a moment and added, "(Niece of Senator Al Moore.)"

Before long a steady stream of people, mostly women in designer suits with carefully coordinated hats, gloves, and handbags, entered the double doors across the hall. Soon, from beyond the closed doors, Jean heard a woman's voice speaking over a microphone. Fearing that Mrs. Roosevelt had entered some other way and had begun her speech, Jean stepped out of the waiting room to peek into the auditorium. As she did so, the outside doors to the lobby swung open and in marched the secret service agents, escorting their famous charge. Two of them immediately placed themselves between Jean and the first lady. They were tall and broad, and Jean could only see Mrs. Roosevelt's feet striding toward the meeting room doors.

"Mrs. Roosevelt! Mrs. Roosevelt!" Jean called, waving her postcard high above her head.

The first lady's feet stopped and turned toward Jean. "What's that?" her high voice demanded. "Who is there? Give me that note."

One man turned, snatched the card, and the next moment Mrs. Roosevelt was peering between two of her escorts. "I'd be delighted to talk with you. Call my personal secretary after 3 P.M. Here." She flipped open her handbag. "Take my card. You'll need it to get past the guards out front. Jim, make sure she has the phone number," she said to one of the men.

"Thank you, Mrs. Roosevelt!" cried Jean.

One man lingered to scribble the secretary's number on the back of the first lady's business card and hand it back to her. Jean retreated to the waiting room and carefully placed the card in a zipper pocket inside her purse. Right now it was worth more than gold.

★

The bus ride back to Union Station took much less time. In the station, Jean settled into a phone booth and tried again to locate a room for the night. Her cash dwindled dangerously as she called one hotel after another. Finally she gave up.

As the time approached for her to call the White House, she began to worry. What if Mrs. Roosevelt had not notified her secretary that Jean should have an appointment? What if the secretary had scheduled a time next week? Jean's funds were limited, and she couldn't call on Uncle Al for help.

At 3:15 Jean nervously dialed the handwritten number on Mrs. Roosevelt's card.

A no-nonsense feminine voice answered. When Jean gave her name, the lady said, "Oh, yes. I can give you fifteen minutes at 11 A.M. tomorrow. Please be here fifteen minutes early. Do not bring a camera or any bags, and be sure to bring Mrs. Roosevelt's card."

"Thank you. I'll be there." Jean's weariness vanished. Although this appointment promised nothing more than a sympathetic hearing, she wanted to leap in the air and shout.

★

Jean reached the White House half an hour early after another miserable night at Union Station. The soldier stopped her on the walk to the entrance, glanced at Mrs. Roosevelt's card, and gestured for her to proceed. At the door another soldier did the same. Inside, she gave her name to the door-man who checked a list, asked her to sign her name in a book, and then introduced her to a young woman in a black pleated skirt and white long-sleeved blouse. The woman greeted her and ushered her down a great hall past a huge room with rich red walls to a wide staircase.

Upstairs, the woman took her into an ornate, old-fashioned parlor. Here, as everywhere, blackout curtains hung inside the lush draperies at the windows, keeping out the edges of early spring sunlight that splashed sideways into the room.

Minutes ticked by. At two minutes to eleven, a woman in a neat navy blue suit appeared and led her quickly down the carpeted hall. At an open door she paused and gestured with one hand for Jean to precede her. Following a step behind, the woman announced, "Mrs. Roosevelt, Miss Thornton is here."

The first lady was seated at a desk that held a neat stack of paper, several fountain pens, a blotter, and a small pot of daffodils. She arose and came with an outstretched hand to greet Jean.

"I'm glad to see you again. Tell me, how can I help you?" she said, leading Jean to a comfortable chair beside her desk. She sat down, picked up a pen and clean sheet of paper, and smiled warmly at Jean.

Jean poured out everything, feeling knowledge of Uncle Al's work was as safe with the president's wife as it had been with the president.

Mrs. Roosevelt made quick notes, scarcely taking her eyes from Jean. When Jean stopped, the first lady asked, "Does Senator Moore know you are seeing me?"

"No. In fact, he forbade me."

"I see. Are you certain all six of these men are as innocent as your friend, Mr. Kagawa?"

"From as much as I know, I believe they are."

Mrs. Roosevelt glanced at her notes and then looked up. "I feel these internment camps have been a great mistake—a terrible injustice. I have said this to Franklin many times, but despite what the newspapers report," she laughed good-naturedly, "he doesn't always listen to me." She sobered. "I have to warn you, I may not be able to do anything for these men."

Jean's heart dropped a notch, but she smiled. "I know."

"But you also believe I'll try, or you wouldn't be here, and you're right. I will do what I can." She made one more note and laid down her pen.

The woman who had brought Jean in appeared to escort her out.

Jean came to her feet. "Thank you, Mrs. Roosevelt. You're so kind. Even if you don't succeed, I'm so happy to have met you."

"And I you. You greatly encouraged me yesterday, Miss Thornton. Keep on sticking up for what you believe. We desperately need young women like you."

Jean stammered, "Thank you. I will. Thank you," as she backed out of the room. The woman walked with her downstairs and turned her over to the first young woman to escort her to the front door.

Just as Jean was about to step outside, someone called, "Miss Thornton!" The woman in the navy blue suit was pursuing her, waving a piece of paper.

Jean turned back.

The woman handed her the paper. "Mrs. Roosevelt wants you to have a good night's rest, and if you can't get on a train immediately, she says, stay on at this hotel as long as necessary. You are to be her guest."

"Oh," said Jean in awe. "How did she know I haven't been able to find a place to stay?"

"You look very tired, Miss Thornton," said the woman gently. "And she knows Washington."

Tears of gratitude sprang into Jean's eyes. "Please tell her thank you again," she begged.

"Certainly." The woman was all business again. "Goodbye."

Jean walked back to the street and squeezed onto a crowded trolley to Union Station. At the station, she asked a ticket agent if her original ticket to Salem, Oregon, was still valid. It was. She put her name on a list for a seat for the next day and then walked to the hotel, looking forward to a hot bath and a real bed.

★

Back in Salem a week later, Jean spent several days catching up on sleep and answering Grandmother's questions. She wrote to Mary, Pastor Ichiba, Helen, and Dr. Langston, but all she could report was that Mrs. Roosevelt had promised to do what she could.

Pastor Ichiba responded with kind encouragement, and Dr. Langston said he was sending her suitcase immediately. Mary wrote that the news of her talk with Mrs. Roosevelt had cheered up Helen, but Helen did not write.

On the last day of March, while Jean was dressing to go shopping, Grandmother called from the downstairs hall. "Jeanie, you have a letter. Looks as if it's from one of your Japanese friends."

Jean ran down expectantly. Helen must have written at last. Taking the letter from her grandmother, she saw immediately that it was not Helen's handwriting. In the upper left corner, the return address said, "Private Thomas J. Kagawa, Camp Shelby, Mississippi." She ran back upstairs with the sealed envelope. With her heart hammering, she sat down at her dressing table and stared at the angular, firm writing. *He's free! Mrs. Roosevelt succeeded. He's free!*

Drawing a deep breath, she cut the flap with her nail file, and pulled out a single white page. She read it fearfully.

"Dear Jean, Helen wrote to me about your trip to Washington. I didn't dare hope anything would come of such a wild idea, but I've been released and exonerated. So have all the men except one, who actually is a troublemaker.

"I don't know what to say, except thanks. I didn't believe you would or could do this. Mrs. Roosevelt sent me a personal note, praising you for how you stood up for the internees in front of those congressmen and army officers. She said I was fortunate to have a friend such as you, and I have to agree.

"As you can see by my return address, I've been accepted for the Nisei Combat Team. Helen was allowed to teach in your absence and will finish the school year at Tulelake. The rest of my family will be going to Chicago. The United Brethren Church has established a hostel there where Japanese people can stay until they locate work and an apartment.

"Thanks for doing what you said you would. Sincerely, Tom."

His words were courteously impersonal, but at least he had

written, and he was not too angry to say thanks. She hugged the letter to her breast and then read it again and again.

Later the same day, when Jean answered the phone, Uncle Al's voice came on from Washington. She braced herself for a tongue-lashing.

"Eleanor told me about your visit."

He was angry, all right.

"I'm not going to go into how I felt about your impulsive actions because in the end everything came out well. But don't you ever pull a thing like that again, openly defying me when I told you how important secrecy was."

"I don't intend to ever have to keep secrets for you again, Uncle Al."

"You're right there. I won't expect you to."

"Mrs. Roosevelt was wonderful," Jean said, changing the subject to something more agreeable. "Even if she hadn't helped, I was grateful to be able to meet her."

"She's an unusual woman and smart. After she checked with me, she was able to do things in a prudent manner. Neither you nor I nor others involved were exposed to undue scrutiny. Nevertheless, I feel betrayed."

Jean cringed at the word *betray.* "It seems that everybody involved in this has betrayed and has been betrayed. I'm sorry."

"Me, too, Jeanie," he said, still sounding glum. After a moment of silence, he said, "Well, it's over. I'd like to put the whole thing behind us. . . . You'll be glad to know I heard from Giselle, but she refuses to leave Claude."

"I can't blame her, but it's too bad the girls can't be sent to us."

"She thinks trying to get them out would be more dangerous than for them to stay. She says the family's cover is good and they have an excellent sanctuary if they should have to disappear."

"I hope she's right. What a nightmare. Can I write to her or send her anything?"

"No. She warned me not to try. It would endanger them." He sighed so heavily the phone picked it up. "They're doing a noble thing for their country . . . and for western civilization. . . . Jeanie, I heard of—and verified—atrocities I never dreamed the German people would tolerate. Hitler is systematically annihilating the Jews. Europe has become a human slaughterhouse. I've decided not to run for re-election. I can do more over there, so I've accepted a position at the embassy in London. Would you like to go with me?"

"To England?"

"Yes. I thought . . . I hoped the opportunity would make up for what I put you through at Tulelake. I've already checked to see if you might be able to teach . . . outside of London, of course. The answer was affirmative. I was thinking of some of the villages where evacuated children have been placed. What do you think?"

"I don't know. Absolutely no spying?"

"None," he said emphatically. "While you think about it, I'll plan as if you were going. It's easier to cancel than to not be prepared. Uhm, Jeanie?"

"Yes?"

"I said some things about your friend Tom that I regret. I . . . ah . . . I realize he was in a bad spot, and we did goad him. You might like to know, if it's important to you, the 442nd—the Nisei Division—will be sent to Europe. If you were in England, you'd be closer to . . . to what's going on," he ended awkwardly. A flood of forgiveness and love for him filled her. She said, "Thanks, Uncle Al. I understand. I just received a letter of thanks from Tom, but I doubt that we'll keep in touch."

"Well, as soon as you decide about going to England, let me know," he said. "Now, is your grandmother there? I'd like to talk to her."

Jean called her and retreated to the kitchen where she turned on the burner under the tea kettle. Grandmother would enjoy a cup of tea and time to chat about Uncle Al's call.

Later while they were still enjoying their tea, the phone jangled loudly again. Jean jumped up and answered.

"Jeanie? Jeanie, this is Rodge. I'm in San Diego."

Jean leaned against the wall for support. "Rodge! It's so good to hear you! Are you all right?" Her voice broke.

"Hey, don't cry. I'm great. I'm fine. I'm coming home."

## CHAPTER 22

On Rodger's first day home, he came to see Jean. Both Jean and her grandmother greeted him with hugs and a few tears of happiness. Then Grandmother fixed them coffee and left them alone in the parlor. Rodge's thin face made Jean want to weep. He was all bony angles and hollows. And yet his gray eyes gleamed with delight.

"It's so good to see you," Jean said. "When I heard you were missing, I was about out of my mind. You're so thin. Are you okay?"

Her question about his health seemed to throw him. The light in his eyes went out, but then his jaw tightened and he cracked a smile. "The doc says I just need lots of good food and a little rest, but let's not talk about me. You're a feast for hungry eyes . . . more beautiful than ever."

He still loved her. He didn't have to say a word. Although she didn't love him, for the first time she considered the possibility of marrying him. She could never marry Tom, and surely in time her feelings about him would fade. She and Rodger could have a good life together. They'd always been such good friends. No one else had been as loyal or as considerate as Rodger, and now his need for her was all over his face.

She said, "I'm so glad you're home. It's like a miracle after I thought I'd never see you again."

"For me too. But, Jeanie, I don't want to talk about what happened to me. Please don't ask."

The haunted look returned to his eyes. Jean wanted to take

him in her arms and comfort away the bad memories. She said, "I won't."

He relaxed. "So how have you been? Why are you home before the school year's out? Was teaching at the internment camp too rough?"

"No . . . yes . . . well . . ." She had to tell him the truth—to let him know about how she'd been misled by her own fear and grief and prejudice, and she wanted him to know the internees the way she'd come to know them. "You must promise not to tell anyone," she began. Cautiously she revealed what she had done for Uncle Al.

"My Jeanie-with-the-light-brown-hair—a spy?" He shook his head wonderingly. "And I was worried about you aiding and abetting the enemy."

"I'm not finished. Wait 'til you hear the rest." She told him about her mission to Washington to obtain pardons for the men she'd betrayed.

"Betrayed!" he cried. "You were doing the American thing. You should be proud of your work. What made you try to get those Japs off?"

"They were innocent. I'd made a terrible mistake, so I had to try to undo the damage I'd caused."

A look of incredulity raised his eyebrows, and then, as if to make her act of restitution acceptable, he said, "Well, you put yourself on the line for your country. What you did was great, no matter how it ended."

She gave up trying to get him to see how prejudice had so easily led her to hurt people. During the months of their separation, the small gap between their ideals had turned into the Grand Canyon. There was no way she could marry him. Her instant relief, once she recognized the fact, confirmed that she had almost lied to herself again.

Now Jean had to be sure Rodger knew the truth. "Rodge, I sent you a letter right before your ship went down. I never knew if you received it. . . ."

"I don't know. What did you write about?"

He sounded too hopeful for Jean's comfort. "Nothing new, but I . . . stated pretty strongly . . . that I couldn't be your girl."

"Oh." He picked up his coffee, finished it, and slowly set

the mug down. Smiling without humor, he said, "The good Lord was taking care of me more than I knew, seeing as how I needed a dream to keep me afloat in that ocean."

She fought a pang of sympathy that he might misread as love. "It must have been awful—"

"It was worse for my buddies. I'm alive and free." Again his eyes looked as if she'd flipped off a light switch.

She changed the subject to remembering happy times: childhood adventures, school days, and Dave. To Jean's surprise, the past they had shared seemed like a lifetime ago. Finally Rodge rose to go home. As Jean walked him to the door, he said, "Be patient with my folks when you see them. They have this notion you and I should marry. I'll try to straighten them out, but don't worry if they still hang onto the idea for a while."

"Thanks for warning me. Will I see you again before you leave?"

He smiled and answered casually, "Sure. I'll be around."

★

After seeing what the war had done to Rodge, Jean desperately wanted to do something for servicemen. She called Mary. "I'm sending in my application to the Red Cross now. I'd like to work in a hospital."

"Good, I'll mail mine now, too, and ask for hospital work. Who knows? Maybe we can get an assignment together. I'm shipping all your things to you tomorrow."

After she hung up the phone, Jean wrote to Uncle Al, explaining why she had decided not to go to England with him.

When the boxes and suitcases arrived from Tulelake, she looked first for Dave's engagement ring and tried to place it on her right hand. Her finger was too big. That afternoon she took it to a jeweler to be enlarged and purchased a service flag with a gold star.

As soon as she returned home, she hung Dave's photo downstairs in the parlor and placed the flag in the front window.

From the parlor doorway, Grandmother watched and nodded in approval but didn't say anything. She seemed to understand that Jean was laying Dave to rest.

During the week Rodge was home, he took Jean out to dinner twice, token dates for old time's sake. Even so, Jean couldn't bear to see him off at the train station. He said he understood.

As the days went by, in spite of herself, Jean began to watch the mail, hoping for another letter from Tom.

The first week of May, Jean received a letter of acceptance from the Red Cross, saying she would be trained to become a recreational therapist. They couldn't promise she and Mary would go to the same hospital, but they would be in training together in September at American College in Washington, D.C.

In preparation for her trip to American College in the fall, Jean shopped for a few personal items, leaving the purchase of new skirts and sweaters and a new winter coat until she went east. With little else to do, idle time lay heavy on her, so she became a nurses' aide at the Deaconess Hospital.

Each weekend she helped her grandmother serve sandwiches and snacks in the canteen of the nearby USO. On Sundays after church, they invited servicemen to a home-cooked dinner. The men noticed Dave's flag and the ring on Jean's right hand and quickly accepted the fact that she was only interested in being a kind hostess.

★

One day in June a letter came from Helen. Hopefully, Jean ripped open the envelope. "Dear Jean, school is out. The children have done very well. They still talk about Miss Thornton with much affection."

Jean smiled wistfully, remembering every face and name, her hopes for each one, and the tears and laughter they'd shared with her. *Will I ever see any of them again?*

Helen continued, "I apologize for not writing sooner. I wanted to be sure Tom wrote first to tell you he is free. He took a while to get back to me and then, after the way I acted last time we talked, I wasn't sure if you'd want to hear from me. I can't tell you how grateful I am for what you did. It means so much to all of us.

"Just as I didn't want you to lie to me, however, I'm not going to lie to you. I'm not sorry for anything I said because you deserved every word. I hope you can accept my honesty as it is offered, with respect and true friendship.

*Oh, Helen, I love your honesty.*

"I don't know what Tom said to you, but if you still love him as you said you did, please write to him. I know he will answer you."

*What can I say to him? How can Helen be sure he will answer?*

"I've decided to stay at Tulelake next school year. There is more unrest every day as the camp moves toward becoming a segregation center for people disloyal to the United States. Many children will have to stay here because someone in the family has refused to answer 'yes, yes' to the troubling registration questions. These kids will need my help more than ever.

"Mary says you will meet her in Washington, D.C., for your Red Cross training. If you should pass through Chicago, my parents would like very much to thank you in person for helping Tom. They asked me to tell you this. I'm enclosing their address and a phone where they may be reached. Please at least write to them.

"In case you're wondering, I never told them or anyone here about your spy job. Even when I was so angry I could have wrung your neck, I could see it might be easy for you to think spying was okay because of the war.

"One thing I've learned from this experience is never to jump to conclusions. I wrote you off as a Judas, and you have proved yourself to be more concerned about doing the right thing than I was. I will never forget that."

It was signed, "Your friend, Helen." Jean smiled and sat down immediately to write to her.

After finishing her letter to Helen, Jean wrote to the Kagawas, and then she addressed an envelope to Tom at Camp Shelby in Mississippi. She got as far as "Dear Tom," and stalled. There was so much she wanted to say that couldn't be said in a letter, and maybe should never be said in person either—the truth about her spy activities, her love for him.

Then she remembered he didn't know about Rodger's

return. After giving him that good news, she told him about her activities at the USO with her grandmother.

Tom answered her letter promptly and described basic training in Mississippi. Helen and her parents also answered. Jean enjoyed their letters and entered into a regular correspondence with all of them.

She swiftly became a mailbox watcher. When Tom's letters came, she took them to her room and read them over and over. No wonder he had gone into journalism. He was a good writer, giving colorful details and spiking his stories with humor. As she read, she remembered the gleam in his brown eyes just before a smile reached his lips and the warm way he'd looked at her in unguarded moments.

As she continued to correspond with him, she relaxed about what to write. His letters, too, grew friendlier. He commended her for joining the Red Cross. They discussed everything from history and politics to religion, the law, ethics, literature, and the Japanese culture in the United States. Their letters flew back and forth almost on a daily basis. As their friendship deepened, Jean began to feel she must tell him the truth about her work for Uncle Al, but she did not dare do so in writing. If she ever told him, it had to be face to face. Then he would see how sorry she was and she could beg his forgiveness.

★

Through corresponding with the Kagawa family, Jean's friendship with them also grew. By the time she was ready to travel to Washington, she arranged her itinerary to stop over in Chicago to visit them.

On a warm September day, shortly after noon, Jean's train steamed into the station in Chicago. She had written to give her arrival time, but she knew none of the Kagawa family could meet her.

When she stepped down from the train, a tall soldier on the platform reached up and steadied her by taking her arm.

"Thanks," she said. She looked up and into Tom's smiling face.

It was like coming home. "Tom." She smiled and couldn't take her eyes from his.

His whole face lighted up with his smile. "I saw you through the windows and ran to get here," he said. "Here, give me that suitcase." He grabbed her small case and led her away from the doorway of the train car. "Do you have any other luggage?"

"No. I sent everything else straight to Washington."

"Well, come on. I'll get us a taxi."

Traffic was not as congested in Chicago as it had been in Washington, but it was just as difficult to capture a taxi.

While Tom waved at one and then another to no avail, Jean's joy became mixed with fear. Now she knew what Rodger had suffered. She didn't know how to handle loving someone when he didn't love her. She didn't want to make a fool of herself by revealing her feelings to Tom, but on a number of other occasions she had failed to deceive him. And then there was the subject of her spying. She must tell him the truth about that. He might blow up and never want to see or speak to her again when he learned that his suspicions had been true.

Could this passionate man ever forgive such a betrayal?

## CHAPTER 23

With her heart in her throat, Jean waited for Tom to halt an available taxi. This was supposed to have been just a friendly little visit with his parents and now, much as she wanted to be with Tom, she dreaded the imminent possibilities.

At last he caught a taxi and helped her in. He had talked two black servicemen into sharing theirs. In the hot cab, Jean was scrunched between Tom and another man. The men chatted over her head until they reached their destination.

When the others climbed out, Jean moved away from Tom, while at the same time wishing she could stay close and feel his arms around her. She avoided his eyes, terrified that her desire might show.

The driver accelerated, lunging the cab into traffic.

Tom leaned back and kept his eyes on the road ahead. "The folks don't have much space, so I hope you don't mind the room we've found for you at the YWCA. You'll understand when you see their place, but it's like heaven to them after Tulelake."

She tensed, wishing he hadn't mentioned the internment camp. "I'm so glad that's over with," she said.

"Aren't we all?" he said laconically. With his head resting on the seat back, he turned sideways and gazed at her so long her cheeks began to burn. He said softly, "I love you."

She must have heard wrong. She must have misunderstood. "What?"

For a fraction of a second he froze. Then he picked up her

hand and kissed her fingers. "I love you, Jeanie Thornton. I'm a fool to say so, but you know I have a hard time keeping my mouth shut."

"I love you, too, but I never hoped you could love me," she faltered.

He threw back his head and laughed. "So we're both fools. Jeanie, let's get out of this hot cab and walk by the lake. We can wade and pretend there's no war and that we're just plain folks in love. We may have no future, so let's take today just for us."

"What about your family?"

"They won't be home for hours. Driver! Can you let us off over there?" He pointed to a tree-lined sidewalk along the shore of Lake Michigan. The cabbie expertly zigzagged through traffic and wheeled up to the curb. Tom climbed out, helped Jean to the sidewalk, set out her suitcase, and handed the man a folded bill. "Thanks, buddy. Keep the change," Tom said.

Jean could see by the look on the driver's face that the tip was generous.

They walked to a shady bench under a tree and sat facing the lake. A breeze brushed their faces.

Tom slipped his arm across her shoulders and drew her close. His gentle manner struck her as almost reverent. She pressed her cheek against his uniformed shoulder. "If we're just plain folks in love, who are we?" she asked.

He leaned his cheek on the top of her head and said, "I'll be Bill Smith and you be Suzy Jones. And we've known each other for years, but suddenly we are in love."

"No. Let's pretend we just met and fell instantly in love and now we have to get acquainted," she corrected.

He lifted his head and looked at her with a quirky smile. "That's too near the truth for pretend." With his hand on her cheek, he turned her face up to his and kissed her.

*Has a kiss ever meant this much before in the whole of history?* she wondered.

He released her. "There. In front of the whole city of Chicago, I kissed you, Suzy Jones."

She nestled her head on his shoulder and gazing up at him,

traced the sculptured curve of his upper lip with her fingertip. To be touched and touchable seemed like a small miracle. "I don't want to pretend anymore. I want you to be Tom Kagawa and I want to be me. . . . When did you know you loved me?"

"Long before I kissed you in the moonlight, and when I feared you were dying, I felt I would die too."

"You saved my life that day. There's so much we need to talk about." She straightened to move away, but he held her close. "You need to know about Dave and the truth about . . . Uncle Al and me. . . ."

"Shh. No need. Helen told me about your fiancé and also about your mission for Senator Moore."

"She did! When?"

"After I first wrote to you from Mississippi."

"You've known all the time we've been writing?"

He nodded, smiling.

"And you forgive me?"

"Forgave," he corrected. "Indubitably." He kissed her on the forehead and then held her tightly. "Jeanie, I was mad as hops at first. But then I got to thinking how I might feel if I didn't know anything about a bunch of people who seemed foreign because of their speech and traditions, and how if I was afraid they could be a threat to national security—with the war and all—I might have done the same as you. I got to thinking maybe you and I are a lot alike. And anyway, I couldn't stop loving you. Now let's get back to the present." He kissed her on the lips again.

When they released each other, he said, "Tell me all the little things you like and don't like, from music and art to how you want your toast in the morning."

While they talked, they strolled down to the water. They took off their shoes and waded and talked and kissed, and sat on the beach and talked and kissed, and threw rocks in the water and talked and kissed. When the sun dropped low over the city, Tom finally said, "It's time to go. Mom and Dad will be waiting supper on us."

Back at the curb he managed to flag a passing cab. They climbed in and sat close together in the backseat. Jean snuggled against Tom, but he only held her close and grew very quiet.

"Penny for your thoughts."

His mouth turned up at the corners, while his eyes stayed sober. "Today is over."

"We will have tomorrows."

"I wish," he said and fell silent.

She rested her head on his shoulder. Pressed against his side, she closed her eyes and prayed for time to stop.

★

Mr. and Mrs. Kagawa, Margie, and Peter all rushed out the door of an old brick apartment building to welcome Jean. They led her inside to their small rooms where the delectable smell of beef and onions wafted from the kitchen.

"Mom used all her red ration points for this week," Margie whispered.

"Margie, I heard that," her mother said. "No, I didn't. We do feel like celebrating though. We can never thank you enough, Jean, and we're so glad you stopped to visit."

Mr. Kagawa added formally, "Please accept our deepest thanks. You risked so much by standing up for us."

"Not anything compared with what you've suffered. I'll never give up trying to show people how wrong the internment is."

"May you succeed," said Mr. Kagawa, "but I fear justice will not come in my lifetime."

"Come on, Dad," Tom said. "Let's keep the faith and dream a little."

Mr. Kagawa smiled indulgently at his eldest son. The rest of the evening they remembered happy times back in Elliston and looked forward with hope to the end of the war and a new beginning.

When Tom took Jean to the YWCA, he did not kiss her in front of the other couples standing on the steps. Instead, he only said, "I'll be back in time for breakfast. We'll have a few hours before your train leaves."

★

When he arrived in the morning, yesterday's glow in his dark eyes was gone.

During breakfast at a nearby cafe, he said, "I didn't sleep much last night. I was thinking about us. . . ."

"And what?"

"I shouldn't have . . . Jeanie, it'll never work. We can't marry, and I shouldn't have said a word about loving you. It only makes things harder for both of us."

Jean laid down her fork. "But I love you."

"You must not. I must not." His voice rose in anger. "Don't you know it's illegal in most states for us to marry?"

His words knocked the breath out of her. "No. I knew a lot of people wouldn't like it, but—"

"In California interracial marriage, especially with a person of Japanese descent, is against the law. I suspect that's the case most everywhere."

Jean went limp. She hadn't thought of such a possibility. "There must be a way, a place where we can . . ." Suddenly she realized he had not even asked her to marry him. They both had accepted unquestioningly that the love they felt for each other was for a lifetime. "We'll find a way," she said.

Tom shook his head. "No. You don't know what you're saying. I've lived with racial discrimination all my life. You haven't. Even if we could marry, I wouldn't subject you to that."

"You have no right to make that decision for me—"

"Both our families would be against our marriage—"

"They'd come around."

"You're showing how little you know. After a few years of discrimination, you'd end up hating me. And mixed race kids, they wouldn't have a chance, especially if their father never made it home from the war. . . ."

Jeanie pressed her lips together to keep them from trembling. She couldn't speak or eat. She sat there dumbly. Tom had become untouchable, unreachable, when all she wanted was to be in his arms.

"Come on," he said, his voice cracking. "Let's get out of here. We've only got two hours before your train leaves." He left money on the table and led her out to the street.

"We'll have to take the bus," he said in an apologetic tone. "It'll get us downtown faster than waiting for a taxi." He tucked her hand under his arm, the way he had at Tulelake when they were walking on icy ground. He steadied her now as he had then. She blinked away her tears.

They rode the bus in the thick silence of too many things to say and no privacy for saying them. When they arrived downtown, Jean said, "Let's get off and walk a while. There's time."

They jumped off at the next stop and, with Tom carrying her suitcase, they strolled along looking in shop windows. "How soon will you go back to camp?" Jean asked.

"Day after tomorrow. I was afraid I might miss you. Maybe it would have been better if I had. " He glanced down at her, and she knew his statement was more of a question.

"No," she answered. "It would not have been better. If yesterday and today is all we have, it's worth it."

"You are a stubborn woman, Jean Thornton."

"Yes, and I intend to marry you."

"Jeanie, please don't—"

Suddenly beyond the glittering shop windows, Jean spied a small stone church huddled between the skyscrapers. "Look, Tom. Let's go in. Let's pray that somehow, someday we can marry."

He hesitated. "Even God can't make our marriage acceptable to other people."

She tugged him by the hand. "From Pastor Ichiba I learned that God can change people. Please."

They entered the quiet, shadowed church and sat together in a pew at the back. Jean closed her eyes and with all her soul silently begged, *Please, God, please.* Other words failed her.

Tom clasped her hand in a firm grip.

He said nothing aloud, but she sensed his prayer, matching hers. After a few minutes, she felt an unexplainable peace.

When Tom whispered, "We must go," she stood up and the peace stayed inside of her.

Out on the sidewalk in the hubbub of the city again, as they walked she asked, "What did you pray?"

"Thy will be done."

She stopped dead and faced him. "That's all? Just, thy will be done?"

"That's what we need most—"

"Well, I couldn't do that."

If people were staring, she didn't care. She twined her fingers with his, white skin and tan skin woven into a beautiful pattern. Lifting their clasped hands, she pressed his against her cheek. "What I did to you and the other innocent people at Tulelake happened because I was willing to lie—first to myself, insisting I wasn't prejudiced and that the end justified the means—and then I lied to all of you, betraying you."

She looked him square in the eyes. "I never want to lie again, especially not to God. I want to marry you, and I'm not ready to just say, 'Thy will be done.'"

Tom's lips twitched; he broke into a laugh. "So maybe I should pray, 'Jean's will be done.'"

They hurried on to catch Jean's train, laughing now as if they were not about to say good-bye, as if nothing could ever part them. In the station, they kissed and clung together like all the other couples in love, but without tears.

When the train pulled out, Tom's smile told Jean that no man-made laws could keep them apart. Somehow, they would have their tomorrows.

# IN GRATEFUL ACKNOWLEDGMENT

It's difficult to find adequate words to express my gratitude to the Americans of Japanese descent who so graciously contributed information and memories of their experiences. Without their generosity, this book could not have been written.

With the best that the word can convey—thanks to Maija Yasui, who put me in touch with so many others; to Frank and Betty Eki; to Min and Bessie Asai; to Mitzi Asai Loftus and her book, *Made in Japan;* to Harry Inukai and his book, *Tulelake Directory and Camp News,* and his generous loan of all the daily copies of *The Tulean Dispatch;* to Roy and Tazu Higashi; and to Kenny and Ruth Namba.

To three women who taught the children at Tulelake I owe a debt of gratitude for their patience in answering my questions and sharing their photos. Thank you, Edetha Keppel, Martha Melton, and Mary Durken.

A mountain-size thank you to my writer friends in my three critique groups who listened, critiqued, and encouraged. Special thanks to photojournalist Gail Denham, my tireless brainstorming partner, to Connie Soth, freelance editor, who helped me polish my words, and to author Linda Shands, ever gentle and right on with her critiques.

I also owe much to several authors I've never met—to Frank F. Chuman, author of *The Bamboo People: the Law and Japanese-Americans;* to Lauren Kessler, author of *The Stubborn Twig;* to Jeanne Wakatsuki, author of *Farewell to Manzanar;* to Yoshiko Uchida, author of *Journey to Topaz* and *Journey Home;* to John Okada, author of *No-No Boy;* to Liam Nolan, author of *Small Man of Nanataki,* the story of the memorable Rev. John Watanabe; to everyone quoted in *Beyond Words: Images from America's Concentration Camps,* by Deborah Gesensway and Mindy Roseman; and to David Brinkley, author of *Washington Goes to War.*

## ABOUT THE AUTHOR

Elsie Larson grew up in Salem, Oregon, and attended Willamette University. A lifelong resident of Oregon, she lives in Gresham with her husband Richard in the home he inherited from his parents. The Larson's three children's families, which include eleven grandchildren, live close enough to come for Sunday dinners.

Elsie enjoys hiking, bicycling, reading, rock-hounding, making jewelry, growing roses and irises, and walking her dogs Jock, a Welsh corgi, and Kodiak, a bear-shaped akita/shepherd mix.